fm
5-
scan
4|17

SEAWEED ON THE STREET

Stanley Evans

D1019146

Copyright © 2005 Stanley Evans
First edition
Second printing, 2008

All rights reserved. No part of this publication may be reproduced, stored in a
retrieval system or transmitted in any form or by any means—electronic, mechanical, audio
recording or otherwise—without the written permission of the publisher or a
photocopying licence from Access Copyright, Toronto, Canada.

TouchWood Editions
#108 – 17665 66A Avenue
Surrey, BC V3S 2A7
www.touchwoodeditions.com

TouchWood Editions
PO Box 468
Custer, WA
98240-0468

Library and Archives Canada Cataloguing in Publication

Evans, Stan, 1931–
    Seaweed on the street / Stanley Evans.

ISBN 978-1-894898-34-8

    1. Coast Salish Indians—Rites and ceremonies—Fiction.
I. Title.

PS8559.V36S42 2005   C813'.54   C2005-905606-1

Edited by Laurel Bernard
Cover photo by Helle Bro/iStockphoto
Interior design by R-house Design

PRINTED IN CANADA

TouchWood Editions acknowledges the financial support for its publishing program from
the Government of Canada through the Book Publishing Industry Development Program
(BPIDP), Canada Council for the Arts, and the province of British Columbia through the
British Columbia Arts Council and the Book Publishing Tax Credit.

Canada Council   Conseil des Arts
for the Arts   du Canada

BRITISH COLUMBIA
ARTS COUNCIL

~: *for Aria, Aila, Zoe, Sophie and Claire* :~

THE WARRIOR RESERVE does not exist. All of the characters, incidents and dialogue in this novel are imaginary. Any resemblance to actual persons, or to real events, is coincidental. Depictions of Native mythology and religion are based on ethnological research and do not necessarily reflect the present-day observances and practices of the Coast Salish people.

PROLOGUE

For spirit quest, Jimmy Scow purified himself by 10 days of fasting and bathing and sexual abstinence. Jimmy Scow then spent one more day picking *Amanita muscaria* — mushrooms common on the northwest coast of British Columbia. Scow's belly was empty when he put the mushrooms into his medicine bag and walked Canoe Cove way.

The moon was hanging halfway up the sky.

Scow lit a driftwood fire on the beach to warm himself. Under the moon, Scow was cold because he was naked. In spite of the cold, Scow covered a large rock with saliva and dived with it into deep seawater. After several dives the powerful spirit Tulmex scornfully informed Jimmy Scow that he deserved no great spirit because his father's father's father had been a slave.

Scow was ashamed. He had not known that his ancestors included slaves. Among the Coast Salish, slaves and their descendants were not merely low-class; they were non-persons, like sasquatches and worms.

Scow had eaten a handful of mushrooms when Moneypower Badger and Healthpower Mouse came to him. Scow slept on the beach with Badger under one arm and Mouse under the other arm. When Scow awakened he was alone again. Badger and Mouse had returned to the Underworld. Scow built up his fire with driftwood, ate another handful of mushrooms and went down the beach to the sea.

Moonlight shone on the waves.

Jimmy Scow squatted on the sand with his feet in the water.

After a while, a raft of wood grounded on the sand.

Jimmy Scow got onto the raft and drifted out to sea. A mile offshore, Jimmy Scow splashed water on his head and, finding a heavy rock on the raft, he covered it with saliva and dived into the sea with it. At the bottom of the sea he chanced upon Wolf's house. Wolf taught Scow how to sing his song. Wolf taught Scow how to make traps for catching salmon and deer. Wolf then offered Scow a stick with a man's head carved at one end. Scow declined the stick. Daughter of Wolf then took the stick and waved it. Twenty humans — half men and half women — dropped dead at her feet.

Wolf told Scow that he would become a great warrior as long as he did not stain his hands with blood. He had to roast the first four enemies that he met over a fire.

Jimmy Scow now accepted the stick and came out of the water.

After this visit to the Underworld, Scow slept for two days and two nights. In a dream, the first enemy that he met was his mother's brother. Scow roasted his mother's brother over a fire. When Scow woke up he got dressed and, with Wolfstick in his medicine bag, he went to the city of Victoria.

CHAPTER ONE

My name is Silas Seaweed. Once I was on Victoria's detective squad. Now that I'm a neighbourhood cop, my office is less than luxurious. There's a tiny cast-iron fireplace with a brass surround and a battered copper coal scuttle that I use as a wastebasket. The fireplace doesn't always work properly, but that's appropriate because I'm a typical cop: I don't always work properly, either. I have an oak desk and a leather swiveller. A hat stand and two metal filing cabinets and a small floor safe. A couple of chairs for visitors. Except for missing-kid bulletins and a picture of Queen Victoria wearing widow's weeds, my walls are unadorned.

The building I operate out of — a three-storey cube of sooty red brick — was erected when the Hudson's Bay Company still controlled most of western Canada. Originally, my room was a harness shop. Sometimes, when it's damp out, I smell old leather and saddle soap.

I'm Coast Salish and I moved in here five years ago. Back then, storefront law-enforcement units manned by Aboriginal policemen were being hailed as bold experiments in social engineering. Nowadays, people complain that I'm running a hangout for the dregs of society. And why not? After all, crooks, drunks, hookers and cops derive from the same socioeconomic group. Cops and killers have similar levels of intelligence and ability, and the average murderer can be as charming as all get-out.

Victoria's evening rush hour was winding down. On the street outside my office, two blonde hookers were standing at the curb in four-inch heels and minis. Sally was wearing a tight yellow sweater. Chantal had on a white shirt. Both women carried shoulder bags large enough to hold a loaf of bread. Why did they need them? A mystery for me to ponder. A middle-aged john cruised by in a newish VW Jetta and the girls gave him the business, jiggling their hips and strutting like pigeons with their chests out. But the john was a hard sell, and he sped off to look at the birds on Bay Street.

Vultures were circling too, cruising the downtown area in shiny black cars. A Viper came around the corner and stopped in a restricted zone opposite my office. Jiggs Murphy got out of the driver's seat, leaned on the car's roof and smirked at the hookers. Murphy crooked his finger. Obediently, Chantal and Sally tripped across the street and had a short conversation with a man sitting in the Viper's passenger seat. The man's name was Alex Cal. After a minute the women reached into their shoulder bags. I saw Cal's big hand appear, then withdraw, full of money. Murphy got behind the steering wheel and the Viper cruised away, but its passage left vibrations in the air that lingered.

Five minutes later, the street was full of johns. Chantal and Sally had got lucky and were turning tricks so they could pay off The Man. There's all kinds of luck.

My phone rang. Somebody with a voice I half-recognized said, "Listen, Seaweed, we've just arrested one of yours. Jimmy Scow. You interested?"

"Sure. What's the problem?"

"Possible contravention of the Endangered Species Act. Suspicious behaviour near the Oak Bay Recreation Centre. Trespass."

The speaker's name came to me. He was a uniform-branch sergeant named George Barton. I said, "Is Scow in the lock-up?"

Barton chuckled and said, "No. He's not in the lock-up. Scow's in Calvert Hunt's house on Foul Bay Road. But don't worry. We won't let him run away."

"I'll be right over."

"Yeah, we didn't think you'd refuse," Barton said, still chuckling when his phone clicked off.

Jimmy Scow, I thought. Well, well.

I was surprised by the depth of my feelings. Jimmy Scow was part of some heavy psychic baggage that I'd been carting around for years. It would, I thought, be nice to get rid of it.

I went across to the lot behind Swans pub, where my car was parked, but I don't remember much about my drive to Calvert Hunt's place. The last time I had been inside that billionaire's mansion, a murdered man had been in there with me.

Back then, I had been a detective with Victoria's Serious Crimes Unit. A 911 call had sent us racing out to Calvert Hunt's place on Foul Bay Road. When we went inside we found Hunt's lawyer, a man named Charles Service, kneeling beside a man with a bullet in his head. Minutes earlier, Service had been working in his office. He heard gunshots, looked out of his window and saw an Aboriginal man driving away in a florist's delivery van. When Service went to investigate, he found the dead man. Valuable paintings and a silver tea service had been stolen.

There had been a rash of lootings in that part of Victoria. Our initial assumption was that the dead man had been a burglar, shot, perhaps accidentally, by a fellow crook. Things became complicated when we learned that the dead man was Harry Cunliffe Jr. The dead man's father, Dr. Harry Cunliffe, happened to be Calvert Hunt's oldest friend.

There was only one Aboriginal delivery man working for Victoria's florists in those days. His name was Jimmy Scow. Scow was arrested promptly and denied all knowledge of the crime. He refused to cop a plea or to name accomplices. The evidence against him was entirely circumstantial. Nevertheless, Victoria's Crown prosecutor charged Scow with involuntary manslaughter and he was convicted — largely upon the uncorroborated statement of a prison informant. Scow got five years, after which he dropped out of sight. The loot was never recovered.

IT WAS GETTING dark when I drove up to Calvert Hunt's mansion. Instead of having a number it had a name: Ribblesdale.

Ribblesdale was a grandiose two-storey showplace, nearly 100 years old, which epitomized a long-vanished way of life. Its ivy-draped half-timbered façade was right out of *Masterpiece Theatre*: Welsh slate roof, long galleries of mullioned windows, a *porte cochère* arching across the driveway. I was crossing a broad flagstone terrace to the front door when it opened and George Barton came out to meet me.

Barton was big. A 50-year-old cop with small brown eyes, a round flabby face and thin dark hair trimmed close to his head. He looked 10 years older than his age, and his expression was of amused benevolence. When circumstances dictated, Barton could be hard-hearted, ruthless and inflexible.

"Good to see you, Seaweed," he said, with bogus heartiness. "Calvert Hunt's housekeeper called us. Told us there was an intruder on the grounds. Native man, she said, and gave us a good description. It turned out to be Jimmy Scow." Barton's smile widened. "Christ, what an idiot. Talk about returning to the scene of a crime. We picked him up near the rec centre and brought him here for the ident."

"Has the housekeeper identified Scow positively as the intruder?"

Barton gave me a look that suggested my question would only occur to a nitwit.

I said mildly, "Why did you bring Scow to this house for the ident instead of taking him to the station?"

Barton's amused expression faded. He made an impatient gesture and snarled, "Because the housekeeper refused to leave this house, that's why. She was the only person on the premises except for Calvert Hunt. He's an old man. She has instructions never to leave him unattended."

I said sarcastically, "The poor housekeeper. She's locked up here like a prisoner too. You never thought to show her Jimmy Scow's photograph, I suppose? It never crossed your mind to get somebody else to babysit the old man while she went away for a few minutes?"

Barton lost his temper and flushed clear up to his hairline. "I *could* have," he hissed, shoving his face up close to mine. "But you know, *pal*, some of us White people see a picture of a Chinaman or a fucking Indian and we can't tell one from another. You all look the same to us."

Barton had about 50 pounds on me. He bunched fists the size of cantaloupes, and I was wondering whether I'd have to break a knuckle on him or kick his ass up into his chest cavity when he came to his senses. He took a deep breath, gave a conciliatory smile and said, "All right, Seaweed, I'll level with you. It was Mr. Hunt's idea. The old man's still got plenty of clout in this town. I guess the housekeeper told him what was going on. He wanted to have a look at Jimmy Scow for himself. See the guy who murdered young Harry Cunliffe. I okayed it. I didn't see no harm in it, but maybe I shouldn't have done it."

"Okay, George, you did what you did," I said, smiling to pretend there were no hard feelings. "Let's go."

We went inside the house. Silver chandeliers hung from high, cross-ribbed ceilings. Old portraits in ornate gilt frames frowned down from panelled walls. Heavy traditional furniture of gleaming dark wood stood on the parquetry floors. A large bowl of freshly cut dahlias sat on a polished oak table.

Calvert Hunt was propped up in a wheelchair at the foot of a staircase, snoring. Iris Naylor, his housekeeper, was sitting in a high-backed chair beside him. There was no sign of Jimmy Scow.

Miss Naylor rose slowly from her chair. Once, she must have been very pretty. But her good looks had been wasted by a habit of constant frowning. Deep lines creased her face from nose to mouth, and her upper lip was stretched tightly across her teeth. Long auburn hair showed wisps of grey, and she wore it swept tightly back from her face and piled up in an elaborate braided crown. Miss Naylor looked confused. Her mouth opened and closed a couple of times, but she didn't say anything.

My encounter with Barton still rankled, but suddenly I felt better. It was as if I'd wandered onto the set of a dramatic farce or an Agatha Christie movie.

"This way," Barton said to me, opening a door off the hall.

"Just a minute," somebody wheezed. "This is *my* house. I'm the one who decides what's what."

Calvert Hunt had woken up in his wheelchair. The old billionaire's face was long and narrow under a sparse crop of white hair. His protruding ears were too large for his head. His big red-veined nose flowed down from his forehead in a long line without the least trace of a ridge. His long scrawny neck disappeared into the folds of silk paisley pyjamas. A red blanket covered the lower half of his body. He blinked his narrow brown watery eyes at me, then at Sergeant Barton, and said harshly, "What's this Indian doing here?"

Barton looked uncomfortable. He said, "Well, sir, it's on account of Jimmy Scow, of course. We generally call on Sergeant Seaweed when there's problems with Natives. We thought you wanted … "

Hunt slammed the arm of his chair and yelled, "I already told you what I want. I want Scow jailed. Why don't you just get on with it?" He listened impatiently to Barton's apologetic mumblings, shut him up with a wave of his hand, then shouted at me, "Are *you* going to jail him?"

"I'm going to talk to him."

"Talk! Talk be damned. Scow's a killer, a menace on the loose. Jail's the place for him, so what the hell are you waiting for?"

Hunt's face was red, his eyes now dry and angry and unfocussed. I laughed at him and said, "We threw out thumbscrews years ago. We've even stopped jailing people without just cause."

"How much cause do you need?" Hunt bellowed. "Scow was just caught trespassing red-handed."

"Was he? It's time I heard Scow's side of the story," I said, turning to Barton. "All right, where is Scow?"

"This way," Barton said. As Barton led me into a reception room, Hunt screeched in the background, "Hear me, Seaweed! That's the last time you'll turn your Indian back on me, you sonofabitch. Don't ever set foot in this house again."

I shut the door on Hunt's bellowing and growled, "Does he ever talk sense?"

"Not often," Barton replied. "He's a right old tyrant."

Jimmy Scow was sitting handcuffed in a chair, being watched over by two uniformed constables. Scow was about 30. Short and skinny, with large black angry eyes. He looked at me with an expression of active disgust. He was wearing a black headband, a red-checkered wool shirt and jeans.

I put my hands in my pockets and looked at him.

Barton unlocked Scow's handcuffs and said unpleasantly, "On your feet, sonny. Sergeant Seaweed wants to talk to you."

When Scow stood up and moved his feet, small chunks of dried mud flaked off his carved leather cowboy boots. His cast-pewter belt buckle was a wolf's head about the size of a baby's fist.

"These guys had absolutely no legal right to arrest me or to hold me against my will whatsoever," Scow said to me, enunciating each word with icy precision. "They confiscated my personal private property. They physically assaulted me without just cause."

Barton threw a small backpack onto a side table and growled, "Calm down, sonny. This time we're giving you a break. But if you know what's good for you you'll stay well away from Ribblesdale. Meantime, you're in Sergeant Seaweed's custody."

The Indian pointed a finger at me, something no polite Native would do to another, and said angrily, "Get me outta this. Any more messing and I'm consulting my lawyer."

I looked at Barton and tilted my head toward the exit. Barton's mouth tightened and his fists bunched again, but after a beat he straightened his shoulders and left the room without speaking. The constables stayed with me until I shooed them off as well.

Jimmy Scow reached into his backpack, took out a small spirit stick and quickly replaced it after checking it for damage.

"It won't get you anywhere, acting the hard-ass," I said. "That your medicine bag?"

Instead of answering, Scow hooked the backpack over his shoulder and marched toward the door. Halfway, he changed his mind. He looked out of a window. Whatever he saw, it failed to please him.

I sat down on a leather club chair and suggested, "Since you're here, why don't you tell me about it?"

He turned glittering black eyes on me and said, "Remember me?" His voice was slow and surly, but a shade less hostile.

"Yeah, Jimmy. I remember you."

He said, "Yah, hey, brother." After thinking about it, he sat down on a chair.

I said, "You want anything? Coffee? I guess they could rustle some up."

"No, I wouldn't take nothing from them bastards," Jimmy said. "This arrest crap. All it was, I've been doing T'sumqalaks ritual."

"On Foul Bay Road?"

"It don't matter where I was doing it. I was minding my own business. Them cops picked me up because my face don't fit. They found an eagle feather in my medicine bag and made a federal case out of it." Scow shook his head and added angrily, "That eagle feather has been in my family longer'n White men have been on Vancouver Island."

"There's a witness outside ready to testify you've been trespassing here," I said, not unkindly. "Trespassing on Calvert Hunt's property? Jimmy, you ought to know better."

"The judge handed me five years. I ironed out three parts of it in William

Head jail and the rest on probation," Scow retorted. "It was railroad city but I've done my sentence. Now I go where I like."

"Fine, I hear you, you're pissed. But I still want to know. Where have you been doing T'sumqalaks ritual?"

"North Saanich way, mostly," Scow said, with less belligerence.

I thought about that. Native origin myths explain witchcraft quite explicitly, and witchcraft stories had been coming out of North Saanich recently. The latest one involved a wolf with a human face loping along a beach near Canoe Cove.

I crossed my legs. Jimmy stared at the fancy silk rug lying on the parquet. I leaned back in my chair and said, "Okay, Jimmy. Keep talking."

Scow shrugged his narrow shoulders. I waited. Scow was good at waiting too. At last he said something in Cowichan, a language I don't speak. Whatever he said, I knew it wasn't a benediction.

But at last he said in English: "I inherited T'sumqalaks ritual and Wolf Song from my dad. The old man had power, but he never used it. Me, I've known I've had strong power since I was a kid. People have been hearing about my power and sending for me."

"Coast Salish people?"

"Salish and Nimpkish. Haidas. Whoever comes to me, I listen."

"These people that you've been working with. What do they want? Wealth power? Gambling power?"

Scow raised his shoulders and showed me the palms of both hands, but he didn't answer my question.

I thought some more: T'sumqalaks Woman gave birth to four children who were wolves. One night, T'sumqalaks Woman was down on the beach digging clams when she heard a noise coming from her house. She tied a torch to her clam-digging stick and looked secretly through a chink in her wall and saw that her young wolves had taken off their skins and were human beings.

"I think you've been eating mushrooms, Jimmy," I said softly. "Tell me the truth: are you trying to witch somebody or burn somebody?"

"Somebody's sick," Scow said evasively. "If he's sick, something made him that way. I'm finding out what it is."

I listened without taking my eyes off his face and said, "This man that we're talking about now. Is it you? Are *you* sick?"

My question touched a nerve. "Evil has been done. I've made it my job to see that things are put right," Scow said defiantly. "If I don't, how can I live with myself?"

Jimmy's face was a study in innocence, but he was working hard to put one over on me.

I said, "Let's quit kidding each other. This is all about revenge."

Scow's cool steady eyes were on mine. He didn't say anything.

"I'm turning you loose with a caution," I said. "If I need to later, how can I get hold of you?"

"You can leave a message with Joe McNaught," he said reluctantly. "I won't guarantee to get back to you in any hurry."

"Forget about revenge. It's a game you can't win." I felt myself scowling and switched on an artificial smile, saying, "I'm not going to ask what you've got in your medicine bag. Whatever it is, I hope you use it wisely. Thanks for telling me all this."

I drove him back downtown and dropped him off at the foot of Johnson Street.

THE FAIRMONT EMPRESS, Victoria's most famous landmark, is an old and typically grand Canadian Pacific hotel, all vine-covered brick and pointed roofs. Located beside the city's Inner Harbour, the Empress is the first thing you notice if you arrive by sea. The Empress's Bengal Room Lounge looks like the inside of a rajah's palace. There's a big tiger skin hanging above the fireplace along with pictures of India from the days of the British Raj. At one end of the room a section of polished floor is set aside for dancing. When I arrived there that night, wearing my best khaki slacks and an Italian shirt, three old guys in black tuxedos were playing Cole Porter tunes with weary professional assurance. I lowered myself into a cane chair and ordered a Foster's, then focussed on the room's main attraction — its silver-and-glass curry table. A fat chef in a tall white hat was presiding over beef and chicken curries, chutneys, garnishes, coconut and pappadums.

Alex Cal and Jiggs Murphy appeared in the doorway — Murphy a subservient half-step behind his boss. Cal was wearing a white linen suit and white kidskin shoes. He looked fit, and he had a lopsided sneer that told us all how good he thought he was. In that setting Cal was as out of place as a frog in a teacup. But he was big and muscular and he moved with the grace of a cat.

Murphy was another big man. He had curly red hair and an Irish-looking face with small blue eyes and a pug nose. Where the skin of his face was not freckled it was pink and raw from sunburn.

After pausing to look around and get noticed, the two pimps sauntered in and sat at a table near the musicians. Alex Cal leaned back in his chair, his body almost horizontal, one leg stretched out, the other bent. People wanting to reach the dance floor had to detour around him. Murphy leaned over their table, the weight on his forearms, grinning as he told his boss something. Cal's eyes swept the room as his driver spoke. When Cal's gaze met mine it slowed for a moment before passing on.

The waiter delivered my Foster's along with silver cutlery wrapped in a linen napkin. I sipped half of my drink, then joined the buffet lineup. American tourists were marvelling about the room, the view, how *English* everything was in Victoria.

I loaded my plate with beef curry, medium hot. Some white rice. Dressed it all with mango chutney, coconut, chick peas, chopped white onion, capers, a couple of peppers, sliced banana and raisins. At the bread table I helped myself to a warm and crispy pappadum, big as a plate.

The food was delicious, the pappadum slightly salty, the way I like it. I'd just finished my first helping and was thinking about having another when the loveliest woman in the world came into the room and took my mind off curry.

She was tall, at least six feet in her high heels, wearing black silk and pearls. About 19. When she stood in the doorway the conversational hum dropped as everybody in the room turned to look at her. Long blonde hair framed an oval face with peaches-and-cream skin, wide-set blue eyes and a pouting mouth with the tiniest suggestion of an overbite. When she saw the pimps she smiled, parting her red lips further, and crossed to their table. Cal remained sprawled, smiling up at her as she leaned forward to plant a kiss on his mouth. Jiggs Murphy fussed around, arranging her a chair, but she didn't even notice him. She was only interested in Alex Cal. They put their heads together and after a minute she took Cal's hand, dragged him upright, and they joined half a dozen other couples on the dance floor. Murphy stood up and walked out of the room, looking pre-occupied as he passed my table.

The pimps were not the only people I had been watching. Charles Service was sitting at the bar. Service had wavy white hair, worn a bit long for a conservative lawyer. A heavy tan made him look younger than his 65 years. He had on a dark-blue suit, a creamy white shirt and was wearing a St. Michael's school tie.

Service was a lawyer with a special practice — his only client was Calvert Hunt. He glanced at me a couple of times, then came over to my table. We shook hands.

I expected him to refer to the encounter at Calvert Hunt's house. Instead he just smiled and said, "Nice to see you, Silas. It's been a while."

"Nearly five years," I said and invited him to sit with me.

"I'd enjoy that, but I can't. Another time perhaps. I'm expecting somebody."

"I was out at Ribblesdale tonight," I said.

Service wasn't paying attention to me. He stared over my shoulder and replied with absent courtesy, "Were you indeed?"

I followed Service's glance. A dark-haired woman was watching us from the doorway.

Service said hurriedly, "I've got to go, Silas. See you around."

He joined the woman in the doorway, took her arm and steered her outside. I paid my bill and went to the washroom. When I came out, I glanced back into the Bengal Room. Charles Service was sitting at Alex Cal's table. Service was in earnest conversation with the pimp, but his eyes were all over the blonde. There was no sign of the dark-haired woman.

I was surprised. What business could Charles Service possibly have with the pimp and cocaine king of Victoria?

LATER THAT NIGHT I was in my sweat lodge, on a high bank above Esquimalt Harbour. Spume coated the shore like the icing on a cake. In the surrounding woods, gently swaying trees were filling the air with creaks and groans and sighs.

I was creating more steam by ladling water onto hot stones when Chief Alphonse walked out of the sea. The old chief was naked except for an eagle feather stuck into his long grey braids. He walked slowly up the beach, ducked inside the sweat lodge and sat on a wooden slab beside me.

I watched the colour of his skin change from purple to red, and then it was my turn to cool off. I stepped outside onto hard-packed sand and hurried down the beach and into the waves. Fifty yards away a huge drift-log was rolling about in back eddies. More loose logs bobbed in the waves. Keeping my eyes peeled for bone-breakers almost took my mind off the north-coast water shrinking my testicles, squeezing my sphincter and giving me an ice-cream headache that started between my eyes and spread through my body like an army of ice worms. Chief Alphonse had stayed in the sea for 20 minutes; ordinary decency compelled me to stay in for at least 10.

My sweat lodge isn't elaborate. It's a dirt igloo. Its skeleton is composed of arched willow wands, poked into the ground at each end and tied together where they intersect. I cover the willows with tarpaulin, shovel dirt on top, and that's it. I heat my rocks in a firepit and when they're hot enough I carry them inside on a shovel.

After a short session in Esquimalt Harbour, that primitive sweat lodge seemed like heaven to me. I carried another big hot rock inside, ladled water over it and got comfortable again.

Chief Alphonse isn't a wordy man. We don't have the kind of relationship that depends on words. We listened to the wind and kept quiet. Then we saw a raven hopping around near the water's edge.

Chief Alphonse said, "Te spokalwets."

The way he spoke told me that no reply was called for.

Te spokalwets. In Coast Salish, the words mean corpse or ghost. The old chiefs are all crazy when it comes to ravens and every time they see one, or hear one, somebody's expected to die.

It's a good thing there aren't more ravens around Victoria.

CHAPTER TWO

The following day, a surprise awaited me at my office. The door was unlocked and a stranger in a VPD constable's uniform was stooped over my desk, writing something in a spiral-bound notepad.

"I'll be right with you," she said without looking up.

After writing a few more words, she turned and raised her eyes. The name tag pinned above her breast pocket told me that her name was Halvorsen. I'd never seen her before. Her welcoming smile faded.

As a neighbourhood cop, I try to look like a man of the people, and my people are punks, drunks and misfits. With my stubble-beard, shoulder-length black hair, plaid mackinaw jacket, caulk boots and Levis, I blend in nicely with the bums on my beat.

Constable Halvorsen said, "What do you want?" As an afterthought she added, "Sir."

I said, "For a start, you can pass me my electric razor from that desk drawer."

She let out a little wordless grunt of realization. "Sorry," she said as colour invaded her cheeks. "They didn't tell me that you were *big*. I was expecting a ... "

"A little drunk in moccasins?"

"Yes. I mean no ... that is ... " She tried to edit the sentence into politeness and then, giving up, stared outside as if the answer might be found beyond the windows. But by the time she remembered to hand me the razor, her composure had returned. She said, "I hope you don't mind me coming in here. I absolutely had to take a pee. Somebody lent me the key."

"Every cop in Victoria's got a key to this place. It's like Grand Central Station in here at times." I extended my hand and said, "Silas Seaweed."

"Denise Halvorsen. I'm new."

Denise was a good-looking woman of about 25 with short blonde hair. She wore no makeup, but while she was moving around I couldn't help noticing her neat little waist and the shapely legs that showed above her highly polished boots.

She said, "Your phone's been ringing off the hook, but I didn't think it right to answer it."

"I don't know what's right either, half the time. This office is a very dubious exercise in social engineering."

"Yes, that's what I've been told," Halvorsen said.

As she was going out I said, "Come back any time."

IN THE CAFÉ next door, Lou was frying eggs and bacon. Two commissionaires in blue uniforms lurked in a corner, resting up before another onslaught on Victoria's dangerous parking violators. Three pipefitters slumped in a booth, unshaven, red-eyed and drinking coffee. They had been partying all night and soon it would be time to clock in at the dockyard.

Lou is a small angry man with a Mexican-bandit moustache. I think he's bald, but I've never seen him without a hat. Lou saw me come in and banged his fist on the counter, saying, "What we gonna do about Iraq?"

I helped myself to coffee. "Bush and Rummy are taking care of it. Everything's under complete control."

"Buncha nonsense," said Lou, flipping eggs on his grill. "What'll it be?"

"Bacon and eggs with everything."

Lou stroked his bushy moustache. "This Iraq deal. It reminds me of the time when I was in the mountains with Tito."

"General Tito made a big impression on you, then?"

"He was a great man!" Lou said, puffing out his chest and staring at me with his nostrils flaring.

"Tito was a street fighter who got lucky," I teased.

Lou turned back to the grill and spoke over his shoulder as he cracked eggs. "Tito was a tactical genius."

I said, "*Rommel* was a tactical genius. Tito was a brigand."

Lou grinned. "You can't fool me, pal. You're just tryin'a get me going. But listen. Tito was something. Guy about my height, looked like my brother. He'd a' known what to do with them Iraqis."

I said, "Oh, yeah? What would he do?"

"He'd ship some of you Salishes and a bunch of Quebec Mohawks out there," said Lou, doubling over with mirth. "Let you bastards fight it out."

Lou turned and shouted, "Come and get it, you guys!"

The yawning pipefitters collected their breakfasts.

I tried to think about Jimmy Scow, until a young Native street kid — wearing a cheap dress intended to reveal as much tit and crotch as possible without getting arrested — weaved her way out of an alley and leaned against a wall across the street. Spaced out on crack cocaine or crystal meth, another little money-maker for somebody like Alex Cal, I figured she had a life expectancy of about two years. It was enough to put me off my food. No wonder I hate pimps and pushers.

I went back to my office and checked my answering machine. Iris Naylor had telephoned several times without leaving any definite message. When I returned her call she said, "It's about last night and that Scow business. Do you think you could possibly come over here again? Mr. Hunt is anxious to talk to you."

I was anxious to talk to Hunt as well.

ALONG FOUL BAY ROAD, roomy old houses stood behind high granite walls and cedar hedges. Oak trees swayed their lofty crowns in a light summer breeze. Fallen leaves, picked up in my car's wake, did a brief dance before resettling. I drove past Runnymede Avenue and turned in to a long driveway bordered by banks of flowering shrubs. An elderly Chinese gardener was steering a self-powered mower around ornamental cherry trees and willows and flower beds. The driveway curved up to Calvert Hunt's mansion. Seen in broad daylight, Ribblesdale looked the same as it had five years previously — when Jimmy Scow went down for Harry Cunliffe's murder.

I parked my Chevy alongside a red Mercedes 280 coupe. Instead of going up to the front door I wandered around for a bit. Ribblesdale stood in at least six acres of prime Victoria real estate. There was a tennis court and a blue-tiled swimming pool where a woman was swimming laps, stroking powerfully and making expert turns. I was in the heart of Victoria, but from the grounds of the Hunt estate no other house was visible. Heavy blue smoke drifted up where garden waste smouldered in an incinerator. The estate's original carriage house — a two-storey miniature of the main house — had been converted into a three-car garage.

I walked back around to the front of the house and across the terrace to the front door. I rang the bell. After a longish wait a young Coast Salish woman wearing an old-fashioned black maid's uniform with a white pinafore over it opened the door and stared at me. With my long black hair and brown skin, I wasn't the usual front-door visitor.

I announced that Mr. Hunt was expecting me. After some hesitation she let me in. The maid looked sullen and her face was flushed, but I didn't think I was responsible. Without a word she showed me in to the reception room where I had spoken to Jimmy Scow. The maid withdrew.

There were fresh dahlias on a refectory table. Morning sunlight, shining through the room's stained-glass windows, picked out the deep red and blue colours in a Persian rug.

The returning maid opened the door and stood aside to admit Charles Service. He turned to watch her go and shook his head. "Damn nuisance," he said, lifting his arms and letting them fall to his sides in disgust. "She just quit on me. A single day's notice. I'll have a devil of a time replacing her. Good help is hard to find. Housemaids get jobs in motels now. Half the work, twice the money."

I doubted that Service's duties as Hunt's lawyer included supervising domestics and wondered why he seemed so upset about it.

"Well," said Service, apparently forgetting the maid and rubbing his hands with a satisfied air. "I suppose you're wondering what this is all about, eh?"

Before I could reply, footsteps sounded and the door opened. A stoop-shouldered, slightly built man with grey hair flattened down on his bony skull came in carrying a black bag. It was Dr. Cunliffe, the father of the murdered man.

Seeing me, the doctor smiled in recognition and extended his hand.

"Morning, Seaweed. Charles told me that you were coming today." He inclined his head toward the upper regions of the house. "I've just been giving Mr. Hunt his weekly checkup."

Service said to me, "Dr. Cunliffe knows why you're here."

The doctor nodded amiably and said, "I plan to sit by the swimming pool and drink coffee. Join me there later if you like." He went out.

Service said, "Funny, us running into each other last night. I hardly see you for five years, then I run into you twice in 12 hours." He stopped speaking and looked grave for a moment before going on: "The Bengal Room. Do you eat there often?"

I laughed and said, "On a sergeant's pay? Are you kidding?"

Service smiled. Choosing his words carefully, he said, "That business with Scow last night. To coin a phrase, it put a bee in the old man's bonnet."

I remembered seeing Calvert Hunt fast asleep in an invalid chair and had to work hard to suppress a smile.

Service said, "It's all nonsense, of course, but Mr. Hunt wants to stir things up. I'm opposed to it, of course. We should let sleeping dogs lie."

I'd heard enough clichés so I looked him in the eye and said, "Why me? If this job is what I think it might be, you need a squad of detectives."

"You're right, we need detectives. However, you were a detective once." He stopped speaking before adding, "Mr. Hunt thinks you have special qualifications."

"Whatever *they* are. From Mr. Hunt's point of view it'll work out cheaper than hiring a private shamus, which is what you did last time."

Service's mouth tightened. Before he said anything, I said, "Not that I mind. This will make a nice change from patrolling back alleys."

Service grunted. "It's nothing to do with Jimmy Scow. It's a missing person inquiry. Mr. Hunt wants you to look for somebody who went missing over 20 years ago."

He stared at me bleakly and slumped into a leather chair. Still staring at me, he put his palms together and touched his chin with his fingers.

I sat opposite, wondering if I would hear any surprises. As a cop, I know plenty of dangerous secrets. Some involved the Hunt family.

Service said, "Calvert Hunt is my boss. He needs help. But first you need to know how he operates." Service stopped speaking and gave me a quick grin. "Calvert loves money. He spent his life making as much money as possible. Now he's a billionaire. He ought to be the happiest man in the world, but he isn't. He lives in self-inflicted misery." An insubordinate ripple moved in the deep ocean of Service's eyes as he added, in a cynical tone, "This is one of those deathbed repentance affairs. An aging parent, smitten with remorse."

I said bluntly, "Then I suppose he wants me to look for his daughter, Marcia."

A deep cleft formed between Service's eyebrows. "Right," he said, apparently astonished. "How did you guess?"

"There's a file on Marcia Hunt down at headquarters. I've read it before. I read it again to refresh my memory before I came out here."

"But why should there be a file on Marcia? She was never reported as missing. At least not officially."

"Police keep files on everything. Calvert Hunt's daughter is not exactly a nonentity."

Service's facial expression went through a series of changes, beginning with outraged indignation but fading to cynical amusement as he said, "What else do you know?"

"I know this isn't the first time you've had detectives out searching for Marcia Hunt. You hired a private eye a long time ago. Patrick Coulton. A retired city cop from Vancouver."

"You're well informed. Yes, we did hire Coulton. But he got nowhere. After wasting thousands of dollars on fruitless inquiries we let him go. By the sounds of things he wasn't even discreet."

"Coulton was a pro. He talked things over with a few city cops, but that's all. He didn't raise a stink, make waves."

"That brings up an important point. We can't afford any scandal. So far, Marcia's name has never appeared in print. It's imperative we keep it that way. As I explained to Mr. Hunt, we daren't risk a full-scale police inquiry. Some glory-seeking cop would run to the newspapers at the first hint of anything juicy."

"Too much secrecy can hamper an inquiry."

"Maybe," said Service. "But we insist on keeping things hushed up."

I said, "Every police matter creates waves. If this were an ordinary case I'd probably set the ball rolling with newspaper ads. Offer a reward."

"Advertisements? Rewards? Are you nuts? Forget it, Silas."

We looked at each other in heavy silence. Service pulled back his cuff, glanced at his watch and said, "Mr. Hunt is probably asking for the impossible. Patrick Coulton couldn't find Marcia when the trail was fresh."

"Just so I'm clear. Am I expected to make a serious effort, or is this a charade? Something to make your boss feel better?"

"We want a decent effort, but we must be realistic." Service pushed himself out of his chair. "Is Patrick Coulton still alive?"

"No. He died years ago."

"Did you ever meet him?"

"Once or twice."

"What did you think of him?"

"Paddy was not very creative. But if he got his teeth into something he was like a bulldog."

"Well," Service said, "let's go upstairs and meet the boss."

I followed Service to the hall. A staggeringly broad staircase curved up to the second floor. As we mounted the stairs a side door opened and the young maid appeared, sobbing and lugging a suitcase. The Chinese gardener was standing in the room she had just vacated, holding a cup of coffee and looking startled, his mouth half open. Still sobbing, the maid ran out the main door and fled down the driveway.

Service, his hand clasping the banister, watched her go. His glance carried to me, a step behind him on the stairs. He gave a barely perceptible shake of his head, his face expressionless. "So much for a day's notice."

I said, "What's her name?"

"Effie."

"Has Effie worked here long?"

"Five years or so. Then something trivial happens, and she's out the door in five minutes." He shook his head in annoyance as we continued up the stairs.

A wide inner balcony encircled the second floor. We stopped outside a big double door. Service knocked. After a muffled reply from within, we entered.

Calvert Hunt was sitting in his invalid chair near windows overlooking the gardens. He pointed outside. "What's going on in this house? Was that Effie running down the drive?" Hunt's deep voice was surprisingly resonant for a man of 85.

"Yes, sir, that was Effie," Service said unctuously, crossing the room to look out of the window himself. "Something upset her. A few minutes ago she told me she couldn't work here anymore."

"Damn nuisance. I liked the girl," Hunt said. He turned his eyes to me. "I know you. You're the Indian cop who came here last night."

I grinned at him. "I'm a glutton for punishment."

He went on, "You were here five years ago as well. The day young Harry Cunliffe was murdered."

"That's right. I was a crime-squad detective back then."

"You're a smartass, but maybe you're the right man to find Marcia. Mr. Service tells me that you quit regular policing to work with street derelicts." Hunt bared long yellow teeth in a wolfish grin. "You may as well tell me. Did you quit? Or did you get pushed?"

"People were lined up in the hallways when I left, throwing rose petals. Maybe they were glad to see me go."

Hunt smiled in cold pleasure. "A lot of people were glad to see me go, too, when I packed up a good job to start my own little business."

He stopped speaking to savour a delicious memory, then added, "I started out in life as a sawmill labourer. My boss was a slave-driving fool. If he'd treated me better I might have stayed with him. If I had, I'd be drawing a nice little pension now."

Hunt gave a bark of laughter and shook his head, pleased with the joke. Hunt's "little business" was Seacoast Pulp and Paper, one of Canada's largest corporations.

The old man rose to his feet shakily, steadying himself with a cane. He was tall and skinny, but had a pot belly. He wore a well-cut grey suit, an old-fashioned wing-collar shirt with a black bow tie, and had a fresh carnation in his buttonhole. Service moved forward, ready to assist, but Hunt waved him away and crossed to the windows unaided.

There was a large oil painting of Hunt's pulp mill hanging over the fireplace. A small green object rested inconspicuously atop the painting's ornate, heavily carved frame. I knew what that object was, but I didn't know what to do about it. Before I could make up my mind, Hunt turned back into the room and looked at me from a distance of two generations.

Abruptly he said, "When you drove up here, Mr. Seaweed, did you happen to notice what kinds of shrubs line the driveway to my house?"

"Rhododendrons. I'm no gardener, but I think there are several different varieties."

"The door outside this room is flanked by two pictures. Describe them."

I said, "There's a picture of a girl wearing a party dress to the left of the door. Looks like a hand-coloured photograph. To the right of the door there's another picture, in a similar gilt frame, of a couple dressed in summer clothes. The woman is carrying an umbrella."

I was being tested and I could see how Hunt had become Canada's wealthiest industrialist.

"You're observant," Hunt said at last. "Unusually so. Probably your Indian blood, eh?"

I don't like being patronized and shrugged my shoulders at him.

Hunt peered into a long dark corridor of history. "The girl in the picture is my daughter," he said at last, pointing outside toward the garden. "I planted those rhododendrons myself, before Marcia was born. When she was little, we used to play hide-and-seek among them. Now she has gone but the plants are still here. I often look at them and think of her. If you live long enough, Seaweed, you'll discover that memory is the curse of old age."

A self-pitying whine had invaded his voice; there was a sudden moist glitter in his eyes. But the lapse was brief. A moment later the old man's teeth were showing in another icy smile. The pride that nourished his anger and bitterness reasserted itself. "Tell me something," he said. "What's your track record? You were with the serious crimes squad and got nowhere with the Cunliffe murder inquiry."

"I seem to recall that a man named Jimmy Scow got five years for it."

Hunt said angrily, "Scow was a joe-boy, just a gormless van driver. Harry Cunliffe's real killers are still out there, somewhere."

This sudden fit of rage exhausted him. His animated expression faded and he slumped. He raised a feeble liverish hand for support and Service helped him to his chair. Hunt's eyes closed and his head drooped toward his chest.

"You'd better leave," Service whispered. "Mr. Hunt needs his rest ... "

"Wait!" said Hunt, blinking his eyes open. "I want this man to find my girl, bring her home."

Hunt roused himself, sitting erect and grasping the knob of his cane so tightly that his knuckles whitened. "Let's get on with it. Dr. Cunliffe has warned me that my heart is weak. I don't have any years left to waste."

Service moved to a chair and sat on the edge of it, leaning forward attentively.

Hunt said, "Marcia is my daughter. I loved her but I make no apologies for calling her a young fool. Sometimes she nearly drove me mad with her wickedness and ingratitude. I devoted my life to earning money so that … "

He broke off suddenly, breathing like an exhausted runner. We waited until this angry spasm passed. In moderated tones he said, "Marcia was headstrong, wilful. She kept running away. Twice from this house, once from her boarding school. To be honest about it, Marcia was more of a trial to her mother than she was to me. I was born on the wrong side of the tracks, came up the hard way. My wife was from a wealthy Westmount family. She had rigid ideas about what well-brought-up young women could do and couldn't do. There were constant arguments about how much effort Marcia should put into learning French, whether she should take dancing lessons. What kinds of friends she should have. Marcia was never easy, but as a small child she was … "

Again Hunt broke off his discourse and stared inward, revisiting scenes that we couldn't know. "Never mind," he said. "By the time Marcia was a teenager, this house was like an armed camp, with Marcia leading a rebellion. She didn't *want* to take dancing lessons. She wanted to run downtown and associate with riff-raff. She'd bring street people home. Beggars, stray dogs, thieves and drunks. She'd expect us to give them money or put them up. She did these things out of kindness, but all it did was make us angry. We were always fighting. Looking back, it's easy to see how Marcia must have hated us."

The old man's eyes were sad as he stared at his feet. Nobody spoke. Then Hunt had another thought and his eyes brightened. "Marcia had one real talent though. She played piano beautifully. Even there she angered her mother and frustrated her music teachers because instead of practising Beethoven and Mozart, she preferred popular music. Marcia loved blues, jazz."

The old man's circling mind returned to a happier time. He was smiling as he said, "She used to play 'Smoke Gets in your Eyes,' sing the words in her lovely, husky voice. Before Marcia left home for the last time she had a rose tattooed on her right shoulder. When Mrs. Hunt found out about the tattoo there was one helluva row." Hunt's voice faded and he looked at his feet again. He looked up and said suddenly, "Ever been hungry, Seaweed?"

"No," I said, after thinking about it, "I never have."

"'Course you haven't," he said gruffly. "A Coast Indian will never go hungry unless he's sick. Lots of your tillikums worked for me in the bush so I know what I'm talking about. They were always bringing game into my logging camps. Deer, fish, edible weeds. Eyes like eagles, the lot of you. You could find my girl if you wanted to. Use tamahnous if that's what it takes, track her down like a wounded animal ... "

Hunt's words trailed away. Smiling vaguely he closed his eyes. His fingers relaxed and the cane slipped noiselessly to the thick carpet.

DOWNSTAIRS IN THE hall again, Charles Service said, "That jargon the old man just used on you. Tamahnous. Tillikum. What's it mean?"

"Tamahnous is a very complicated word. The closest I can come is magic, or spirit. Tillikum means people."

"Interesting," Service said, sounding as if he didn't mean it. "Find your own way out to the swimming pool, Silas. I have a couple of things to take care of. I'll join you quick as I can."

Service went off toward the back of the house.

I didn't have much time so I went upstairs immediately and returned to Calvert Hunt's room. I grasped the doorknob firmly and eased the door open. The old man was snoring in his chair, his head back and his mouth half open. Floorboards creaked as I tiptoed across his room to the fireplace, took a sharp pencil from my pocket and poked it into the small green fragile object, about the size of a mouse, resting atop the picture frame. Nobody saw me carry the object outside the house and into the sunshine.

"Who the devil are you?" a voice said imperiously. "What are you doing here?"

I turned. It was the dark-haired woman Charles Service had met in the Bengal Room the previous night. She had an assured manner and a boarding-school accent and was wearing a two-piece bikini. Her hair was still wet from her morning swim. She was more than pretty; she was stunning, and she had a sensual mouth.

But I scowled at her. Lovely socialites ride roughshod over many, but not if they're hard-nosed cops. "I'm here on police business, ma'am," I said heavily. "I'm Sergeant Seaweed, Victoria PD. Who are you?"

"Why, I'm Sarah Williams, Mr. Hunt's niece. I'm staying here at the moment," she said uncertainly. "I'm sorry, I thought you were another bloody prowler."

Her eyes turned to the thing impaled on my pencil. Her poise returned and she said, "What's that you've got in your hand?"

It was a tough question. I resisted a temptation to become lost in the interstices of thought and tackled it head-on. "It's an effigy," I said bluntly. "A Native shaman made it out of bulrush stalks. Grass effigies are almost universal. In England they're made out of wheat stalks and are called corn dollies. I found this example in Mr. Hunt's room."

"Corn dollies? Shaman? What the hell? … Here," she said and held out her hand. "Let me have it."

I moved the effigy beyond her reach and shook my head. "Sorry, Miss Williams, touching it may not be a very good idea. Come with me, please."

I walked around to the back of the house and dropped the effigy into the garden incinerator, along with the pencil. Miss Williams and I watched them burst into flames.

She said, "I hope you've got a good explanation for destroying my uncle's property."

"It's property that Mr. Hunt never knew he had. Believe me, your uncle wouldn't thank the man who planted it on him."

"Perhaps so. But I want answers."

The rush effigy and the pencil had turned to ashes.

I said, "How much time have you got?"

"Oh, God. I *do* hope you're not going to be tiresome," she said wearily. "I'm really not ready to hear another litany of Native grievances, going back generations. I'm *sorry* that your ancestors were wiped out by smallpox. I'm *sorry* about the residential schools fiasco. I *deplore* the ancient theft and the modern clear-cutting of tribal lands, all right? Now just simply answer my question or I'll phone your supervisor and have *him* explain it to me."

"I suggest you go into the house and get dressed. I'm not going anywhere just yet. We can take this matter up again later."

She turned on her heel without speaking and walked to the house. She'd impressed the hell out of me. Sarah Williams possessed in abundance that air of well-bred self-containment for which middle-class posers strive in vain.

DR. CUNLIFFE WAS seated beneath a patio umbrella by the pool. He had a large vacuum flask of coffee beside him and seemed cheerfully indifferent to the many wasps buzzing around a tray of doughnuts. He pointed at the flask. I nodded and he poured me a cup.

The sun was already hot enough to fry eggs, but the pool looked cool and inviting. Dr. Cunliffe guessed my thoughts and said hospitably, "If you feel like a swim, go ahead. You'll find swimsuits and towels in that cabana over there."

"Thanks, but I'll pass this time." I tasted the coffee and said, "Mr. Hunt wants to involve me in a private search for Marcia Hunt."

"Yes, he told me. Is that within your mandate?"

"Possibly. It might be a bit of a stretch, but on the other hand, nobody has fully defined the duties of a neighbourhood cop. I get dragged into all kinds of private mischief."

"Lucky you. But this is a waste of your time. Marcia's dead."

"Mr. Hunt doesn't think so."

"He does, but he won't accept it."

"What makes you so sure?"

"Because I know Marcia. I knew her from infancy. As a little kid, Marcia was hell on wheels, but she's a Hunt. That means she inherited a love for money and power. She would have been back here years ago if she were alive."

"Mr. Hunt didn't say much that was really useful. He fell asleep after telling me about naughty Marcia's tattoo."

"Calvert tells everybody. I think he was secretly proud of Marcia's rebellious streak. It was a trait he thought she got from him. But Mrs. Hunt took the tattoo as a personal insult. Wanted me to remove it surgically against the girl's will." The thought made Dr. Cunliffe frown. "I refused, thank God, but I did worse things later. Things I'm ashamed of now." He flapped his hands at the wasps and offered me doughnuts from the silver tray.

Dr. Cunliffe said guardedly, "I don't suppose anything was said about Marcia's committal?"

My mouth was full of chocolate doughnut. I shook my head.

"Marcia was headstrong. If she got an idea into her head you couldn't move it. From an early age she was just an unhappy little rich kid. She hated her boarding school but was forced to go. The Hunts never listened to her complaints. They expected her to do what she was told and keep quiet. Marcia detested most of the *proper* girls she had to associate with. Girls who were the daughters of Mrs. Hunt's Junior League friends." He grinned icily. "Marcia was the first person to shake Calvert's absolute belief in the power of money. Until Marcia reached puberty, he thought money could buy anything."

I raised my shoulders an inch, thinking about that poor little rich kid, born with every advantage. A healthy, good-looking girl who spent her summers at a cottage by a lake and her winter vacations skiing, but who liked to hang around on street corners with people who had nothing.

Dr. Cunliffe said, "When Marcia was little, Calvert gave her everything she wanted. Then she was suddenly 14 years old and they had a spoiled monster on their hands."

A cloud of starlings landed on one of the oak trees, their combined weight sagging a sturdy branch.

Dr. Cunliffe looked at the starlings and said, "At heart, Calvert is a roughneck. He was born poor. Calvert scrapped his way to the top. He battled with unions, governments, competitors. And he had virtually no schooling. For years, even after he became a billionaire, he'd go to his office in plaid shirts and caulk boots. Don't get me wrong. Calvert is a clever, ingenious man. But he has no patience with theorists. I told him that Marcia needed psychotherapy but he laughed at the idea. If she'd been born a male, Calvert would have put her to work in one of his sawmills. Or she might have gone off to sea in one of his lumber freighters, knocked about a bit. Sowed the wild oats, then settled down. But Marcia was a girl and a girl's options were limited back then. Instead of running off to sea she married a biker. A fellow called Frank Harkness."

"More fool her," said a voice behind us.

Charles Service had walked across the grass and arrived unheard.

Service sat down and said, "As soon as Mr. and Mrs. Hunt found out, they did everything they could to have the marriage annulled."

The doctor nodded in reluctant agreement and said, "They tried, and failed. The courts wouldn't intervene. The bottom line is that, while still a teenager, Marcia cleared off for several weeks. She came home with a motorcycle ruffian and introduced him as her husband." He frowned and added, "Marcia was also pregnant."

Service shook his head, not in denial, but in reaction to the memory.

Dr. Cunliffe said, "That was the final straw for Mr. and Mrs. Hunt. After a family conference it was decided that Marcia's pregnancy be terminated."

I said, "How did Marcia respond to that?"

Dr. Cunliffe's eyes were bleak. He said, "Marcia wanted the child. When told she'd have to give it up, she was prostrated. Frantic with grief."

I tried to consider these facts without rancour and conceal my disgust. A Salish's first priority is to take care of his family. To injure a relative is to violate the most sacred of tribal taboos. It is the kind of thing that witches do. I said, "The forced abortion. Was that legal?" I cocked an eye at both men in turn. The doctor watched the starlings. Service frowned.

Cunliffe answered first. "What we did was immoral and stupid. I'm ashamed of my part in it."

"Now look here ... " began Service, but the doctor interrupted.

"We've gone through this a hundred times, Charles. We were wrong, there's no getting around it."

Impatience rose in Service's voice. "It's easy to be wise after the event. Mrs. Hunt was raging. Half crazy with panic and anxiety. She wanted Marcia to marry into her own class. Frank Harkness belonged to a criminal gang. He had a police record, for God's sake!"

I said, "A record for what?"

"He'd been arrested for trafficking and possession more than once. He could afford good lawyers, though, and kept getting off," Service said.

"He did serve three months for assault causing bodily harm."

Cunliffe said quickly, "That sounds worse than it is. Harkness was a rough diamond, no question. The man Harkness assaulted was a pusher. Harkness smoked dope and probably sold it too, but the police were wise to him."

"What police? I'm a cop. I never heard Frank Harkness's name before today."

"Harkness was from up-island, Wellington. Not Victoria. Rode around on a big Harley Davidson, dressed in black leather and asking for trouble. The Mounties gave it to him."

"That's baloney," said Service. "You're too lenient. Harkness wasn't just messing around with a bit of marijuana. He owned a chemical factory. He was brewing speed by the gallon. Marcia was probably on it when she brought him to this house."

Dr. Cunliffe said, "Let me tell you something, Silas. You can listen too, Charles, because it's something you've never acknowledged. Calvert didn't object to the marriage because Frank Harkness was a roughneck. It was because Harkness was a kindred spirit. He was a tough, hard-nosed man who wouldn't bend his knee."

Service shrugged. "Maybe. You're entitled to your opinion. But the main point is, Marcia went to bed with this biker, got pregnant, and they were married. False documents were used to procure the union. In my opinion, they were never legally joined."

Dr. Cunliffe opened his mouth to argue the point, then thought better of it.

I remembered something and said, "You spoke earlier, Doctor, about a committal?"

Cunliffe's face hardened. "Yes," he said, uncomfortably crossing and recrossing his legs. "We decided to have Marcia removed from circulation. Taken off the streets and away from Harkness. I arranged to have her committed to the mental hospital. The idea was to terminate the pregnancy and to wean Marcia off drugs while lawyers argued whether she was really married or not. It was a stupid idea and I'm ashamed of it. There was nothing wrong with Marcia, either mentally or physically, and we all knew that. She was just an unhappy young woman."

Service didn't like that. His lower lip went under his teeth, and his chest rose and fell rapidly with his breathing. "That is a medical *opinion*, it is not a medical *fact*. Two of your colleagues … "

"For God's sake!" Dr. Cunliffe exploded. "Let's be honest!" He turned to me. "The medical fraternity is like the legal fraternity or a plumbers' union. It's a club for people with similar prejudices. I telephoned two of my colleagues, described Marcia's history, her actions and her mental state, and I strongly suggested that she was certifiable. My colleagues agreed immediately and without reservation. Marcia was committed to hospital that same night."

I said, "Did that abortion go ahead as planned?"

"No," Service said. "There was no abortion because Marcia escaped. Nobody has seen or heard from her since."

"You're forgetting this," said Dr. Cunliffe, reaching into a pocket. He handed me a postcard and added, "This arrived a few weeks after Marcia disappeared. I dug it out when I learned why you were coming here today."

The postcard was an advertising freebie. One side of the postcard showed a photograph of five musicians clustered around a seated pianist. A sign on the piano top identified the group as the RayBeams Orchestra. I turned the card over. It was addressed to Dr. Cunliffe and had been mailed from Seattle. The message, written in faded blue ink, read: "*Dear Doc, I'm feeling better now, resting up and thinking things over. Maybe I'll see you in a couple of months.*" The card was signed, "*Marcia.*"

I said, "Let me get things straight. When Marcia came home with this biker, Frank Harkness, there was a family council consisting of you two and Marcia's parents?"

"The council also included Phyllis Williams, the late Mrs. Hunt's twin sister," Service explained. "Phyllis's daughter, Sarah Williams, was swimming in the pool a few minutes ago."

I said, "Does Mr. Hunt have any other living relatives?"

"He has no *blood* relations apart from Marcia," said the lawyer. "Calvert Hunt is the only child of immigrant parents. Phyllis and Sarah Williams are Calvert's only legal kin. They are of course related by marriage, not blood."

"Who will benefit from Mr. Hunt's estate?"

Service said reluctantly, "Most of it goes to a foundation. A sizable amount goes to the Williamses."

"How much is a sizable amount?" I asked. Service frowned at the question but said, "Phyllis will inherit about $50,000. Sarah gets a million, plus this house."

I said, "And if Marcia is found?"

My question hung in the air.

Service said, "Marcia left the family in bitterness and anger. The Hunts disinherited her to prevent Harkness from getting his hands on any Hunt money. If Marcia ever shows up, Mr. Hunt would probably change his will. As his lawyer, I'd certainly advise it."

I said, "But if Mr. Hunt dies tomorrow, Sarah Williams will be a rich woman?"

"I'm rich already," said an amused voice.

It was Sarah Williams. I didn't pay much attention to her clothes. They had probably been made by Chanel or some other Parisian haute couturier, but on the whole I'd liked it better when she was wearing her bikini. When she sat down and crossed her legs I could see almost as much as I wanted to see, and she knew it.

The other men stood up politely. I stood up too, more slowly, because I hated to lose the view, even for 10 seconds.

Service said awkwardly, "I'm sorry, Sarah. I had no idea you were listening."

"That's all right, Charles. I broke in before you said anything naughty about me." Still seated, she laughed and leaned toward him, puckering her lips to be kissed. Her eyes were closed and she had a dreamy expression.

She broke away and extended her hand to me. "I'm Sarah Williams," she said, acting as if we'd never met. "You must be Silas Seaweed, the mysterious detective."

"Mysterious?" I said. Sarah's fingers were cool after her swim.

"Well, it's very hush-hush isn't it?" she said, recrossing those long, beautiful, suntanned legs. She turned to Dr. Cunliffe. "Be a pal, Harry. Pour me a coffee and pass those doughnuts. I'm famished."

"Calvert's asked the sergeant to have one more look for Marcia," said Service. "We don't want everybody in town to know what's going on, but we have no secrets from you."

"I'll bet!" she said, arching her eyebrows and taking a doughnut from the tray. She took a bite and said to me, "I hope you do find Marcia. I've been hearing stories about her all my life. How bad she was and all that. I only met her once, when I was nine. We lived in Montreal then and the Calvert Hunts came east for a visit. Marcia was only a bit older than me, but she acted very grown-up. She got into trouble for wearing eyeshadow and lipstick against her mother's wishes, but she looked very pretty too." Sarah laughed. After taking a sip of coffee she added, "Poor Marcia, staying away all these years. Such a waste."

Sarah Williams's arrival put an end to our conference. Small talk dragged on until Service tried to pour more coffee and discovered that the flask was empty. He said, "If anybody wants more, I'll run into the kitchen and get this refilled."

"Forget it," Sarah said hotly. "The servants are ready to mutiny because of that bloody creature Effie."

In a jittery voice Service said, "Don't upset yourself. It wasn't your fault."

I rose to my feet and said, "Well, I'll be going."

"Heavens," Sarah said. "You're not leaving this lovely company? Don't you have things to talk to *me* about?"

"Another time perhaps. If you don't mind."

"Mind?" she said, looking into my eyes and giving me a smile I felt all the way down to my feet. "Why should I mind?"

Dr. Cunliffe said, "I'll walk you to your car, Silas."

As the doctor and I strolled off, Service and Sarah put their heads together and began a whispered conversation.

When we were out of earshot I said, "*Somebody* must have helped Marcia escape from that mental hospital. Was it you, Doctor?"

Surprise made Cunliffe's eyes widen. "Yes. Conscience got the better of me. That postcard she sent me from Seattle was a thank-you note." In a thoughtful voice he added, "I suppose you know that Marcia was traced to Seattle by a private investigator?"

"I know that Patrick Coulton was on the case for a while. I don't know how much progress he made."

"What you also may not know is that hiring Coulton was Calvert's idea. Mrs. Hunt knew nothing about it. Her cold-hearted attitude toward Marcia was pathological. The breakup with her daughter, when it came, was total. She was completely unforgiving. She went to her grave 10 years ago, still hating her own child."

We reached the doctor's red Mercedes and he stood with his hand on the door. More things were troubling him, but he wasn't ready to tell me what they were just then. He flung his medical bag onto the passenger seat and got in the driver's seat. He looked like an old man, slumped forward over the steering wheel. He said, "Ever been married, Silas?"

"Uh-huh. Once."

He stared past the rhododendrons. "There's a lot of pious nonsense spoken about the blessings of family life. As a doctor I see its curses. I see lives wrecked by ignorance and pride." He got into the car and waved toward the big house. "To Marcia, this place was a prison. Her parents were a couple of jailers." He poked a skinny arm through the car's window and we shook hands. The doctor's skin felt dry, withered, but his grip was firm. He said suddenly, "That man, Jimmy Scow. Did he kill my son?"

"No."

Dr. Cunliffe released my hand. I watched him drive off, the back of his white head contrasting sharply with the Mercedes' red leather upholstery.

I got into my battered Chevy with its ripped leatherette seats and its stained roof lining. The car needed work. It needed new shock absorbers. The passenger seat was defective. Half the time the seat was stuck; the rest of the time it slid around without restraint. The last time my ex took a ride with me, she flew forward when I jammed the brake on suddenly and banged her nose against the dashboard. I needed a new car. I needed a lot of things. I felt a vague uneasiness. Half-captured ideas were struggling to be comprehended.

A hand came through my car's open window and tapped my shoulder. The hand belonged to Sarah Williams. It was a very nice and beautifully manicured left hand, with a diamond ring adorning its fourth finger. She said, "You're amazingly good-looking, aren't you?"

I grinned at her and got out of the car.

She said, "I'm still waiting for you to explain the effigy thing."

To give myself time to collect my thoughts I said, "Let's go back to the pool."

She shook her head.

I said, "In the religious life of the Coast Salish, the most important element is the concept of personal spirits."

Sarah smiled.

I said, "Am I boring you already?"

"Not at all. I took a course on Indian mythology at McGill and found it quite fascinating."

"There are two kinds of personal spirits. *Skaletut* and *shzudab*. Skaletut is the spirit of the layman. It brings luck in gambling and in the acquisition of wealth. A few other things. In the days when Coast Salish were still warring with other tribes, skaletut spirit helped us to win battles. In general, skaletut spirits are harmless, or at least not dangerous." I looked directly into her eyes. She didn't blink: she was listening attentively. I went on, "It's impossible to obtain any kind of spirit without doing something to earn it.

"Shzudab spirits are shaman spirits. Shzudab spirit is powerful, and it is exceedingly difficult to acquire. The only people who can explain or describe spirit properly are those people who actually possess it."

"I suppose you have shzudab spirit, do you? You being big and powerful and all."

I ignored this sarcasm and went on, "All spirits have songs, with unique words and tunes."

"What about that effigy?"

"I'm getting to that," I said. Thinking hard, wondering how much to tell her. "Salish spirits travel around the earth. It takes them a year to complete a circuit. On these journeys, spirits gamble or trade among each other, their owners' fortunes rise and fall accordingly, depending how much luck these spirits have with their endeavours. Spirits return to their owners at Winter Dance. At this time, everybody with spirit gets sick. When he begins to get sick, he has to sing his song, perform his dance, some other things. Spirit sickness can last for several days during which a man fasts and goes without sleep. At this time a man needs a lot of friends to help him."

"A *man*?"

"Women have spirits, but female shzudab spirit is rare."

Sarah reached out and touched my arm.

I said, "A shaman's power comes from shzudab spirit and it can be lethal. It is never used for killing game, only men. In olden times, when a warrior grew too powerful, people became afraid of him and would have a shaman secretly kill him with his power. Sometimes the shaman sent spirit snakes or spirit lizards into people's bodies. Shamans with powerful shzudab killed people by hanging rush effigies on their house poles."

Sarah's eyes widened. She let go of my arm. "Somebody is trying to kill Calvert Hunt?"

"No. Calvert Hunt is perfectly safe. So are you."

"How about Calvert's employees? How about Charles Service?"

"They'll be all right."

Sarah was satisfied, I think. Turning away, her face darkened. She said coldly, "You don't fool me, Silas. I've met men like you before. You're one of those dark dangerous bastards. You have no more sympathy for people like us than a fox has for a rabbit."

She was right. Frankly, I didn't give a damn for Marcia's family. They struck me as being completely worthless human beings, and that went double for Charles Service. The only person I had any real sympathy for in this whole deal was Jimmy Scow, a convicted killer.

I SPENT THE REST OF THAT DAY reviewing the file on Jimmy Scow and transacting routine business. Darkness had fallen by the time I cleared my desk and left the office. It was the height of Victoria's tourist season. Double-decker sightseeing buses and horse-drawn carriages passed back and forth beneath the city's ornamental street lamps. Sailboats and canoes drifted about the harbour.

The nocturnal hunting cycle had begun. It was the time of the owl and the coyote — and the greedy pimp. Halfway down Waddington Alley a woman screamed. I froze, staring into the darkness, and saw two people scuffling near a big metal garbage bin. A sharp curse rang out and the couple fell down together. I moved forward and came across Chantal, the prostitute, lying in the dirt. Jiggs Murphy was kneeling over her, slapping her with his meaty hand.

Rage set my pulses hammering. "Back off," I said and grabbed Murphy's shoulder. The pimp turned an angry face. From a crouch he drew back his arm and threw a fast punch. I sidestepped, grabbed his wrist, pulled him close and hit him in the stomach. He went sprawling. I circled until I felt the bin against my back and watched as Murphy, on all fours, sucked air. He reached inside his coat, and metal glinted. I kicked his arm with the hard toe of my shoe. He squealed, and a pistol fell to the ground with a clatter. He made a grab for it but I seized a handful of Murphy's hair and shook him like a rat. When I let go he fell backward and his head hit the ground with a thud.

Chantal had picked herself up and was leaning against the bin, massaging her neck. Angry tears spilled from her eyes but she made no sound until I took her in my arms and hugged her close. Her voice breaking, she said, "You didn't kill him?"

"I didn't try to. He just fell. Guys like Murphy are harder to kill than a virus."

She began to sob.

I said, "Come on, I'll take you home."

She shook her head and pulled away, looking up into my face. "It ain't that easy," she whispered hoarsely. "You don't just walk away from pimps, Silas. Not when they're Alex Cal and Jiggs Murphy."

"There's an easier way than this, Chantal. Why don't you lay charges against those bloodsuckers? You know I'll protect you."

Her eyes met mine in an instant of shared knowledge. She knew and I knew that even if I drowned Murphy in a sewer, other parasites would crawl out of the slime and take his place immediately.

"You're such a bloody romantic, Silas, but I hope you know what the hell you're doing," Chantal said and walked off, a little unsteadily, her high heels clacking on the dark pavement.

I felt my rage returning as I knelt beside Murphy to frisk him.

He was carrying two thick envelopes full of money, collected that night from Alex Cal's stable of hookers and addicts. A leather billfold made Murphy's hip pocket bulge. I stuffed the envelopes inside my shirt and flipped the billfold open. It contained half a dozen credit cards and a driver's licence with photo ID identifying the pimp as Jason Murphy. Inside was another stack of money in 20s and 50s. I pocketed all of the cash and tossed the billfold into the Dumpster. Then I poked around in the dark until I found Murphy's pistol. It was a .30 Ruger Blackhawk. I jammed it inside my belt. I thought about running Murphy in, but I knew he'd be back on the street inside of four hours and I wanted more. I'd deal with this business in my own way.

Somebody came around the corner of Waddington Alley. It was a rummy. He faced the brick wall and began to fumble with his zipper. Murphy was groaning and nursing his head now, so I went out of the alley.

I walked to the place where I had parked my Chev and forced myself to breathe deeply, calm down, stop thinking about that filth in Waddington Alley. I unlocked my car and stood there, my arms resting on the roof. My racing thoughts turned to the beautiful woman I had seen with Jiggs and Alex Cal in the Bengal Room the night before — another filly being broken in for the pimps' stable of hookers.

Murphy staggered out of the alley, stooped forward, holding both arms across his gut. He steered a wobbly line up the street. My anger started coming back as I got into my car.

CHAPTER THREE

The next morning I got out the money that I had lifted from Jiggs Murphy and put it on my desk. After admiring it for a while I took two manila envelopes from a drawer and stuffed $500 into each. I still had about $3,000 left over that I didn't know what to do with. For the time being, I locked it in my office safe. I wrote Chantal's name on one envelope and Sally's on the other, then went next door to Lou's Café.

When Lou brought me coffee, I ordered bacon and eggs and gave him the two envelopes. I said casually, "Give these to the girls next time they come in. Don't tell them who the envelopes came from. Okay?"

Lou seemed preoccupied. He nodded absently and slipped the envelopes under his counter.

I used my cellphone to call a man I know in the parole branch and asked him about Jimmy Scow. I had to prod his memory: "Scow's the guy got five years for the Cunliffe killing."

"Yeah, right. Calvert Hunt's house. What's it called again?"

"Ribblesdale."

"Right. I knew it was something goofy. Hang on a minute."

After a while he came back and said, "Scow's probation ended months ago. He behaved himself and is now free to sleep on the streets or do whatever else he wants to do."

I thanked him and hung up.

Over breakfast I composed a personals ad. When I was satisfied with the wording, I phoned it in to Victoria's *Times Colonist* newspaper, which has good distribution on Vancouver Island.

✴

JOE McNAUGHT RUNS the Good Shepherd Mission in Victoria's Chinatown. His declared mandate is to succour the hungry and bring muscular Christianity to the street people of Victoria. Noble ideals, but I have misgivings about McNaught and he knows it. When I went around to the mission, McNaught didn't want to be found. The place was jammed with people wanting free breakfasts, so it was easy to hide from me. I gave up looking and spoke to a kitchen volunteer instead. He was a short, skinny, middle-aged Kwakiutl man. His jacket fitted him like a Doberman's kennel fits a chihuahua. Six inches of bare ankle showed between the bottom of his jeans and the top of his Nikes. His laces were undone. He had a face like Boris Karloff with jet lag.

"Jimmy Scow?" he said thoughtfully, not looking at me. "Yeah, we know him. When he was in prison he followed the Jesus Road. When he came out he prayed with us for a while. Till something happened."

"What?"

"I don't know." He lifted a cigarette from an inside pocket but didn't light it. "There's things we don't do in the Lord's house," he said, and shuffled outside. The volunteer lit his cigarette, filled his lungs with smoke and let it dribble out through his nostrils as he leaned against a wall in the sunshine. I noticed that his nails were bitten down to the quick. His small black eyes were like black knobs sunk in his face. He said, "You're a cop, you got your ways of looking at things. I tell you this though. Jimmy Scow got a very raw deal."

"It wasn't my case. But the way I remember it, Scow got legal aid."

"Sure he did," the volunteer returned savagely. "Scow's brief was just out of law school. A pipsqueak pretending to be a big noise. Jailing Jimmy Scow was like giving a raccoon five years for being furry. He'd been a White guy, he'd never done day one in jail. Not day one. Jail turned Jimmy sour. Now he's worshipping Dokibatl and doing Wolf ritual."

I looked at my watch. It was getting on toward noon. I said, "If you happen to run into Jimmy, will you tell him that Silas Seaweed says to lay off what he's been doing at Foul Bay Road. It's dangerous."

"I'll tell him, brother. But all Jimmy wants to talk about now is Wolf God, so I doubt he'll listen."

A boy went by in an unmuffled '29 Chevy kit car; the noise hurt my ears. I thanked the volunteer for his help and went on my way.

I WAS THINKING about Wolf ritual when I chanced upon Chantal. She was patrolling her corner, doing an exaggerated loose-hipped walk and pouting her lips toward passing cars. When she saw me coming she forgot about business and ran my way, tripping along in the knock-kneed, short-stepped style of women wearing high heels. Beaming, she threw her arms around my waist and said, "Guess what? Sally just left town!" Chantal cocked her head to one side, to gauge my reaction.

"So she left. Is that good?"

"For Sally, yes. One minute she's here, the next minute she's outta here. We had coffee together at Lou's. After coffee she went home, packed her bags, kissed me goodbye and took off."

Chantal was wearing a high-necked blouse. I put my finger inside her collar and gently eased it open. There was an angry red bruise where Jiggs Murphy had manhandled her the night before.

I said, "Did Sally say where she was going?"

"I didn't ask. If somebody wants to find her, it's better I don't know."

"Wherever Sally ends up, I hope it's not back on the street. You should quit too, instead of wearing yourself out for bloodsucking pimps."

Chantal gave me another long look. "I can't figure you out. You act hard-ass, but you're a big softie at heart," she said, adding, "A girl pounding the pavement, no way she can make it on her own. No way, José."

She stood there, grinning at me. That's why she was a great hooker: she was capable, resourceful, happy in spite of everything. Why wasn't she selling real estate, managing a dress shop? "Get off the street, Chantal," I said, giving her hand a squeeze. "You're smart, you could be a winner at anything you wanted."

"You kidding? I quit school in Grade 8, been hawking my ass since I was 15. Besides, I like hooking, the hours suit me. Can you see me behind a counter, or sweating in a laundry?" She shook her head. "Sally was different. She was scared every time she got into a car with a john. Somebody beat her up six months ago."

"I know. That bastard she was working for."

"Oh, sure," said Chantal. "Cal beat her up all the time, but that was just business. She got clobbered by a bad date too." Chantal's expression clouded for a moment before she brightened. "Anyway, she's gone, who knows where? Maybe she went back to the Kootenays to be with her mom. Sally had this picket-fence dream. I hope it comes true."

"You got a dream, Chantal?"

"Sure, Silas. I keep dreaming you'll come cruising by sometime in your Chevy, give me the high sign. We'll have a few drinks at Laurel Point. Hold hands and watch the moon come up over the Inner Harbour. Then you'll take me upstairs and I'll give you my in-house special. I'll even buy the drinks."

She grinned at me. I grinned back.

Chantal said, "You'd be getting 500 bucks' worth, Silas."

I pretended to be mystified.

"You don't fool me," she said. "Lou gave Sally and me money this morning, and I know who it came from."

She walked off, smiling, holding her head up, a gutsy broad.

I let myself into my office and switched on the answering machine. There was a message from my sister. Canadian Blood Services wanted more of my blood. A message from somebody named Eunice asking me to call, but leaving no number. I didn't know anybody named Eunice. Then there was a brief insulting monologue from somebody who spoke street and called me a chicken-fat motherfucker.

I phoned Mallory, Victoria's police chief, and asked him about travel expenses for a possible trip to Seattle. Mallory was unusually cooperative. He agreed to the expenses and only raised his voice a little bit when he nixed my request for an unmarked car. Mallory told me that the police budget didn't run to cars for lowly neighbourhood cops. I was supposed to walk, get to know people, and if I pushed my luck he'd shut down my whole operation.

Next I telephoned my sister. Sis gave me her number one lecture: how stupid I was not to settle down with a good woman. Why couldn't I be smart like her and her industrious husband, Dick?

Dick was a fisherman who moonlighted as a house painter when he wasn't trolling for salmon off the west coast. Every year Dick and Linda spent two weeks at Qualicum Beach in their state-of-the-art camper, relaxing in the shade with gin and tonics. And later in the year, another two weeks in Las Vegas playing the dollar slots and watching Wayne Newton and Celine Dion. In a steadily rising voice Sis told me that she and Dick had a quarter of a million dollars in their savings plan already and weren't even 40 years old yet.

I could just imagine her at the other end of the line, chest heaving, eyes flashing, as she said, "And what do you have to say about that?"

"Nothing," I said in my humble-pie voice.

"That's what I figured," she said. "No wonder I get mad at you!" She slammed the phone down.

Maybe she was right. What was wrong with me? Why couldn't I settle down with one woman? Why couldn't I enjoy lining up outside the Bellagio in the Nevada desert with Sis and Dick, waiting to see Wayne Newton? Maybe I should see a shrink or something, investigate the reasons why I had absolutely no desire to sit in a trailer park for two weeks in the shade of my very own awning, shooting the breeze with ramblers from Oklahoma. If I had a million bucks in savings plans, what the hell would I do with it — buy a camper? Shit. Maybe when I was old.

I went home.

HOME IS A TWO-ROOM cabin on the beach. I built it with my own hands. Chief Alphonse selected its location. There is a monument nearby commemorating the spot where our ancestors greeted Manuel Quimper — the first European to set foot on local shores.

Quimper arrived in a great white ship, stayed for a couple of days, then sailed away, leaving the Coast Salish people in undisturbed possession for another century or so. Quimper is supposed to have buried a bottle on the beach somewhere. It allegedly contains documents claiming the whole country for the Spanish Crown. Sir James Douglas arrived next. He claimed everything for the British Crown. Now that we've found out what Canadian real estate is worth, we Natives are claiming it all back.

Everything that a Coast Salish chief does has symbolic overtones, so the location of my house has a deeply significant meaning, if only I could figure it out. I was the first Indian in these parts to work for the White justice system. Maybe the chief chose this site as a compliment, maybe not. In any case, I like it here. There's no hot water unless I light my wood stove. My outhouse is a classic one-holer half-hidden beneath a big cedar tree. But the house is wired for electricity. One wall is covered with bookshelves, racks for my blues records, and an outmoded stereo system. From my sleeping room I can see the Warrior longhouse. It sits in a grove of fir trees, with a moss-covered roof and black-and-white killer-whale paintings covering its walls. From my front room I can see the Olympic Mountains, 30 miles away.

I showered, then pulled on jeans, sneakers and a red-checkered logger's shirt. For my intended overnighter in Seattle I packed a canvas shoulder bag with razor, toothbrush, a change of underwear and a Gore-Tex shell in case it rained. It's always raining in Seattle.

I thought about making an omelette. In my dinky refrigerator I found some mouldy cheddar, half an onion that had been in there long enough to delaminate, three eggs and an open can of sardines that smelled a bit funny. Come to think of it, the whole refrigerator smelled bad. I should put deodorant in there. What did people use, baking soda? On the bottom shelf, a full carton of milk had turned solid. I closed the fridge door. Then, with a sigh, I opened it again, grabbed the milk, dumped it into the sink and rinsed it down the drain. I was thinking about Sis, that's what it was — sometimes her lectures scrambled my brains.

The next ferry to Seattle left Victoria in 45 minutes. I could still catch it if I hustled.

TWO HOURS LATER I was devouring a ferry hamburger. Whidbey Island drifted by. Mount Baker's snow-covered peak gradually emerged from the heat haze blanketing Puget Sound. A fellow passenger pointed to a pod of killer whales. A dozen of the big mammals, led by an orca with a dorsal fin as big as a windsurfer sail, plowed alongside the ship for 10 minutes before veering off toward Port Townsend.

Matters great and small nibbled at the edges of my mind. What kind of double-entry moral bookkeeping had led a B.C. Crown prosecutor to railroad Jimmy Scow into jail? The evidence tying Scow to Harry Cunliffe's murder consisted of 1) Charles Service testifying that he had seen an Aboriginal man driving a florist's van away from Ribblesdale and 2) shaky testimony from a snitch who told a cock-and-bull yarn about Scow's alleged jailhouse confession. The testimony of a career crook and known liar that Scow had vigorously denied. But the Crown prosecutor did a Johnnie Cochran number on a jury that bought the whole package, and Scow drew five bullets.

I'd been ordered to find Marcia Hunt, but at that point in my investigation, I was more interested in settling the Cunliffe murder. One of the many puzzling aspects about it was that the thieves had stolen half a dozen so-so paintings — landscapes, a still life and a nice watercolour of a fishing smack leaving an English harbour. But they had ignored a very valuable Emily Carr oil painting. Why? The likeliest explanation was that the crooks didn't know good art when they saw it. None of the stolen items had been recovered. The murderers had either dumped them in a panic after the killing or had … What?

Another small anomaly: Why had Effie the maid chosen to quit working at the Hunt mansion at this particular time? I dislike coincidences. Somehow, a grand equation was being worked out. With the right formula, Harry Cunliffe's murder, Marcia Hunt's disappearance and Effie's departure would integrate into a perfect whole.

In Seattle I would try to get a lead on Marcia Hunt. I had one clue — the postcard mailed to Dr. Cunliffe. The card showed a picture of a dance band, the RayBeams Orchestra. Marcia had been a pianist; maybe she was playing in a bar somewhere?

FOR 10,000 YEARS my ancestors have been crossing and recrossing Juan de Fuca Strait without passports. A U.S. immigration inspector took one look at me and waved me through the barriers. In the old days we came to wage war against the Natives of Puget Sound — enslaving their women and killing their men. Now we come to watch the Mariners.

I took a cab from the Seattle ferry terminal to a public library near Pioneer Square. The reference librarian was a thin woman close to retirement age named Miss Brighton. Miss (please don't call me Ms!) Brighton had grey hair twisted into a coil and pinned on top of her head with tortoise-shell pins. She had grey eyes, grey skin and blue granny glasses perched on the tip of her nose. One stiff Seattle wind and she'd be swept away. She looked harried and despondent, but when I told her that I was looking for a missing girl, she cheered up and we searched the city directories together.

I was looking for information on the GoodTimes Club — the place the RayBeams played in 1980. We found no listing for the club in any recent directory, but Miss Brighton went into the stacks and we checked out some old ones. The GoodTimes Club was listed in the 1982 and 1983 directories — it was a basement bar on Water Street. But we drew a blank on the RayBeams Orchestra. Nothing. There had never been a listing anywhere. I wasn't surprised. The RayBeams had probably been a pickup band — a group of musicians who got together for a season, played a few gigs, then drifted apart.

Seattle has several long-established booking agents and music promoters, and the Musicians' League also had offices in town. I noted likely telephone numbers, thanked Miss Brighton for her help and taxied across town to Water Street to check out the GoodTimes Club. But it had vanished: in its place was a gleaming 50-storey office tower.

The Elliott Bay Bookshop was only five minutes away. I hiked over there and went down to the basement coffee shop. The daily feature was Kona Gold. I bought a cup, settled at a table in a corner and used my cellphone to call the Musicians' League. Zilch. The girl who answered knew nothing and was interested in nothing.

I said, "May I speak with the business agent?"

"Nah. The business agent is at a conference, can't be reached."

"What are the business agent's regular office hours?"

She said indignantly, "Hey. What's your name, mister? You a paid-up union member or some smartass looking to stir things up?"

I thanked her and started working through my list of booking agents. They take calls politely, 24 hours a day, but nobody knew a thing about the RayBeams. I spent nearly an hour making calls and still nobody could help me. Nobody, that is, until a woman with a voice like Laura Bush's said the band was something that Ray Smith might have dreamed up.

"Ray Smith?"

"Ray's an old retired guy, plays tenor sax and clarinet. Sometimes he sits in with Dixieland jazz bands when he isn't laid up with arthritis. You might check with the Banjo Club."

I phoned the Banjo Club and was told that they were open that night for dinner and dancing. I said, "Do you know whether Ray Smith is playing tonight?"

"Yeah, probably, because today's Friday. Ray Smith generally comes in on weekends. Who's asking?"

"I'll come over and introduce myself," I said.

THE BANJO CLUB was a low-ceilinged room with a horseshoe-shaped bar. There was a small space for dancing and a foot-high stage for the band. A sign on the piano announced that tonight's band was the Seattle Stompers. Photographs of Louis Armstrong, Bix Beiderbecke and 50 other jazz greats decorated the walls. Lighted candles stood on tables draped with checkered cloths. The room's air conditioner was an open door facing a back lane.

A good-looking woman in a yellow shirt was polishing glasses behind the bar. I approved of everything I could see above the counter. She was brushing her blonde-streaked bangs with one hand now; the other rested on her hip as she said something to a drunk.

The drunk was flipping a quarter with his thumb, catching it in his left hand and checking to see whether it came down heads or tails. Then he flipped it again.

It was the happy hour, but nobody looked happy except the bartender. Two construction workers in hard hats stood at the end of the bar, eating salted peanuts and watching the Seattle Mariners taking a beating on the big screen. In the background, Louis Armstrong was singing "St. James Infirmary Blues."

I sat on a stool at the counter and ordered rum and coke with a twist of lime over ice.

The bartender said, "You're Canadian, right? I just spoke to you on the telephone." A lapel pin said her name was Barb.

"That's right, Barb," I said. "How did you know I was Canadian?"

"Easy. Your accent is different, for one thing. For another, if you were an American you'd call that a Cuba Libre." She placed the drink in front of me and leaned on her elbows.

"But if I was a real Canadian I'd have ordered rye and ginger. It's the national drink."

"You're real, mister," she said, eyeing me up and down. "That'll be four bucks. You want to run a tab?"

"I may not be staying long," I said, putting a five spot on the counter.

"Coulda fooled me." She took my money to the cash register and rang up the sale. "Guy comes in packing an overnight bag, I figure he's here indefinitely."

"That's what I like. A good-looking woman with brains. Uses five-syllable words. In-def-in-ite-ly. You working your way through college?"

"Not me. I'm working my way through my second alimony settlement. Two losers I met in this very bar, sitting exactly where you're sitting now."

Barb dropped my change on the counter and settled herself beneath a neon Stroh's sign. I watched her fold her arms, and when our eyes met she smiled easily. "You want me to stash that bag where people won't fall over it?"

I passed my bag across the bar. "You've had two bad marriages. Want to try for third time lucky?"

"Not until I know you better."

"Hey, Barbie!" a slurred voice said. "You working or not? Get your ass over here, we're dyin' a' thirst."

It was one of the hard hats. Barb rolled her eyes, gave me a menu, switched on a smile and walked down the bar.

Louis was coming to the end of "Infirmary Blues," laying the dead gambler out with a 20-dollar gold piece on his watch chain so the boys would know he'd died standing pat.

Checking the menu, I learned that the club specialty was a Bessie Smith steak, but they had a Billie-Burger, a Nat King Coleslaw, a New Orleans patty melt. They were also plugging a Benny Goodman Surprise for dessert, and I knew what it would be — two scoops of vanilla ice cream with a stick of black licorice.

Two middle-aged couples came in and took a table next to the dance floor. The women wore elaborate silk flapper dresses, silk stockings with garters, and carried umbrellas decorated with bits of coloured ribbon. The men had on straw boaters and elbow garters. The drunk with the fedora was crawling around the floor now, looking for his quarter.

When Barb came back I said, "Are you expecting rain?"

Barb pursed her lips as she watched the women with umbrellas. "They got a deal here," she explained. "When the band leader figures everybody's drunk enough, he breaks into 'When the Saints Come Marching In.' The women in flapper outfits parade around the room, twirling umbrellas and kicking up their heels, showing off their garters and lacy knickers. Guys follow, mugging with their hats. It's a Dixieland tradition, don't ask me why." She pointed beneath the bar. "I've got the company umbrella stashed there. When the procession starts rolling, I have to join in. It's in my contract."

"Fun, eh?" I said.

"You bet," she said, with good-humoured resignation. She watched the drunk find his quarter and reseat himself. "You want another rum and coke?"

I shook my head. "Gimme a Cuba Libre this time."

A waitress dressed like a flapper appeared and started taking orders at the tables.

Barb leaned closer. "You're a cop, aren't you?"

"Yeah."

"Vancouver?"

"Victoria PD."

"You going to make life hard for Ray Smith?"

"Just the opposite. If he can tell me what I need to know, there might be money in it."

"A reward?"

"Could be."

"I hope you're not trouble. Ray is coming to the end of the road and it's been a bumpy ride. Time hasn't treated him well. He's got this arthritis that acts up so he can't play much anymore. Even at his peak, Ray was never exactly a household name."

"Just a working musician."

"That's right, a working stiff like the rest of us. What did you say your name was?"

"Silas Seaweed." I looked into her eyes. "If I'm gonna make a proposal later, I'll need to know your name."

"Barbara Scarborough. Awful, right? Kids at school used to call me Barb Scarb, made me sound like an automobile part."

"Ever think of changing it?"

"I did, twice. One of my husbands was called Yastremkowich."

"Lucky his name wasn't Dwyer," I said.

She grinned. "Barb Dwyer? That's nearly as cute as Silas Seaweed."

It was my turn to grin. I said, "There's a hundred R. Smiths in the book. You know Ray's number?"

Barb shook her head and moved away to take another order.

I liked her already. Liked her easy wit and the way she didn't get mad when the hard hat told her to get her ass moving. And I loved the way she'd put her head to one side when she was being droll about the company umbrella. I liked her because she cared enough to worry about a tired old musician.

Barb uncapped a Miller Lite. A man sat next to me and she placed the beer on the counter in front of him. Without a word the man picked up the bottle and held it admiringly for a moment. Barb and I watched him empty the bottle without taking it away from his lips for air. The drinker was a skinny dude of about 35, dressed in a red-and-white striped shirt and white pants, with a straw boater and white loafers. His Adam's apple bobbed up and down as he swallowed.

"Man, I needed that," drawled the newcomer, smacking his lips. He looked at the menu in front of me and said, "Stranger, my name's Hugh Baines. I wouldn't feel right if I didn't warn you about the food here."

"Shut up, Hugh," Barb laughed. "The food's great and you know it."

"They've got a Delta Blues sauce here that's really something. I use it to remove paint from my boat," said Baines. "But if you like it hot … "

Barb lifted her eyes in sardonic prayer and smiled. "Hugh's a musician. Plays piano with the Seattle Stompers."

"I don't play the piano here, no sir," Baines said, picking up his second beer. "I beat the hell out of it. I murder it with my foot on the loud pedal all night long. People in this place like their tunes *loud*. They're hoping that one night I'm gonna pound the 88s so hard the frame will collapse and ivory keys will fly across the room." He grinned at me. "You a music lover, or do you like Dixieland?"

"I think 'Gimme a Pig's Foot and a Bottle of Beer' is the greatest song ever written."

"Me too. Let me buy you a drink?"

"Rum and coke," I said.

"Give the gentleman his heart's desire," said Baines.

Smiling, Barb reached for the rum bottle.

"My name's Silas Seaweed. Thanks for the drink. I'm looking forward to hearing you play."

We shook hands and Baines stood up, holding his beer. "Glad to meet you, Silas, but I've gotta circulate, keep everybody smiling. You sticking around for when the dancing starts?"

"Sure. See if I can borrow an umbrella, join in the fun."

Baines ambled away and sat with a foursome. The place was filling up.

"Nice guy," I said.

Barb nodded. "He's part owner of this place. When he isn't playing piano he's an aerospace engineer with Boeing."

The hard hats had gone home. Now the TV was running a videotape of the Hollywood Greats playing "Calico." A starlet with a cigarette in one hand and a microphone in the other was enthusiastically belting out the lyrics.

Barb nodded toward the entrance and said, "Here comes Ray."

An elderly black man wearing a black derby hat, starched white shirt and black pants limped in slowly, favouring his right leg. He carried a clarinet case and lowered himself carefully into a seat at the back of the room. He mopped his face with a large red handkerchief. He looked tired, old.

"What's Ray's drink?" I asked.

"Diet Pepsi," said Barb, pouring one. "Take this over to him and introduce yourself before the place is too full. You won't be able to hear yourself speak in here soon."

RAY SMITH TOOK his time before answering my question, lighting a cigarette and leaning back in his chair with a thoughtful expression. "Sure, I remember Marcia," he said at last. "She was the sort of girl you don't forget." He smiled. "You ain't the first guy been looking. There was another detective came after her, a long time ago."

"Patrick Coulton?"

Smith's gaze turned inward to the past. "Yeah, that's it. Coulton said Marcia's daddy wanted to see her."

"Marcia's daddy still wants to see her. If he doesn't get his wish soon, it'll be too late."

"That right?" said Smith, giving me a hard but not unfriendly look.

I said, "I'd be grateful if you could help me find her."

Absently, he stroked the swollen knuckle joints on his left hand. "What if she don't want to be found? Marcia deliberately turned her back on her family, didn't want no part of it. That's what I told the Coulton guy."

"I can promise you this. It wouldn't hurt Marcia to be found."

"Maybe, but like I said, I ain't talking."

I handed over a photograph. It showed Marcia Hunt posed for the camera with Frank Harkness. When Smith saw it, he nodded. "That's her. How a nice girl like Marcia ever got tied in with that biker is one of nature's mysteries."

"Marcia's family didn't think much of Frank either."

"That figures. But for some reason, Marcia was in love with Frank, crazy about the bastard." Ray shook his head. "That girl, she was something. She could play the piano, sing like Peggy Lee."

"Did she ever sing in a band?"

"You kidding? She *sang*. She played piano with me and my orchestra. The RayBeams we called ourselves. Before she came along we were nowhere. Just five guys hustling weekend gigs in taverns, high-school dances. Marcia filled in one night when our regular piano player took sick. Soon as we heard her, the other guy was history. Afterwards, the band took off like a rocket. We were in demand, played all the fancy lounges, the lodges." Ray smiled, forgetting his arthritis as he remembered old times. "I trimmed the band down to a quartet. Marcia on piano and vocals, me on tenor sax and clarinet, Tubby Brown on drums. Bob Kessler played bass. Yeah, we were a team, all right. Marcia was a dream come true for an old hacker like me, but it was too good to last. If she'd stayed, we could have gone straight to the top, to Hollywood even."

"What happened?"

"What happened was that Frank Harkness had this formula for speed," said the old man bitterly. "He used to brew the stuff in his bathroom and sell it on the street or trade it for smack. Also, he was feeding smack to Marcia." Ray scowled. "Goddam tragedy. Another Janis Joplin, see? It was cool to be high all the time, and she was also doing this rebellion number on her parents. She got so wired that she couldn't play straight. What made it worse, she was pregnant. Pretty soon we couldn't rely on her."

The room was full now, crowded with noisy beer drinkers. People were jammed three-deep around the bar. A waitress in a flapper outfit came over and asked us if we'd mind sharing our table.

I said, "Give me another minute with Mr. Smith first," and leaned forward, speaking urgently now. "Mr. Smith, if Marcia had a child, it couldn't lose by meeting its grandfather."

"Oh, Marcia had the baby, all right. Little girl, cute as a button. I saw her a few times."

"Help her. That child deserves to get what's rightly hers."

"You talking about an inheritance?"

"Yes. If Marcia doesn't get it, or that baby, most of her family's money will go to charity."

He looked around the room as if for a portent. "I gave my word, friend. Guy breaks his word, what's left?"

"You gave your word to a strung-out woman, 20 years ago. Marcia wasn't even making sense then. I think it'd be very ethical to help me find her. She and her child will gain by it. You'd gain too. There's a reward for information."

The old man nodded, eyebrows lifted. "Yeah? You may be right. I dunno."

His resolve was weakening so I kept pushing. "The other thing is, Marcia could be dead. It's one thing to get mad at your folks, run away after an argument. Another thing to stay away forever. But Marcia's child could still be alive."

Ray shrugged. "Let me think about it, okay?"

The band broke into its opening number, "Swanee." The people who wanted to sit with Ray stood nearby, waiting.

I got up from the table. "Okay if I check with you later? I'm going back to the bar now."

"Sure. Hugh Baines will ask me to play a few numbers after, when the band takes a break. Maybe we can talk then."

THE BANJO CLUB regulars were mostly middle-aged, but they knew how to kick up their heels. They crowded the dance floor all night, doing '50s jive, '30s Charleston and fancy two-steps I had never seen before. As Hugh Baines had promised me, the music was loud and the beat was fast. Waitresses served non-stop as the band worked through its Dixie repertoire. After a brief intermission, Baines introduced Ray Smith and some other guest performers, and the regular musicians took a breather. The new band broke into "Melancholy Baby." Ray was good, squeezing clear sweet notes out of his horn. The crowd, grateful for a slower number, again filled the floor. Somebody turned the house lights down. Watching, I felt a tap on my shoulder.

Barb stood right behind me. "I need a change from pouring drinks. Can you dance, big fella?"

"You bet." I took her hand and we went onto the floor. She closed her eyes, rested her cheek against my shoulder, and we held each other close, matching our steps effortlessly as if we'd been dancing together for years. We kept holding even after Ray finished his number. It was there, that old magic. I knew that she felt it too. During the applause her arm tightened around my shoulder for a second before she pulled away.

"Gotta go." Her voice was low, husky.

"One more," I said, still holding her around the waist.

"I'm a working girl. They need me at the bar."

"I need you here," I said as Ray, urged on by the enthusiastic crowd, began to play "A Sleepy Lagoon."

Barbara smiled; we danced again. I said, "If I let you go now, can we continue this later?"

She nodded.

By now it was standing room only. Ray left the stage to loud applause. I ordered a beer. Hot from dancing, I drank half of it before looking around. Ray was not at his table. I crossed to where he had been sitting. People at the table looked up. I said, "What happened to Ray?"

Somebody said, "Aw, he went home. His rheumatics is acting up. Guy's great, ain't he, playing like that with his problems?"

I didn't wait to reply. I brushed through the crowd to the exit.

The street was empty in every direction. To my left was a row of stores with boarded-up windows, but that direction led into an industrial area. There were more lights and activities the other way, so I sprinted to the corner. Down the street, rock music blared from a tavern. Patrons had spilled outside and were drinking beer on the sidewalk. Ray Smith came into view as he passed through the crowd and turned another corner. I was panting when I caught up with him.

Ray stopped walking and we gazed at each other across the chasm of age and experience and male loneliness. His eyes were empty, and suddenly, I didn't have anything to say.

"I been thinking about that stuff, all that old misery," he said finally. "I just didn't want to hassle with it."

"You're the only real lead I've got. I guess I'm pushing you too hard."

"Yeah, man, I can't blame you for that. You've got a living to make." Ray switched the clarinet case from one hand to the other. "The thing is, I can't tell you much about Marcia, even if I wanted to."

Ray resumed his walk. I fell into step beside him. "Funny," he mused. "Stuff that didn't bother me none when I was younger, it keeps me awake nights now. Conscience. It's a bastard, ain't it?"

"Man does what he thinks is right at the time," I said. "Looking back, you think about what you could have done better. That stuff can drive you crazy if you dwell on it."

"You tell me how a man can stop dwelling on it? I get to tossing and turning with my aches, and the pain in my mind, the pain in my joints, I dunno which is worse."

"I tell you something," I said, and pointed to his clarinet case. "You can play that thing."

He smiled at that. "Yeah, I'm starting to get it, after 60 years. It's in my fingers, the music. I think of the note and there it is."

"I used to go to blues clubs in Chicago, years ago," I said, walking slowly to match the old man's halting stride. "South Halstead Street. You know it?"

"Know it? Brother, I *lived* it. Knowed every one of them rooms. I gigged with B. B. King, Howlin' Wolf, Muddy. I go way back, man. I sat in with all them dudes." Ray's face softened. "Them niggers give you a hard time in Chicago, an Injun guy from Canada?"

"Nothing serious. They knew I was a music lover."

"Man need to be serious, he mess with you," said Ray, eyeing my shoulders.

We came to a side-street hotel. Ray stopped walking. It was a roach joint, one step up from a homeless shelter, and it was named The Astoria. To enter you passed through a battered door sandwiched between a taxi office and a newsstand. A sign said: ROOMS $18. TRANSIENTS WELCOME. Visible behind a glass panel was a grubby, pint-sized hall and a flight of uncarpeted stairs.

"This is it," said Ray in a thin voice. "I get tired of crime on TV, I just look through my window, watch the real thing."

"Nice meeting you, Ray." I found a 20 in my billfold and handed it over.

Ray looked at the money but he didn't take it. "I got something for you, mister, but not much."

He turned his back on the hotel entrance as if hating the sight. "Marcia, the last I seen of her, she was living at Point Matlock. You know where that is?"

I shook my head.

"South of town," he explained. "A little old army fort. Bunch of artillery installations and houses was built for the military, years ago. In them days the government was worried the Russians would come down from Alaska, claim the whole coast. Then when the military stopped being worried of that, they took their guns away but left the houses. Had a nice view, if you like water and seabirds and logs spread out on the beaches."

Ray put his clarinet case down and massaged his swollen knuckles absently. "Marcia had this house on the cliffs, her closest neighbour was 200 yards away. Whether she owned the place or just moved in without asking nobody, I don't know. She made herself at home, her and the baby. From Marcia's front room you could see the Point Matlock lighthouse. Nighttime, the beams would shine through the windows, through the curtains. Light up the whole place. In the winter, the foghorn, it sounded so loud it like to shake the house foundations. But Marcia loved it there. She musta done, she stayed there for a long time." He smiled at some memory, then held out his hand horizontally, palm facing down. I took it gently, feeling his knobbly knuckles hot under my fingers.

Ray said, "I'm busy right now, got things to do, a little business.

You want to come back in a couple of days? Get a car, we take a nice drive. I'll show it to you, Marcia's house."

"Today's Friday. I can come back any time that suits you."

"Lessee." Ray pondered. "You be along here Monday, not too early, sometime after lunch. Okay?"

"I'll be here."

A tall man dressed in rags lurched out of an alley and staggered toward us. He walked like somebody crossing uneven ground. His rheumy, streaming eyes, sunk deep in a ruined face, had a vacant look and he carried both arms before him, raised like a sleepwalker's.

Ray picked up the clarinet case and watched the rummy pass by. "My neighbour," he said, with a harsh laugh. "Saving a place for me, a nice soft piece of cobblestone for when I can't afford the Astoria no more."

I said, "Ray, you're going to help Marcia, and when you think back on this in a few years, you won't be sorry." He turned his head and reached for the doorknob.

Ray tightened his lips. "You got that right, friend. A few years, there won't be nothing troubling this old turkey. Nothing at all." He shuffled inside the hotel and laboured painfully up the grubby stairs, out of sight. He hadn't taken the $20.

I stood on the sidewalk. What was I going to do now — pick up my bag at the Banjo Club, go home? Or make the moves on Barb Scarb? Maybe she was tired of it. Guys like me coming on non-stop. Lounge hustlers with their wisecracks, on the make, kidding around but hoping for a little sack time at the end of all the kidding. But I remembered how it had been, holding her on the dance floor. She fitted just right, head on my shoulder. Yeah. It would be nice. Wait for the bar to close, go somewhere together for a nightcap. Then what? We take a cab to her place and make love. Afterward I shake her hand, thank her for a lovely evening, go back to Victoria? Barb's here in Seattle polishing glasses and wondering what's going on, is he going to call?

I went back to the Banjo Club and ordered a beer. The band had gone. The only noise came from the chef, still rattling pans in his kitchen. Instead of pouring my drink, Barb pulled her apron off and leaned on the bar. She blushed a little and it made her prettier; our faces were about four inches apart. "There's this place I know," she said, in a low voice.

"It's right around the corner from my apartment. They serve Szechuan food."

"That I like. I'm not crazy about the atmosphere, though."

"You'll love the Blue Yangtze," she said. "It's candlelit, and they're big on Billie Holiday, Django Reinhardt and the Hot Five. Think you could handle that?"

I knew I could handle that.

Over dinner we talked inconsequentially and held hands and were the restaurant's last customers. The woman who had served us stood smiling in the shadows.

Barb had a little townhouse on a well-travelled street near Lake Washington. It was toward two in the morning and Seattle's sidewalks were shiny after a sudden rainstorm. Barb was wearing patent-leather pumps and we stepped carefully under the street lights to avoid puddles. When we entered her place she turned on all the lights, took a bottle of Gewürztraminer from her refrigerator and left it on a side table with two glasses and a corkscrew. While she was in the bathroom I opened the wine and engaged in the usual guessing game. Had I misinterpreted her signs? Were Barb's hopes and thoughts and intentions similar to mine? I filled the glasses and took a sip.

She came out of the bathroom and switched on her radio. The radio was tuned to KPLU. Sam Taylor was playing "Harlem Nocturne." It's a song of loneliness and despair and Taylor's rendering of it almost overwhelms me every time I hear it.

Barb was looking at me now with an expression I couldn't decipher. But whatever it was, she smiled and picked up her glass and said, "To us."

After we drank I took the glass from Barb's hands and put it with mine on the side table and put my arms around her. She hung her head from some reflexive modesty so I put my hand under her chin and lifted her head. She opened her mouth and I kissed her and somehow the buttons of her blouse came open and there was more of her to taste and feel and touch. She was trembling when I looked into her eyes. She smiled at me and that's when I knew she felt the same way I did.

CHAPTER FOUR

When I got back to Victoria there was still no word from or about Jimmy Scow. I used my key to let myself into my office, but I suspected Constable Halvorsen had been there before me. I had left the toilet seat up and now it was down. I spent a couple of hours lolling about, ostensibly reading reports and answering e-mails, but what I was actually doing was combatting a vague feeling that I'd let Barb down, behaved badly, taken advantage of somebody decent.

At ten o'clock I grew tired of twisting knives into my vitals and salting the wounds. In a fit of moral fervour I shoved files and forms and other police bumf aside, took up a sheet of lined paper and a Pilot Fineliner pen and had just written "Dear Barbara" when the phone rang. It was Dr. Cunliffe.

He said, "Morning, Silas. How did you make out in Seattle?"

How did he know I'd been in Seattle?

I said, "Not bad. I'm making some progress."

"*Some* progress?"

"Who told you I'd been in Seattle?"

"I'm not exactly sure. I think Charles Service might have mentioned it."

I scratched my head with the wrong end of the pen.

Dr. Cunliffe said, "I'd like to get together with you sometime, explore a few ideas. How about coming to my place?"

"Fine, I'd enjoy that. Today?"

"Not today. I have hospital rounds at the Royal Jubilee. Maybe tomorrow. Thanks, Silas. I'll call you."

Dr. Cunliffe hung up.

My most important priority at that point was finding Jimmy Scow. I wanted him to know that I had reopened the Cunliffe file. I wanted to ask him to forget about trying to exact personal justice and to give the White man's law one more chance.

I stared at *Dear Barbara* for a couple of minutes, wrestling with troublesome ideas concerning love and death and effigies. Then I had another brainwave. I went out.

JOE MCNAUGHT OPENED the envelope that I had just given him, gazed at the contents and laid it all down on his desk. With a long sigh he swung around in his swivel chair and looked out of his window. McNaught was a burly man, and when he spoke his voice was slow and suspicious.

"A thousand dollars?" he said at last in tones of incredulity. "*You're* donating $1,000 to my church?"

"The money isn't a donation," I said. "It's a bribe. You can keep the money if you tell me where I can find Jimmy Scow."

"Funny thing, Silas. I never knew you were a Christian."

"I'm not a Christian. I'm Salish."

"Salish isn't religion. It's pagan witch superstition."

I don't mind being kidded, but I wasn't going to be kidded about that. I didn't answer him. He swivelled around and stared at me. I still didn't say anything.

McNaught pushed a button on his desk. A young volunteer poked his head in at the door. McNaught said, "Ask Jimmy Scow to come in here."

The volunteer's face registered extreme inner confusion. "Jimmy Scow?" he said in a puzzled voice. "I've never even heard of him."

"Thanks," McNaught said.

The volunteer departed. McNaught put both hands on the arms of his chair and heaved himself upright. He gave me a long sideways look. "See? Nobody here knows anything about Jimmy. If you need him, you'll have to look elsewhere."

"I spoke to a man in the kitchen here, couple of days ago. He knew Jimmy Scow."

McNaught shrugged, and I had counted to 10 before he added slyly, "Can I keep the money anyway?"

"You can't think of a single thing that'll help me find Jimmy Scow?"

McNaught looked at the envelope and sighed. "Well, there *might* be something. Somebody did say they'd seen him fuelling a boat at the Canoe Cove marina."

"When?"

"It's a complete blank."

"See," I said. "There's no telling what a Christian can do when he tries hard. So keep the money, Joe. If you hear anything else, give me a call."

"Go with God," McNaught said. "A thousand dollars, that's extremely generous. It'll keep this mission going for two whole days."

I WENT TO my office and checked my answering machine. A man with a fake street-jiver voice was now calling me a candy-assed chicken-fat motherfucker. Brian Gottlieb wanted to talk to me about Native artifacts. Detective Sergeant Bernie Tapp wanted to talk to me about a robbery in Waddington Alley. Somebody called Fred was interested in the reward that I'd advertised in the *Times Colonist*.

I called Fred first. A woman with a tentative voice answered the phone and said, "Hello?"

I identified myself. She made me wait and put her hand over the mouthpiece. Twenty seconds later she came back on and said, "This reward. How much money we talking about?"

I said, "It's negotiable."

She said, "You better not be jerking people around."

I said, "Look, I'm busy. If somebody has news and wants to sell it, let's talk directly."

She grunted deep in her throat. I overheard a muffled conversation between her and somebody else. Then she said, "Can you meet Fred in the coffee shop at Fisherman's Wharf in an hour?"

"Yes. What does Fred look like?"

"Like a biker," she said, slamming the phone down.

Boots clattered and Denise Halvorsen came in. The edges of her mouth were down. I looked up from my desk and said, "Hi, Denise, good to see you. How are you enjoying the foot-leather patrols?"

"We need to talk, Sergeant."

"Okay. I've got a few minutes to spare. Let's go to Lou's for coffee. I'll tell you a few things you need to know about these streets."

"No thanks," she said. "No offence, but I think your MO needs an overhaul, frankly."

Taken aback I said, "I may be out of date, but nobody can say I'm not results oriented. If I wanted routine I'd still be on the detective squad."

She let out her breath, making an impatient, angry noise. "Results oriented?" She planted her feet wide and put both hands on her hips. "If you think that punching guys out in back alleys, intimidating taxpayers, and socializing with known prostitutes is the way to get meaningful results in this neighbourhood, you're wrong."

"Is that right?"

"Yes, Sergeant, that's right!" She was leaning forward, her pretty head poised above me like a hammer over a nail.

I tried to ignore the contours of her body and said, "Where did you learn about policing? Cop college?"

"No!" she barked. "*Police* college, where scientific research shows … "

"Forget other people's research and do your own," I said. "First thing you need to do, Halvorsen, is put your old ideas away and get to know real people." I pointed through the window. "In this neighbourhood, a traditional cop affects some people the way a red flag affects a bull."

"Bull?" she snorted. "Bull, Sergeant, with all due respect, is what you're talking."

"Another thing," I said. "Your face is dirty."

She stamped out of the office and locked herself in the bathroom.

I opened the office safe, retrieved the Ruger Blackhawk I had taken off Jiggs Murphy and put it in my pocket.

DETECTIVE SERGEANT BERNIE TAPP was waiting for me at Lou's. Tapp is a tough-looking guy with hair a quarter of an inch long, an 18-inch neck and eyes the colour of coal. He has the same hard leanness as men who chop down trees for a living. He was wearing a white shirt with the top button undone, a maroon necktie that had been slackened off and a pair of green twill pants. His red golf jacket had burn marks on both pockets. The first thing he did was repeat some of the bad things Constable Halvorsen had been saying about me.

"All this discipline," I said. "What happened to *esprit de corps*? It beats me."

Tapp gave me a gloomy look and began to fish around in his coat pockets. Dragging out a stubby pipe, he pressed the ash down with a calloused thumb and rammed fresh tobacco into the bowl. "So you don't know a thing about a recent mugging in Waddington Alley, Silas?"

"Would I lie to you?"

"You'd lie to your grandmother." Tapp struck a kitchen match with his thumbnail, lit his pipe and puffed smoke in my eyes.

I batted the smoke with my hand and said, "I don't know why you're worried. A pair of pimp-traffickers get hijacked and one of them is roughed up. What do you care?"

"I don't care if they get roughed up, pal. I don't even care if they get rubbed *out*. It's just that I don't like unsolved mysteries."

"Speaking of unsolved mysteries, Bernie, what's the latest on the Cunliffe murder? You making any progress there?"

"Brazening it out, eh?" said Tapp, showing his teeth in a wolfish grin. "Think you'll change the subject, take my mind off Jiggs Murphy."

"Jiggs Murphy?" I said, putting on a blank look.

"Yeah, Jiggs Murphy, Alex Cal's driver. The guy you mugged and robbed in Waddington Alley."

He drank some coffee and stared at me. "You heard something about the Cunliffe case I should know about?"

"I was just taking a polite interest in your career."

"Yeah, that's the thing about you, Silas, always the gentleman. Did you apologize to Jiggs Murphy before or after you hit him?"

"Give me a break, Bernie."

"I'll give you a break, but I dunno about Jiggs Murphy and Alex Cal. You mess with those animals, you'd better get yourself a bullwhip and a steel chair or they'll claw you to death."

"I'll keep it in mind."

"What is this, a personal vendetta?"

"I hate those fuckers, Bernie. I hate traffickers and I hate pimps. Every time I see a wasted young life I hate 'em more."

"Who doesn't? You think you're the only cop in town with a social conscience, for Chrissake?"

Tapp thought for a while and said, "The Cunliffe case, eh?" He tipped his head sideways like a bird and stared across the table without blinking. "That was DCI Bulloch's case and he got zapped on it. You know as much as I do. The murderers drove off in a florist's van with some stolen paintings. Aboriginal driver. Nobody saw them except that lawyer ... " Tapp fumbled for the name. "Service, Charles Service. Then they vanished."

"And no leads since?"

"I told you, nothing. Those paintings never showed up again either. Every once in a while I pull the Cunliffe file out, take a look at it."

"Even though it's DCI Bulloch's case?"

Bernie's face was about as expressive as an Easter Island statue.

I said, very carefully, "There are people, I've met some, who think that somebody, I won't say who, put pressure on the department. What happened was, Jimmy Scow might have ended up in a frame."

That went nowhere. Bernie had gone wooden on me.

I continued doggedly, "If you have a detective with some free time, this would be a good time to take another look for those missing paintings."

Bernie gave me a blank look.

I said, "The paintings stolen from Calvert Hunt's house."

Bernie nodded. "So that's what you want. Even though this is Chief Detective Inspector Bulloch's case? Even though Bulloch hates Nosy Parkers almost as much as he hates you?"

"Even so."

"Okay, we'll take another look. But what will you do for me?"

I brought Jiggs Murphy's pistol out and slid it across the table. Tapp stared at it for a moment, then slipped it into his pocket. "There you go," I said. "A nice little Ruger for you. I found it in an alley near my office."

"Waddington Alley?"

"I think that's what it's called."

Bernie stood up. He paused to relight his pipe, and as he was leaving I asked, "What's the deal on Halvorsen?"

"She's beautiful, smart and has a master's degree in criminology."

"Maybe," I said, "but what kind of cop is she?"

"The best kind."

"All she's done so far is use my office as a comfort station and spread malicious gossip."

"So what? You're a bad person and your office is a disgrace."

"Street people feel very much at home in there."

"Yeah, no doubt. It reminds them of a back alley." Bernie nibbled his bottom lip with nicotine-stained teeth, trying to maintain his artificial bad humour, but we had been friends for too long. He said, "I *know* you hammered Jiggs Murphy, and you need a new brain if you think you can rob him and get away with it." It appeared that he wanted to add something. After hesitating, Bernie changed his mind and left the café.

AT FISHERMAN'S WHARF, sunlight glinted off the water. Seagulls screamed. Fishermen mended nets, scraped paint or idled in the sun. One rusty old ship of a type that I did not recognize rode at an outside berth. It looked like a big ocean-going tug, but stood higher out of the water and lacked the usual towing equipment at the stern. Three men were using a gasoline-powered winch to load it with stores.

Every few minutes noisy float planes took off from the Inner Harbour, bound for the Gulf Islands or Vancouver or Seattle. The departing planes thrashed along slowly at first, throwing big rooster tails and rocking in the choppy waves. Then the rooster tails diminished and disappeared as the aircraft accelerated and became airborne. Freed from the water, the planes banked to the west and disappeared into the sun. The tang of salt, tarred ropes and creosoted pilings filled the air.

Mom's Café was an old clapboard and corrugated-iron building overlooking the marina. A telephone-repair vehicle and several pickup trucks stood in the café's gravelled parking lot. I parked my Chevy alongside the telephone truck and went inside. Two men wearing orange hard hats were at the lunch counter having coffee. Other customers occupied vinyl-upholstered booths. An old-fashioned Wurlitzer was belting out Elton John's "Goodbye Yellow Brick Road." Inside the kitchen somebody rattled pots and pans. The hum of conversation in the room subsided when I entered, then picked up again as I sat at the counter. A chalkboard advertised Mom's world-famous homemade pies. A girl came out of the kitchen and, without being asked, put a plain white mug in front of me and splashed coffee into it.

"I'd better have one of those world-famous pies. What kinds you got?"

"Cherry, banana cream, blueberry and apple," the girl recited mechanically, wiping dishwasher-red hands on her apron.

"Make mine apple. À la mode."

The two men in hard hats went outside. Moments later the telephone truck's engine started with a roar and the heavy vehicle lumbered away, spinning its wheels on loose gravel until the tires bit.

A rough, wheezy voice said, "So I took the stuff, jammed it in a paper bag and fired it through the window." Laughter greeted this remark.

Across the room, two men and a woman occupied a window booth. The person who had just spoken was a stocky, middle-aged man with long dark hair, streaked with grey, receding from a high forehead. He wore a black woollen shirt with Harley Davidson patches. The shirt had an attached hood that, resting on his shoulders, gave him a slightly humpbacked appearance. The woman sharing his booth crossed to the Wurlitzer and began feeding it coins. She was about 25 and had a mane of yellow hair, noticeably darker at the roots. Heavy breasts and nipples were prominent beneath her white T-shirt. Blue stretch pants strained across her buttocks. She had a cheerful face and exuded a raffish sexuality. After making her selections at the Wurlitzer she returned to the booth. As she sat down, the Beach Boys started on "Surfer Girl."

The second man at the booth was also about 25, very overweight, with a bushy moustache. He seemed intimidated by his companions and grinned shyly when anyone spoke. When he opened his mouth, I saw that all the teeth were missing from one side of his upper jaw. Eavesdropping on their conversation, I learned that the woman's name was Patty Nolan; the fat man was called Sidney Banks.

The waitress arrived with my pie and slid it in front of me. I watched as she crossed her arms and leaned behind the counter, gazing into space with a rapt expression. I tasted the pie and said, "This is good."

The waitress stared at me dully. "What?"

"Great pie."

She raised her shoulders an inch. In a second I was forgotten as she listened to the Wurlitzer. She was 1,000 miles away, on a California beach with golden-haired boys.

The biker's two companions went out. I finished the pie and carried my coffee cup across to the old biker's booth. "Hi, Fred," I said, and slid into the seat opposite.

Fred's lips tightened and his eyes were suspicious. "Do I know you?"

"Silas Seaweed."

"Man sits at my table, I don't know him, he'd better have a good reason."

"Somebody left a message for me. That's a reason."

"That's a reason, mister, but I said you'd better have a *good* reason."

I made myself comfortable, moving slightly on the seat, taking my time about it. "I've known people," I said, "sweet young boys, never missed choir practice. I've seen these boys led astray, their heads turned by shiny motorcycles. Threw a leg over a hog and thought they were shitkickers and tough guys. I heard about one who walked into a bank, packing a loaded revolver. Ten years later he was still packing a broom in William Head penitentiary, along with a bunch of other losers."

"Yeah," said Fred, smiling without parting his lips. "That's me. Fred Eade, bank robber."

He dragged out some tobacco and rolled a cigarette. Instead of lighting it, he stuck it behind his ear. "Hey, Pearl, bring that coffee pot over here, will ya?"

He waited until Pearl came over and filled our cups. He was working something out in his mind. At last he said, "So, you done some checking on me already. That's quite an act. How'd you do it?"

"I recognized you as soon as I walked in."

"You a cop?"

"I'm here to *ask* questions."

Fred bared his teeth. "You look like an ex-cop. What happened? They kick you off the force for stealing apples?"

"No, Fred, they didn't kick me off the force. Not yet, although that day may come. See, I get special consideration. I'm the token Indian. Long as I don't show up for work in war paint and feathers, I'm safe.

But I'm tired of punks. I'm tired of wasting my time with guys who don't know their ass from their elbows."

Fred nodded, sipping his coffee. "So, you want to lay some cash on me?"

"I might, if you give me something I want."

"How do I know you won't cheat me?"

"I won't cheat you, but I won't take any crap either. If you've got something, talk."

Cunning made his face furtive and ratty. "Buddy, I got what you need. You're looking for a woman, went missing a long time ago. I know where she is."

"Where is she?"

Fred Eade shook his head. "First, I got to know how much money we're looking at."

"Information like that, it could be worth something if nobody else knows about it. But I figure an asshole like you knows something, other people must know it as well."

"That's right. Lots of people know this lady, but there's a snag. The woman we're talking about, she's a basket case. She's what you call confused. She doesn't even know her own name half the time."

Things were beginning to add up. I said, "Tell me something. Prove you're not conning me. If it sounds good, I'll talk to the Man, get money for you."

"Maybe I can talk to the Man myself, make my own deal."

"That's what I'd expect, from a two-bit grifter. Go ahead and try."

Fred scowled, dragged a commando dagger from its sheath and began to rake dirt from beneath his fingernails. "This woman we're talking about. In the newspaper you said you was looking for Marcia Harkness, right?"

"That's right."

Fred had a copy of the *Times Colonist* with him. He passed it across the table. One of the personal ads had been circled with black ink.

REWARD OFFERED FOR INFORMATION

PRESENT WHEREABOUTS MARCIA HARKNESS

MARRIED WELLINGTON 1980S.

Fred took the page back and said, "Here's something for you. The ad says the woman's name was Harkness, but the guy she married, his name was Turko."

"Wait a minute. What are you saying? That her name was Harkness before her marriage?"

"Don't go jumping too fast, give me a chance to explain." Fred had a confident smile now.

"It's like this," he said. "In the late '70s, sometime around there, this American guy, name of Frank Harkness, comes up to B.C. from California. He was running away from something, I never found out what. Trouble. Anyway, he come up and got tied in with us bikers, in Wellington. We was disorganized then, stealing bike parts, hubcaps, dealing a little grass. Pretty soon Frank took over, changed a few things. He was tougher than hell, man, and a good organizer. Been with the Angels in Oakland, suppose to be a friend of Sonny Barger's. Suppose to be. Leastways, he was a tough monkey. He kicked ass around the club and soon made president. He was king a' the fuckin' hill, nobody messed with him."

Fred scratched his whiskers with the dagger handle and took another drink of coffee. He was enjoying my attention. "But this tough guy, he had, what you call it? A blind spot, or maybe a better word, weakness, for classy broads. There was good-looking chicks around the club all the time. Mamas with big tits and tattooed asses. Frank wasn't interested. He liked class. Used to vanish for a week at a time, hang out in a suite at the Empress Hotel, get his rocks off with college girls and all like that. Then he meets this one, Marcia. He met her in a fuckin' tea room!" Fred shook his head as if he still couldn't believe it.

I said, "You were a member of the same club?"

"Sure. I was a punk. I got my patches under Frank, he was my fuckin' hero, man. I seen that guy duff it out with two soldiers from the Burnaby club who come over to show us how things ought to be done. They was using iron bars. Frank took 'em on with his bare hands. When they carted those two bastards out of the clubhouse, the place looked like a slaughterhouse." Fred shook his head, remembering. "Frank was something, all right. Like a maniac when he got mad. Maybe it was his Russian blood. But that Marcia, she had Frank wrapped around her little finger."

I said, "What was *she* like?"

"I don't know what she was like *then*. He kept Marcia under wraps."

"You never met her?"

Fred shook his head reluctantly. "Not then. He didn't introduce her. She never come into the clubhouse."

"So you didn't know who she was, anything about her?"

"I knew she was called Marcia, that she come out of Victoria, and she married Frank Harkness in Wellington." He cocked his head. "You think that more than one broad called Marcia married guys called Frank Harkness in Wellington?"

"No. It sounds like you've identified her."

"So how's about it? You satisfied I know what I'm saying?"

One thing still puzzled me. I said, "Tell me about this Harkness-Turko connection. How does that tie in?"

"Frank Harkness's name was really Frank Turko. I told you, he was on the lam from stateside, changed his name when he crossed the border, lots of guys done that."

"Let's get this straight. You know where Marcia is now, and you can take me to her?"

"Correct. She's living in a place, you can be there in about four hours." His sly look returned. "How much is this reward, anyway?"

"A few hundred bucks," I said, snatching a figure out of the blue.

Fred rolled his eyes. "You shitting me?" he mocked. "This is some kind of inheritance deal, got to be. Either Frank's money is looking for her, or her family's."

"How do you know her family has money?"

"I don't. But it's a fair guess. I told you. Frank was interested in class acts. Girls who wore fancy clothes, dressed nice, went to college and all like that."

"Frank had money too?"

Fred laughed. "He had a licence to *print* money. Bought it off a guy that lived in Ladysmith. It was a recipe for brewing speed."

"Speed?"

"That's right. Speed. *And* MDA. Frank learned how to make it. That's how the club earned its money. We was dealing acid, grass, heroin, meth. You name it. We had it all."

"What happened to Frank Harkness?"

Fred slid the commando dagger back into its sheath and said

impatiently, "I said enough already. I ain't saying no more until I get cash laid on me. You check with the guy who's pulling your wires, then report back with some serious coin."

"Fair enough."

"I want 5,000 bucks," Fred said, standing up and leaning his weight on the table as he shuffled sideways out of the booth.

I said, "Don't aim too high. Five thousand is a lot of money."

"Let me talk to the Man myself, maybe I'll cut you in out of my piece."

"That's not the way I work."

"Yeah? Well, I'm flexible, maybe you should be. Think about it." He nodded toward the marina. "I live on a boat with my old lady. You want me, come find me."

I said, "Wait a minute, I need to ask you one more thing. The woman I'm interested in had an identifying mark on one arm."

"I know she did," Fred said. "A rose tattoo, up on her right shoulder. Frank told us about it. The rose was put on by a guy in Nanaimo."

I watched Fred walk away. The old biker had a limp and was much shorter than he'd appeared when sitting down. He was probably about 50 — perhaps younger. But with his seamed face, greying hair and limping stride he looked a lot older. He'd lived fast but hadn't died young. The hard life had caught up with Fred Eade.

THE WHARFINGER'S OFFICE was a small wooden building at the end of a pier. Inside, ship models stood on window sills, pictures of sailing vessels covered the walls. A telescope in a corner was aimed at Spinnakers pub. The wharfinger sat in a captain's chair, watching the scene outside his window. When I entered, he spun around and grinned at me. A plastic sign on his desk told me that this was Captain Thomas Bloggs.

"Nice day, ain't it?" Captain Bloggs said cheerfully. "What can I do for you?"

He was an elderly, bearded man with skin like old leather. He wore a uniform cap and, in spite of the warm weather, a thick pea jacket with brass buttons. He would have looked right at home on the deck of a three-master.

I produced a photograph of Harry Cunliffe Jr. and showed it to him. "Ever see this man around the marina, Captain?"

The wharfinger studied the photograph and nodded. "Who are you, mister, and what's your business?"

"Silas Seaweed. I'm a city cop," I said, giving him my card.

Captain Bloggs settled back on his chair. "Sure. I knew Harry, he was a favourite of mine. Dr. Cunliffe's house is on Dallas Road, only a few blocks away from here. The boy was crazy about boats, used to hang around my wharf all the time. Goddam shame, him being murdered." The captain raised his bushy eyebrows. "What's your interest, Sergeant?"

"It's a confidential matter, Captain. I can't say much. Be obliged if you'd keep this under your hat."

Irritation reddened the old man's face, but before he could speak I added, "No offence, but we don't want this stirred up, out of respect for the boy's father."

Mollified, the wharfinger said, "I saw Fred Eade just now. You were talking with him in the café. You ask him about Harry?"

Evidently, not much went on around the marina that escaped the old man's eye. I said, "Did Harry know Fred Eade?"

A nerve twitched in the captain's face and his eyes flicked toward the south end of the marina. "Everybody knows Fred Eade." He spoke with disgust. "Fred's been living on my marina for years. Always behind paying his mooring fees. Complains he's broke, but he can find money for booze easy enough. I ought to run him off, but if I did, where would he go?" He sighed and added, "But you were asking about Harry."

I said, "A boy of Cunliffe's background, I'd expect him to spend his time around the Royal Victoria Yacht Club."

"Harry was interested in sailboats, sure, and he did a bit of racing out of the yacht club, but he loved commercial boats. Worked summers on fish packers and suchlike, sailing up the coast to Alaska. Lots of workboat skippers gave Harry work."

Our conversation was interrupted by a loud crash outside. A winch cable had broken and a pallet-load of stores had dropped onto the wharf alongside the rusty-looking ship that I had noticed earlier. Three men were surveying the damage.

The old seaman narrowed his eyes. "Greenhorns playing at sailors!"

he snapped. "That ship's falling apart. They think they're gonna take that wreck to Guatemala. Some hopes! It'll either founder in the first gale or they'll pile her up on a lee shore."

"What's going on?"

He pointed at the ship. "That's an Atlantic trawler, an old rustbucket. Been laid up in St. John's for years. Engine's worn out and you've just seen how good the rigging is. Some guy bought it, thought he'd use it as a crab boat here. Anyway, he went broke. Now she's been bought by a bunch of dreamers. They're aiming to ship out on some get-rich-quick scheme." The wharfinger turned away from the window. "You got any new leads on this Cunliffe case?"

"What do you mean?"

"Everybody in town knows that Indian kid wasn't acting on his own. He was just the driver. The guy that pulled the trigger is still running loose."

"The case is still open," I said.

"I've got a theory on it." The old man crinkled his forehead.

I waited.

"I figure Harry was murdered by somebody who knew him." The old man leaned forward. "Makes sense, don't it? Harry's out there at Calvert Hunt's mansion. He hears or sees something suspicious and goes to investigate. Finds a burglar lifting the paintings off the walls and recognizes him." The old man stopped speaking to gauge my reaction.

I nodded encouragement.

"It's the only thing that adds up," he said. "The paintings, what are they worth, a few hundred? Not worth a killing. Not unless the robber is recognized and panics. He knows he's not going to get away with it so he shoots first and thinks second." His glance drifted toward the live-aboard boats and he added slyly, "Perhaps you don't need to look too far for a suspect, eh?"

I stifled a grin and said, "That's a possibility. Thanks for sharing your ideas."

"Glad to help," said the captain. Then he was seized by another idea. "One thing I don't understand. What was young Harry doing at Calvert Hunt's place in the first place?"

"Calvert Hunt and Dr. Cunliffe are close friends. Family friends. Harry spent a lot of time there, swimming in their pool, playing tennis."

The captain nodded wisely.

I said, "The summer that Harry was murdered. Did he work on boats as usual?"

The old man pushed his cheek out with his tongue and wrinkled his nose, thinking. "I believe he did. I wouldn't swear to it, but he probably crewed with Taffy Jones."

"Where can I find Jones?"

"Taffy's fishing up at Adams River, won't be back for a few weeks." The captain sighed. "Goddam shame, ain't it, the way things turn out. The world's full of deadbeats like Fred Eade who just go on and on, creating misery. A nice feller like Harry dies young. It don't make no sense to me."

The wharfinger rose ponderously and fastened the buttons of his jacket. "I better get down there, see if those dreamers damaged my dock."

A STIFF ONSHORE BREEZE was blowing when I parked my Chevy outside Dr. Cunliffe's house on Dallas Road. It was a '50s cedar-and-brick bungalow with a steeply pitched roof, built around three sides of a cement patio. I rang the doorbell, turned my back on the house and watched a couple of sailboats, heeled over to their gunnels, as they raced upwind along Juan de Fuca Strait. Across Dallas Road, a broad expanse of parkland extended to steep cliffs. Dense thickets of low bushes and trees dotted the park; mallard ducks floated on a pond. Hikers strode along the trail at the edge of sandstone cliffs. A big freighter, inward bound from Asia, was picking up a pilot. The ferry from Port Angeles was rounding Ogden Point.

A minute later Dr. Cunliffe appeared from the backyard. He gave me a cheery smile and said, "I've been messing about in my greenhouse, don't always hear the bell. Been waiting long?"

"Just got here."

Dr. Cunliffe looked out to sea. "I hope those sailors are wearing survival suits. That westerly must be blowing over an icefield," he said with an exaggerated shiver.

He opened the front door and invited me in. Passing him in the hallway

I caught a whiff of his breath, pungent with alcohol. We went into the front living room. He grinned at me and said, "I've already started. What's your poison?"

"Scotch."

He congratulated me on my taste, waved his hand toward a chair and busied himself with the bottles and glasses set out on a side table. Through the French windows that opened onto the front patio I heard a murmur of voices as two men walked past the house with their heads together.

Dr. Cunliffe came up behind me, his footfalls soft on the carpet, and gave me my drink. We clinked glasses. After tasting it I tilted my head appreciatively. It was Glenlivet.

Dr. Cunliffe gazed out across the strait toward the distant Olympic snowcaps and said, "It's a big country out there. Plenty of room to hide in."

Moving slowly and somewhat erratically, Dr. Cunliffe crossed the room again and sat in a leather club chair. I knew what he wanted to say, and I also knew that he wasn't quite ready to say it yet, so I took a chance and said quietly, "You're Calvert Hunt's doctor. Is Charles Service your patient as well?"

"Not really, although Charlie consults me from time to time. Why do you ask?"

"I'm curious to know how long Charles Service has been addicted to cocaine is all."

Dr. Cunliffe's face closed up in thought. He shrugged and said, "Coke? Charles has been on the stuff for a few years now. Off and on, that is. Sometimes he gets into a 12-step program and stays clear of it for a while, but he always goes back. A smart fellow like that, I'm damned if I can understand it."

So my guess was right, but I didn't feel good about it. How many times have I sat with people, smiling and lying, tricking them into telling me the truth?

Dr. Cunliffe screwed up his eyes and mouth in concentration and went on. "Damn shame. Charles is a decent sort. God only knows what possessed him to dabble with the stuff in the first place. Bloody foolishness. When I think what it must have cost him, over the years … "

Dr. Cunliffe looked at his glass and discovered that it was empty.

Moving with difficulty, he got up and went unsteadily to the side table for a refill. Speaking over his shoulder, his voice half muffled, he said, "The reason I called you. It's about my boy, Harry."

He turned toward me and said awkwardly, "I don't know how to put this, but the thing is, I've never been satisfied. About Harry's killing, I mean. The real reason for it. What I wanted to ask you, Silas, as a favour ... Since you're working on that Marcia Hunt thing, maybe you could keep your eyes and ears open ... "

His voice trailed off. He was quite drunk. He went to a sideboard, pulled open a drawer and took out an unframed four-by-six photograph. "Here," he said. "You can keep this."

It was a photograph of Harry. I turned it over. A pencilled caption read: "Harry Cunliffe. 1978–2000."

Sudden drops of moisture glistened in Dr. Cunliffe's eyes. He brushed his face with the back of a hand and said, "Sorry. Unforgivable. I'm getting maudlin in my old age, but he was my only son. There's just me now."

I felt like I was mainlining on wretchedness.

He said, "I asked you a few days ago if you thought Jimmy Scow had killed my boy. Remember?"

"Yes, and I remember the answer I gave you. It was no."

"Were you just guessing, or do you have evidence?"

"Let me put it this way. The evidence against Scow was tainted."

"I know it was, because I attended every day of Scow's trial. I was hoping that the prospect of a jail sentence would soften Scow up. Encourage him to rat on his accomplices."

I didn't say anything.

Dr. Cunliffe sat down and said gamely, "How's your tipple? Help yourself, old boy. I'm a bit legless, myself."

"We'll find him, Doctor. Find the guy who killed your son, and that's a promise," I said. I meant every word, but by then I was thinking with my heart instead of my head.

I had another Glenlivet and then left him to his desolation.

CHAPTER FIVE

I met **Chief Alphonse** in the Warrior band office. Smoke wisped from the briar pipe hanging between his front teeth. He looked at the raindrops running down his windowpanes and said cryptically, "First Woman is crying and bringing rain to our lands. Pretty soon, First Son will bring the west wind, dry the tears of his mother if she weeps too long."

That was fine with me.

The chief burned more tobacco and continued solemnly, "George Putty is getting the heebie-jeebies from too much drinking. We've got to do something before he runs away."

"Gregarious George?" I said. "What's George been up to this time?"

"Passing out in the street, panhandling. Making a nuisance of himself at Gottlieb's Trading Post. It's pathetic. George Putty is a Black Tamahnous. That man was respected from Seabeck to Fairbanks at one time. Now he's a disgrace. Never goes home, doesn't talk to his family." The chief sighed and added, "Little Sam thinks that Little Earths have taken George's soul."

"I suppose Little Sam wants to do some medicine."

"Yes. Little Sam said he'd throw bones in the air and do Earth Dwarf Song. The very mention of bone throwing and Little Earth conjuring scared George out of his wits."

"Well, drinking, Chief. I drink myself."

"Not like George Putty. Getting drunk is all he does now."

"I could lock him up long enough to dry him out, but that won't correct George's underlying problem."

"Little Sam and me, we know what George's underlying problem is," the chief said dryly. "I want you to think about it, Silas. George Putty has a lot of respect for you."

"I wish Jimmy Scow had respect for me as well," I said. "*He* seems to think I'm a halfwit."

"Little Jimmy Scow," Chief Alphonse repeated thoughtfully. "Now there's a *name*."

I waited. The chief added, "He's spending a lot of time Canoe Cove way, diving into the sea."

"Wolf ritual?"

"Wolf ritual is right." Chief Alphonse took the pipe out of his mouth and looked at it. He put it back in his mouth again, took a few puffs and said, "I'll tell you this, though. I knew Jimmy Scow's dad. He had real power."

"Jimmy told me his dad never used it."

The chief frowned and said, "I heard Jimmy's dad sing Wolf Song in Haida Gwaii 15 years ago."

That gave me something else to wonder about. I told the chief I'd think about George Putty.

The chief's prediction was being fulfilled. The wind had swung to the west and a rainbow was bridging James Bay.

I WAS IN BARTHOLOMEWS, drinking Foster's draft at the bar and fretting about Barb. A philosopher on the adjacent stool was bemoaning the collapse of western civilization. Its ultimate achievement had been the 1955 Chevrolet Bel Air. Since then it had been downhill all the way.

"They don't make cars now," the philosopher said with alcoholic belligerence. "They make shit. Give me a '50s Bel Air, give me any kind of iron built in the '40s, '50s. That's my idea of wheels. You telling me any Jap heap's the match of a full-size Chev?"

"I'm driving a 1982 Chev," I answered, referring to my rustbucket parked across the street.

"Put it there, pal." He extended his hand. "I wanna shake hands with a guy knows cars."

He signalled the barman and ordered pints for each of us. "An '82 ain't no '55, but it's better'n a Mazda. You seen them Hyundais? Made outta recycled plastic and sardine cans. Shit. Ain't even got a carburetor, they got a fuel injector." After a disgusted snort he lapsed into stuporous silence.

I stared at the liquor bottles arranged on glass shelves behind the bar and thought about my day.

After talking to Chief Alphonse, I'd driven north up the Malahat highway. Traffic was thin and I made good time. By six o'clock I was approaching Nanaimo, driving past a pulp mill. The mill's belching smokestacks and sulphurous stink were like a foretaste of hell, plunked down on the forested shores of B.C. by a satanic jokester.

Half an hour later I entered a room full of large men wearing wide-brimmed hats and showed my ID to the RCMP sergeant in charge. Within five minutes I was seated across a desk from Inspector Fred Wells. The Mountie was a man in his late 50s with a clipped moustache and the rigid bearing of a regimental sergeant major.

I said, "I'm looking for a woman called Marcia Hunt. She disappeared years ago after marrying a member of the old Wellington motor-cycle gang." I explained what was going on.

Wells' air of polite attention sharpened noticeably when I mentioned Frank Harkness's name. He looked at me through half-closed eyes and said, "Frank Harkness was a hard case. I remember him well. He was clever, good-looking and tough. Local kids destined to pump gas and sweep floors for a living joined his gang, and Harkness made motorcycle goons out of them. His bunch raised hell around here for a few years and kept this detachment pretty busy. When we put him out of business the gang disintegrated."

I said, "Does the name Fred Eade mean anything to you?"

Hearing these half-forgotten names made Wells thoughtful, and his relaxing facial muscles drooped in the pull of gravity, making him seem older and less cynical. "Fred was a gofer. After Harkness bailed out, small-timers like Fred turned to other crimes. Without leaders they weren't very successful. Fred Eade pulled a clumsy bank holdup and we put him away. Hell's Angels rule the roost here now. Harkness's old-time biker buddies are either dead, in jail, pumping gas or on social assistance."

"What happened to Frank Harkness?"

The inspector made the slightest movement in his chair and the tendons in his neck twitched, pulling down the edges of his mouth. "The file is still open. I'll tell you a story, and you can decide."

Wells collected his thoughts and said, "Harkness was an American. From Oakland, California. One of those who came to Canada after the Vietnam War. Before the war, Harkness studied chemistry at UCLA until he was conscripted into the U.S. Marine Corps. At war's end, Harkness didn't return to civilian life with his comrades — he was serving time in a military prison because of some black-market scam."

Wells fell into a glum silence for a moment, absently tapping the edge of his table with his fingers, then continued. "But in 1977 Harkness was living on a rented farm a few miles north of Nanaimo. Ostensibly, he was supporting himself as a construction worker. Harkness soon had enough money to buy the farm. He grew vegetables and raised a few sheep. To all appearances, Harkness was just another hobby farmer living on a half-cleared woodlot out in the boondocks."

Wells stopped speaking and stared out of the window, looking at the night sky where a distant yellow glow marked the pulp mill. He said, "Harkness's farm was surrounded by an electrified fence, which seemed a bit elaborate for a few sheep. He discouraged visitors. People who got into his place found an inner fence, 10 feet high, topped with barbed wire. Harkness let it be known that he was breeding Doberman guard dogs inside the second fence. We found out that members of the Wellington motorcycle club often called on Harkness, so we started to keep an eye on him. Harkness had a hobby — flying. He took flying lessons. After getting his pilot's licence he bought a new Cessna, which he kept in a hangar at the Cassidy airport. We wondered how a struggling immigrant, paying off a mortgage from his earnings as a casual construction worker, could afford all these expensive toys. So we got a search warrant and raided his place. But our timing was off, nobody was home. We penetrated the second fence, shot the Dobermans and investigated Harkness's outbuildings. Concealed in the bush, we discovered growing sheds full of marijuana plants, as well as a well-equipped chemical laboratory. Our technical experts proved that Harkness had been making speed and MDA in large quantities. We mounted a stakeout, but Harkness never showed up.

"Months went by. Gradually we pulled officers off the case. One day, long after our raid, somebody replaced the distributor caps on Harkness's impounded Cessna and the plane took off. When it was airborne, heading toward the mainland, the pilot radioed that he was having engine trouble, losing altitude, and was preparing to ditch in the ocean. Then the radio went dead. Within minutes a tugboat captain reported seeing a plane nosedive into the sea near Sandheads. The tugboat crew salvaged bits of floating debris. Nobody could have survived such a crash. We listened to tapes of the pilot's conversation with Vancouver's air-traffic controllers and we recognized Harkness's voice. It was assumed by one and all that Harkness had drowned. Case closed."

Wells smiled, savouring these memories. "But some of us weren't completely satisfied so we spent a ton of money and salvaged that wrecked Cessna. There was no body strapped into the pilot seat. One of the aircraft's doors had been removed prior to takeoff."

Wells stood abruptly and faced the window, clasping his hands behind his back. He said, "We think that Harkness took the Cessna from Cassidy airport and flew to another landing strip, where he unscrewed the door from its hinges. He then took off again, wearing a parachute. After establishing course and contacting Vancouver's air-traffic control, he put the Cessna on autopilot and bailed out. If our guess is right, Harkness was faking his own death so that we'd quit looking for him. He's has never been seen since."

Wells walked outside to the parking lot with me. We stood in silence by my car and looked at the glowing sky. Wells' voice dropped several decibels and he added, "Harkness has been on the run for over 20 years. Keep this under your hat, Seaweed, but at this point I'm not sure I really want him. It would be a bit unsporting to jail him now."

THE BARTENDER AT Bartholomews said, "You want another beer?"

I shook my head and got down from the stool, stiff from sitting too long. The philosopher was long gone. Half a dozen new drinkers separated me from the door now. Outside the door, a passageway led to a dining room and to Bartholomews' oyster bar. I felt hungry and was wondering whether to have dinner when a tall, gorgeous blonde appeared in the doorway. I froze. It was the woman I'd seen in the Bengal Room with Alex Cal and Jiggs Murphy. The blonde hesitated on the threshold, then turned away and walked on toward the oyster bar. The two pimps were right behind her. Somebody tapped me on the shoulder and I turned. It was Sarah Williams. Dark glossy hair brushed prettily across her shoulders in a slight forward curve. She wore a short, layered silk dress and matching patent-leather pumps. Her voice was beautiful, too, with deep, mysterious undertones.

She said, "Well, well. Silas Seaweed."

I grinned at her.

"I've been looking at you for half an hour. You were gazing at those bottles behind the bar. I thought you were drunk at first."

"I'm a deep thinker."

"I know you are. I've been making inquiries about you."

"It's supposed to be the other way round. Need I be alarmed?"

"I don't think so. But there's more to you than meets the eye. You're not exactly the pemmican-chewing savage you sometimes pretend to be. In fact, you're quite a scholar."

"You've obviously been misled."

"Don't be modest. Face it, Silas. Your dad was a Salish chieftain and you were a scholarship boy at St. Michael's. That's Charles Service's alma mater. As B.C.'s boarding schools go, it doesn't get much better than that. After St. Michael's you studied law at UVic."

"Anthropology."

"Really? Well, you played rugby, I know that for sure. They called you Sacker Seaweed." She laughed and shook her head. "Weren't you on the team that played the All Blacks?"

"Listen," I said, "have you had dinner?"

"Not yet."

"Let's drop by Thrifty's. Pick up some groceries, a bottle of Gala Keg. We'll fry something up."

"*Fry!*" Sarah frowned at the dirty verb. "Tell you what. Why don't you buy me a drink and we'll review your entire history? Afterward we can go to my condo. I've got smoked salmon, other things."

"You've got a condo? I thought you lived at Ribblesdale."

"At the moment I do. But I like my privacy sometimes."

"Don't we all," I said and signalled the bartender.

Sarah asked for a champagne cocktail. I ordered another Foster's.

Sarah said, "Somebody told me you have a wife somewhere. A podiatrist."

"*Had* a wife. Nancy was a dentist. But that's enough about me. I'm trying to imagine you as a schoolgirl. I'll bet you were a skinny kid with big horn-rimmed glasses who played clarinet in the school band."

"No way. I was an ugly fat broad with pimples. Teeth braces and no tits, an absolute horror," she said, smiling. "My idea of a good night out was coffee and cakes with sorority sisters, discussing the history of existentialism or something equally light-hearted."

Sarah put her hand on my thigh and gave it a playful squeeze. "Then I discovered boys. I stopped reading Kierkegaard and whadda you know? My pimples cleared up. What I find attractive about you, Silas, is that you're impetuous. I've always liked that in a man."

We finished our drinks and went out. We planned to stroll along the causeway. Instead of a condo smorgasbord we were going to have dinner at the Ocean Pointe Resort. After that, who knew? Sarah took my hand. Another Harlequin Romance was beginning its maiden voyage.

Suddenly a gang of Sarah's friends spilled out from the Union Club and swept us up in their merriment. They were all going to a house party in the Uplands and insisted we join them, wouldn't take no for an answer. Giggling and flirting, they all piled into a stretch limousine waiting for them at the curb. I didn't know any of them.

I had been slightly drunk, but now I was sober.

What the hell was I doing with Sarah Williams? Didn't I have enough dramatic fantasies complicating my life already?

I sidled away and hid like a thief in the Union Club's grandiose shadows until the limo drove away with its cargo of fun-seekers. I walked to the McDonald's on Douglas Street and ordered a Quarter Pounder with fries and enough Pepsi to dissolve my tooth enamel. It tasted great.

CHAPTER SIX

I woke up feeling like I had a stoker's sweat rag in my mouth. After an inch of toothpaste, two cups of black coffee and five minutes with a Mach3 Gillette razor, I probably looked about normal. I drove through the Oak Bay village and at Monterey Avenue, past the Blethering Place tea room with its fake-Tudor façade. I wondered whether Frank Harkness had rendezvoused with Marcia Hunt in there — softening her up with cups of tea and hot buttered crumpets. Him in a leather biker's jacket and black leather boots. Her in pearls, a grey dirndl skirt, white cotton blouse, a navy-blue blazer with a St. Margaret's crest on its breast pocket.

The village of my schooldays had all but vanished. The Oak Bay Cinema and most of the old houses were long gone, replaced by upscale dress shops and galleries and places selling antiques. A bulldozer was flattening a once grand, now shabby Victorian house near Yale Street to make room for another brick and concrete condominium. A girl in a bright yellow vest was directing cars around the site, and traffic stalled for a minute. I glanced in my rear-view mirror and noticed a green Toyota Corolla right behind me.

An elderly gentleman wearing a dark business suit came skateboarding down the avenue with a briefcase tucked under his arm, weaving gracefully as he swept past stationary cars. Where was he going? Who was he? Maybe it was the mayor, trying to jazz up Oak Bay's image as a little bit of eccentric Olde England. I got past that obstruction at last, but a minute later came to a halt behind a vintage Bentley that had stopped on a winding section of Foul Bay Road. The Bentley's driver, a tiny, ancient woman with a lace shawl across her narrow shoulders, had yielded to a family of mallard ducks. The ducks waddled fatly across the road, but what they were doing so far from the ocean was a mystery — they should have been a mile away, paddling around the Oak Bay Marina.

The green Toyota was following two cars behind me now.

A man raking leaves in a nearby yard gave me a friendly nod. He pointed at the ducks and said, "Wonderful, isn't it?"

I said, "What beats me is how baby ducks can walk this far into town without getting killed by dogs or raccoons."

The man grinned. "There's probably an Oak Bay bylaw against it."

Somebody honked impatiently. The ducks had gone and the Bentley was moving. The gardener laughed and said, "People! What's their hurry?"

I drove a couple of blocks and turned up Calvert Hunt's curving sun-drenched driveway. The Chinese gardener was absent. This time when I rang the bell the front door was opened by Iris Naylor. There was something pathetically drab about her today. Her clothes seemed second-hand and she looked as if she'd recently drenched her hair in ultra-strength black coffee. Her nostrils flared in a sneer. She was letting me know that she wasn't accustomed to opening doors for anybody, and certainly not to Natives wearing jeans and open-necked shirts.

"What do you want?" she said, drawing in her chin and staring down her nose.

I didn't get it. Iris Naylor was acting as if she'd never seen me before. I gave her my card and said sweetly, "Is Mr. Service here today?"

"No. Mr. Service has been away for a day or so."

Her eyes were hostile, and the door began to close in my face. I tried to think pleasant thoughts and smiled. "I've heard Mr. Service say how much he relies on you, Miss Naylor." This was a lie, but it had the desired effect.

The door stopped closing. She put one hand to her neck and touched an imitation pearl necklace with long slender fingers. She didn't smile, but I sensed layers of glaciation melting. She glanced at my card.

"As you know, I'm doing some work for Mr. Hunt."

"I believe somebody did mention something of the sort, but I wasn't expecting ... "

She stopped speaking and gazed at her feet.

I smiled some more and said, "I'd be grateful, Miss Naylor, if you could spare me a few moments of your time."

Curiosity overcame her. She unbent a fraction and said primly, "I don't think we can discuss this on the front doorstep, do you?" The door opened wider. "Perhaps you'd care to come to my apartment? I've been frantically busy and was just about to have a cup of tea."

Iris Naylor's "apartment'" turned out to be a modest bed-sitting room in the basement. To reach it we first passed through a spacious lounge where a valuable Emily Carr painting was hanging over a carved marble mantelpiece.

She stopped before it and said, "That's an original. *Totems at Cormorant Island.* Magnificent, isn't it?"

"Yes. And I've seen it before. On the day Harry Cunliffe was murdered."

At the word *murdered* she shuddered. Her right hand went to her throat. But the gesture was studied, phony. She collected herself with a visible effort and said, "Such a horrid day. But I'm afraid that I don't remember much about it."

"There's no reason why you should," I said. "If memory serves, you were on vacation at the time."

She seemed bereft of speech.

"That's right, isn't it?" I said, pressuring her for a response.

"Sorry," she said, in a tone that implied the opposite. "You were one of the policemen on the case?"

"Initially. But that was a busy time for us. We had an arsonist on the loose. Plus there'd been a killing over in Vic West, so the detective squad was spread thin. I was assigned to other duties. Detective Chief Inspector Bulloch was in charge of the Cunliffe homicide."

"Is that the way it works?" she said, turning away without waiting for my answer.

The single room was sparsely lit by two tiny windows. No sunlight could enter because the panes were crowded by thick shrubbery. A narrow bed lay half-hidden behind a folding bamboo screen. Beside the bed was an immense mahogany wardrobe, an unmatched dressing table and a couple of bamboo side tables. A worn Axminster rug did what it could to hide the room's cracked linoleum floor tiles. Two lumpy armchairs flanked a glass-topped coffee table where a tea tray was set for one.

Apart from a few cheap etchings of the *Stag at Bay* variety, there were few pictures, books or personal touches. Evidently the room had been furnished with random cast-offs from upstairs. It was a depressing, gloomy place and I wondered why Iris Naylor chose to live in it. Suddenly I felt sorry for this stern-faced woman.

She said, "Please sit down. If you'd like to join me with tea, I'll fetch another cup and saucer."

I accepted and sank into one of the lumpy armchairs. As soon as she went out, I rose from the chair and went behind the bamboo screen. A silver picture frame lay face-down on her dressing table. I turned it over and saw a photograph of a young Charles Service. He was standing on a tennis court holding a racquet. The picture was inscribed, "To dear Iris. Love and kisses, Charlie." I replaced the picture and put my hand on the dressing table's drawer knob, but was overtaken by a sense of shame. What did I expect to find? Faded love letters wrapped in pink ribbon? Contraceptives? A gun? Miss Naylor's footsteps sounded outside so I sat down, relieved.

Iris Naylor poured tea from a large bone-china pot into mismatched cups and saucers. She said, "I think morning tea is so much better than coffee, don't you?"

"It makes a change," I said, without enthusiasm.

"I found these cups and saucers at a Sunday flea market. Paid 50 cents each. They're Royal Worcester." She had an offhand air.

"I'm sure they're worth much more than you paid for them."

She gave a satisfied smile.

I turned down a chance to share her bran muffin.

"I don't keep extra tea things here because I generally eat with the family," she said and immediately corrected herself. "I mean, when there *was* a family. Now there's just Miss Sarah Williams, when she's here, and Mr. Service. Mr. Hunt takes most of his meals alone in his room."

"Is there a large staff?"

"Adequate, hardly large, it's nothing like it was in the old days. We have a live-in cook, and another woman who comes in to do the cleaning. There's Mr. Hunt's old chauffeur-gardener-handyman. The butler is on vacation at the moment. Usually we have a maid. At present we have no maid so I'm answering the door and running about."

"What happened to the maid?"

"I really can't say," she said, looking at her hands. "Some fracas involving Miss Sarah Williams, I'm told."

"I know you've been with the Hunts for a long time. Did you know Marcia Hunt well?"

"Pretty well."

Miss Naylor sliced her bran muffin into precise halves with a pearl-handled knife and buttered it sparingly. She said, "I was close to Marcia's age, and our relationship was, I like to think, quite intimate." She put an embroidered napkin on her lap and began to nibble the muffin.

"Were you surprised when she married Frank Harkness?"

She sipped tea before answering. "I'm not sure what I thought of Frank Harkness then. I was probably shocked. But I've thought of it often since. In hindsight, I shouldn't have been surprised, of course, because Marcia was impulsive, headstrong."

"Was she intelligent?"

"Intelligent?" Miss Naylor echoed, as if my question demonstrated ill-breeding.

"Sure. Intelligent, bright. Quick on the uptake."

"She was all of those things."

"It looks as if she had a pathological lack of judgment." I waved a hand at the surroundings. "Turning her back on all this to marry a roughneck."

"But Marcia was in love," she said, as if this explained everything. "People in love don't always show good judgment, do they?"

"You're right," I said, thinking of the face-down picture of Charles Service lying on her dressing table. "What did you think of Frank Harkness?"

"I almost liked him. Frank was a breath of fresh air." For the first time she laughed unaffectedly. "I didn't approve of him, not at all. He was, well, earthy."

"Coarse?"

"A rough diamond, but he was well-mannered. At least he was well-mannered around me, and he loved Marcia." She dabbed her lips with a paper napkin. "Manners make up for such a lot, don't you think?"

"Do they?"

"Of course," she said, with a heartiness that sounded a bit forced to my ears.

I said carefully, "I understand that you're the one who saw Jimmy Scow prowling on the grounds recently and reported it."

"Yes, I did," she said. She dropped her gaze and added, "I was a bit on edge at the time."

"May I ask why?"

She looked at me, her expression revealing a curious mixture of nervousness and bravado. "As I say, I was a bit on edge at the time. Perhaps I overreacted. Something happened here one night. Something odd."

Miss Naylor dropped her gaze. She said softly, "This will sound ridiculous. I've never spoken of it till now. The fact is, I saw something. It frightened me terribly at the time. Even now I don't like to think about it. But the thing is, I'm perfectly sure that I saw a wolf on the grounds."

"You're sure it wasn't a large dog?"

"I'm *sure*. I spent two years in the Northwest Territories. But all the same, perhaps I should describe the thing that I saw as wolf-*like*."

She poured herself another cup of tea. Her hands were shaking; drops of tea slopped over into her saucer. In her nervousness, she forgot to offer me a refill.

I waited a minute and said, "How long have you been with the Hunt family?"

Her face smoothed itself out into blandness. "Getting on for 25 years."

"You haven't been the housekeeper all that time, surely?"

"I began as Mr. Hunt's private secretary, when he still kept offices on Douglas Street. After he gave up day-to-day control of his business there was still plenty to do, so he asked me to stay on." She held the cup and saucer above her lap and pulled down her skirt in a ladylike way. "Mr. Hunt was a good employer, but he was *very* demanding. Often we'd be working nights until long after the last buses had gone. I don't drive, so this room was set aside for my use when necessary. Eventually, as Mr. Hunt aged and his involvement with business affairs diminished, my duties changed. The Hunt family evidently found me agreeable because I ended up as housekeeper-companion to Mrs. Hunt." She laughed, but not with amusement. It was a sudden, unbidden bray of bitterness. She raised the tea cup to her mouth, her little finger pointing daintily.

"Tell me about Mrs. Hunt. I understand that she was quite a martinet."

"She was in some ways. She had very high standards. It was hard for people to live up to them at times."

"Well, this is a beautiful house."

"It is," she agreed. "This was one of the last houses designed by Francis Rattenbury. Rattenbury was cheating on his wife while this house was being built ... I suppose you know the story?"

She didn't wait for me to answer, just launched in to the tale.

"It was horrible. Rattenbury deserted his wife to marry somebody else. He was old and she was far too young so the marriage was doomed from the start. Soon the new wife was cheating on him. One of her lovers murdered Rattenbury. Sex and murder and scandal. Maybe this house picked up some of that bad energy. It's cursed with ill luck. People are never happy here for long. When Mr. Hunt dies, I'll leave here too."

"You won't stay?"

"Certainly not. I shouldn't be welcome in any case. I'm only tolerated now because Mr. Hunt likes me. As soon as Sarah Williams gets her clutches on the place, I'll be out." A note of hysteria invaded her voice, and another suppressed emotion rattled the teaspoon in her saucer. She put the cup and saucer on the table and tried to smile. "Yes. I shall move on. Find myself some nice rooms in James Bay or somewhere."

"And Mr. Service?"

"What about him?" she said sharply.

"When Mr. Hunt goes, there'll be no need for him to stay here either, will there?"

She looked down and lifted her shoulders once, but did not speak.

I said, "You are the first person I've spoken to who has said anything positive about Frank Harkness."

She looked up. "I don't want you to think I approved of him as Marcia's husband. I assumed he was a fortune hunter. But still, as I said before, he made Marcia happy. That counts for a lot."

"Do you think Marcia is still alive?"

She shook her head. "I haven't the least doubt that Marcia is dead.

Frank Harkness probably kept her happy for a while, but Marcia's a Hunt, remember. There's no possibility that Marcia would have stayed with him permanently."

She saw me smiling and said in chilly tones, "Did I say something to amuse you?"

"Sorry, I just thought of something. If Marcia came back it would stir things up around here, wouldn't it?"

"What do you mean?"

"I'm speaking of the inheritance. You've been close to Calvert Hunt for a long time. You're part of the family, almost. Do you know about his will?"

She hesitated before replying. "In a general way, not the specifics."

"If Marcia returned, it would change everything."

Hope shone in her eyes. She leaned forward, clutching the arms of her chair. "But Marcia's been disinherited!"

"Marcia would contest the will."

"But Charlie ... Mr. Service, he said ... " She broke off.

"Yes," I urged her, nodding encouragement. "Go on."

"Mr. Service said that Mr. Hunt's will was unshakeable. I asked him."

"There's too much money involved. If Marcia shows up before Mr. Hunt's death, he'll have to change his will. Either that or die knowing that his estate will be tied up in endless litigation."

"But," she exploded, "Calvert is practically senile. He has a few lucid moments in the morning, but much of the time he doesn't know what's happening under his nose. He's transferred the affection he once had for Marcia to that bitch, Sarah Williams!"

Iris Naylor's hand flew to her mouth in consternation. Losing all self-discipline, she burst into tears and fled behind the screen, where she flung herself upon the bed and sobbed.

I watched her in an awkward silence, seeing a woman whose repressed sexuality had aged into affectation and bitterness. But Iris Naylor's emotions could still burn brightly, given the right stimulus.

I left her weeping.

Alone in the main lounge I stared at the Emily Carr painting again — five moss-covered cedar poles standing before a Native longhouse.

The sort of house that my ancestors lived in for thousands of years. My reverie was broken by the sound of gravel crunching on the driveway outside. Charles Service was arriving in a Lincoln town car. I let myself out of the house by a side door and walked quickly down the driveway toward the road. Instead of going through the gates I cut through shrubbery and looked across a stone wall. That green Toyota Corolla was parked on the tree-lined street. I wrote the licence-plate number in my notepad and walked to the front door of the house.

Charles Service was unloading luggage from the Lincoln's trunk. He turned when he heard my footsteps and his features stiffened. Then he smiled with an effort and said, "Silas! What are you doing here?"

"Waiting for you. As long as I was here I thought I'd walk in the gardens for a minute, admire this house again. It's a beautiful place."

"Yes," Service agreed amiably. "Well, it is a showplace. Francis Rattenbury was the architect. He was responsible for the Empress Hotel, amongst other things."

"But people think this house is unlucky."

"Who told you that?"

"Well, isn't it true? The story is that Rattenbury's wife was fooling around and somehow … " I broke off and changed the topic. "You've been away?"

"Yes. Say, I've got things piling up. What did you want to see me about?"

"I need $5,000."

Service's eyes narrowed. "Are you serious?"

"I've found somebody who knows where Marcia's hiding."

Service was visibly, almost comically, startled. Gnawing his bottom lip, he glanced back at the house, then strode toward the pool, saying, "Follow me."

We stood next to the swimming pool, out of earshot of the house. Me with my hands in my pockets, Service with his arms folded. His manner had hardened. Now visibly angry, Service snapped, "All right, let's have it, mister."

I said, "I put an advertisement in the *Times Colonist*. Maybe it paid off."

"Cut the small talk. What about this $5,000?"

"Reward money."

Service's face grew red, his breathing was shallow and fast. He said, "Is this some kind of shakedown?"

"The money isn't for me. I'm paid by the city. I need to pay an informant."

Service calmed down, but he stood there for a full minute, drumming his fingers against his upper arms. At last he said, "I apologize. For a moment there I thought you were trying to extort money. I see now that I was mistaken."

"Think nothing of it," I said. "Here's the deal. A man who claims to know Marcia Hunt called me. He said he knows where Marcia's living. He'll take me to her for $5,000."

"And what did you tell him?"

"I told him he was greedy."

"You've got that right. Anyhow, he's probably an imposter."

I waited.

"Well come on!" said Service, his voice rising. "What do you think?"

"I think the man has genuine information about the life and times of Marcia Hunt-Harkness. I'm not so sure whether he knows where she is now, though. Still, you never know. It wouldn't hurt to give him something."

"I don't like the sound of this," Service snapped. "I thought I'd made it clear that we don't want our business broadcast all over town. Now strangers are making outrageous demands. This is the sort of thing I was afraid of. There'll be reporters knocking on these doors next." He caught the edge of his upper lip between his teeth and worked his jaw from side to side.

"If reporters arrive, it won't be because of anything I did."

"I'm disappointed," said Service.

"Me too."

"Damn your insolence! Who the hell do you think you're talking to?" Service unfolded his arms and clenched his fists.

"Up your ass," I said and turned away. I hadn't walked five yards before Service called out. "Wait a minute," he said. "Let's try this again."

I turned and said, "Would you like me better if I wore a cedar cape and dentalia beads?"

My words were wasted. Instead of listening, Service was trying to get a grip on his temper. He moved closer and said, "There are things going on that you don't know about. Actually, I'm under a bit of pressure. Maybe I need a holiday."

"I assumed you'd just had one."

"Think again. That was no holiday." He jammed his hands deep into his pockets and stared at the ground. "It's too much to deal with now. We'll have to leave any decision on the reward for a couple of days." His smile was as genuine as a 50-cent pearl. "This man with the so-called information. Will he wait?"

"I don't see why not."

Service was still uneasy, but he was under control now. "Anything else?"

"Not much. I have a so-so lead in Seattle. Maybe that will go somewhere, maybe it won't."

"That's not very specific."

"Well, in this business it's generally just a question of putting one foot in front of the other. Most of the time I'm doing it for the exercise; occasionally things fall into place. So far, apart from the guy who answered my newspaper ad, I've got nothing much to tell you."

"Your informant. Is he a local man?"

"Yes," I said evasively. "He lives in Victoria."

"Whereabouts?"

"He's got a mobile home."

Service wanted more, but things had gone badly and he didn't push it. He said, "Sorry, Silas. I guess I blew my stack."

"Sure. No problem. Guy in the snoop business, people assume he's an asshole. I'm used to it."

"Well, if there's nothing else I'll be getting along."

"There is something else, actually," I said.

Service waited.

I said, "It's about that maid, Effie. Why did she quit?"

"Effie?" Service shook his head. "I honestly don't know why she quit."

"I'd like to talk to her."

Service's eyes narrowed again.

I said, "Do you have Effie's address, phone number?"

"Not offhand. I've got it in my office, though. This way."

I followed Service back to the house and through the front door.

We went down the hall, through a butler's pantry and along a passageway, and came out in a library. Service's office was next door. We went inside. Service poked about in a filing cabinet while I looked through the windows. Wisps of smoke dribbled from the garden incinerator. Today the three-car garage's doors were all open. There was an ancient Silver Ghost in one bay and a white Mark v Jaguar in another. The third bay was empty.

Service finished rummaging in the filing cabinet, slammed the drawers shut, locked them and went behind his desk. He wrote Effie Yokwats's address and phone number on the back of one of his business cards and handed it to me.

I said, "About Paddy Coulton. You told me he got nowhere with his inquiries."

"That's right," Service said, sitting down and drumming his fingers on the edge of his desk. He seemed agitated now; drops of perspiration glistened on his forehead.

I said, "According to you he spent thousands of dollars before you let him go. He must have made some kind of report. I'd like a copy of that report, if I may."

"Believe me, Silas, Coulton came up with absolutely nothing." He smiled and said, "Sorry I haven't been more helpful."

He noticed me looking at his drumming fingers and put his hands on his lap. When I looked into his eyes, his glance fell away but not before I noticed that his pupils were dilated. This was a man in dire need of a tranquilizer. Or a fix.

I said coldly, "Believe me, Charles. You've been more helpful than perhaps you realize."

I drove out of the gates slowly to give the man driving the green Toyota a chance to follow me. Nothing happened. Maybe, I thought, I was becoming like Charles Service — a bit paranoid.

THERE ARE AT LEAST A HUNDRED souvenir shops in Victoria where you can purchase West Coast Native masks, miniature totem poles, handwoven baskets, drums, beadwork, Cowichan sweaters and the rest of it, a good percentage of which is imported from Asia. Folks interested in genuine Native artifacts — modern or antique — gravitate to Gottlieb's Trading Post on Courtney Street. Gottlieb buys his stuff at auction or from Native artists. He pays well and is generous to carvers down on their luck. I was walking past Gottlieb's when he came out and grabbed my arm. "Silas," he said, "we need to talk."

I followed Gottlieb through his trading post into a storeroom-cum-office at the back. Somebody had used a double-bitted axe to hack through an exterior wall from the back lane. Two women were cleaning up the mess. Gottlieb had nailed a sheet of plywood over the hole. Bits of splintered lumber lay everywhere. A thick coating of powdered gyproc overlaid Gottlieb's desk and everything else. Gottlieb ushered the cleaning women out, shut the door and invited me to sit. After eyeing the dust-covered chairs, I declined.

Gottlieb was nervous. He said, "A carpenter's on his way to fix things. A couple of days and nobody will ever know what happened here."

"What *did* happen?"

"Gregarious George did it."

That sounded improbable. I said, "Did you see him do it?"

"No. But I know it was George."

"How?"

"I just know, believe me. George is the one, he did it," Gottlieb said adamantly. "George and me, we've been having problems for about two years."

"Gregarious George has been having problems with *everybody* for about two years. What makes you so special?"

Instead of answering, Gottlieb took a clean plastic garbage sack from a package and laid it on a chair for me to sit on. His chair already had a sack on it. "Go on," he said. "Take the weight off your feet."

"I'd rather stand."

Gottlieb sat down and mopped his forehead with a handkerchief. He said, "I won't lay charges because George is nuts. I won't add to his problems. But George took something and I want it back."

"What's that?"

Gottlieb shook his head.

I've known Gottlieb for many years. This was the first time I'd seen him blush. He also coughed, sighed, hemmed and hawed, and finally managed to say, "It's confidential, Silas. Very."

"Gottlieb," I said, "you're being disingenuous. It's not like you."

Gottlieb was still flushed to the roots of his hair. He took a deep breath and said, "Two years ago, George sold me an earth dwarf manikin."

My heart jittered. Gottlieb's words hit me right down to my toenails. I sat down without taking my eyes off his face.

"An *earth dwarf manikin*," Gottlieb said. "I didn't know what it was at first. All I knew, it was old."

"You kept an earth dwarf manikin in this shop for two years?"

"No. And like I said, I didn't know *what* it was. Not then. George brought it in. It was obviously old, possibly valuable. I asked George how he came by it, what it was. George said he didn't know what it was. He'd found it lying on a bunch of kelp weed on the beach at Gonzales Bay. George asked $100 for it. That's what I paid him, I didn't argue."

Gottlieb stopped talking. He was shaking. When he calmed down he said, "I phoned Peter Wool, asked him to drop in here and take a look at it the next time he was passing. You know Peter Wool?"

"Sure," I said. Peter Wool wrote the book on Coast Salish artifacts.

"Right," Gottlieb said. "Peter came in here and saw it a day or two later. He thought he knew what it was but wouldn't commit himself."

I said, "What's the manikin look like?"

"It's a slab of cedar, painted with red-earth pigment and creosote. About a foot wide, an inch thick, three feet high. The colour is very faint. You can still make out a wolf's-head design on the front side. There's a half-inch-diameter hole drilled more or less in the centre of the slab. There's a wooden peg, about four inches long, projecting from the bottom edge. I took digitals of the thing and e-mailed them to the Smithsonian. I showed the same photographs to Theo Durksen at the provincial museum. Durksen said it didn't even look Coast Salish to him. He suggested I bring the actual artifact in for a proper examination."

Gottlieb's blush had faded. Now his complexion imitated Hamlet's father's. I waited.

Gottlieb said, "That's when things started to get weird. I left the museum, came back here to get the manikin and *couldn't find it*. It had gone." Gottlieb pointed a finger across the room. "I know damn well I left it leaning against that wall. Right there. I *know* I did."

"Somebody took it?"

"I don't know. That's the hell of it," Gottlieb said. He came out of his chair, opened the door to his office and asked me to check the lockset. There was a good Yale on the door, plus a TrustBankers lock with a hefty deadbolt.

Gottlieb sat down again and said, "This is exactly the way it happened. I lean the dwarf against that wall, lock it in here and walk to the museum with my photographs. When I get back here that door's still locked, but the dwarf isn't where I left it. It's gone. But that dwarf came back."

I thought I knew where we were going. I didn't say anything.

Gottlieb said, "I can still remember the number of every telephone I ever owned. I know my social insurance number, my library card number, and the licence number on the Hertz Rent-A-Car that I drove on my honeymoon in 1954. I know my children's birthdays, my grandchildren's birthdays, the birthdays of my entire extended family. I can recite the Old Testament, not excluding the begats. Plus, I'm one helluva bridge player. What I'm getting at, I don't have Alzheimer's. When I put things down, I remember where I put them down."

"I believe you," I said. I meant it.

"The next thing happens, George comes barging into my shop with the $100 I'd given him. He's excited. Waving his arms, wants the manikin back. But George is drunk. He knows my rule, I kick him out."

I know Gottlieb's rule as well. Every Native carver in Victoria knows it: if you've been drinking, even a little bit, he won't do business with you.

Gottlieb said, "It's lucky George *had* been drinking, because I couldn't have sold the manikin back even if I'd wanted to. Like I told you, it had disappeared."

Gottlieb spread his arms with a helpless gesture and looked at the ceiling. He shook his head, lowered his arms and looked at me with eyes that seemed to recede and diminish. He said, "My friend at the Smithsonian gets back to me. He's excited as hell. He tells me it's an earth dwarf manikin — there's one that's almost identical in their Myron Eells collection. My friend tells me another thing. That earth dwarf manikin is priceless. It's one of a pair made by a Twana carver in 1858. Theirs is a moneyfinder manikin. Mine is a ghostfinder manikin.

"In the meantime, Gregarious George is driving me nuts. He's pissed from morning till night. He won't give me a minute's peace till I give him the manikin back. I can't give it back because I don't have it anymore. Two years go by like this. Then something happens.

"Yesterday's my regular day off. I'm at home, in my garden shed, taking out my mower. Ready to cut my lawn. So I take the mower out and check the oil level. I check the mower blade to see if it's still sharp. Everything's Okay. My mower's a good one, it starts the first time I yank the cord. I leave the mower running and go back to the garden shed for my grasscatcher attachment. And there it is. The earth dwarf manikin. It's leaning against the wall in my fucking garden shed."

I had been holding my breath.

Gottlieb said, "I started to take the manikin into my house, but something stopped me. Don't ask me to explain it because I can't. I just didn't want that thing in my house. What I did, I wrapped it in newspaper, taped it into a nice neat parcel and drove it downtown to my store. My store's open, of course. My manager keeps it open seven days a week in the tourist season. I park my car on the street, take my parcel into the store, unlock my office and put the manikin on my desk. Then I turn around and there's Gregarious George, drunk. He'd seen me get out of my car and followed me in. Wants to know what's in the parcel. I tell George it's none of his business. George calls me a thief. He reeks of booze. I gave him the same lecture that every drunk gets and he backed down, for once. Went out onto the street and staggered off. That was last night.

"Today I've got no manikin, and no wall. What're you gonna do about it?"

CHAPTER SEVEN

Vancouver is British Columbia's best-known and largest city. Victoria, B.C.'s provincial capital, is a city of about 250,000 people built on an island about 20 miles from the mainland. It's been obvious for a hundred years that Vancouver is where the money and the power are, but instead of erecting new legislative buildings in Vancouver, B.C.'s legislators, after much deliberation, decided to leave the legislative buildings where they were and build the world's largest ferry fleet.

At 6:45 on Monday morning I drove my Chevy aboard the *Spirit of Vancouver Island*, left it on the lower parking deck and walked up three flights of stairs to the ship's dining room. I found a window seat and looked up at the sky to the east, where the sun was rising above the Gulf Islands. One oddly symmetrical white cloud shimmered on the horizon. I narrowed my eyes. It was no cloud. I was looking at the *Pallada*, a magnificent full-rigged Russian sailing ship, en route to Victoria for a sea festival.

Three and a half hours after leaving Victoria I was crossing the Canada–U.S. border at Blaine and heading south down Interstate 5. In the ever-changing pattern of southbound traffic, certain companion vehicles began to distinguish themselves as I passed them and they repassed me en route. One was a U-Haul truck driven by a bearded young man. Another was a Mazda Miata convertible driven by an older woman with grey hair and a long silk scarf fluttering from her neck. The third was a dust-covered black Buick with tinted windows. I lost the Buick and the U-Haul when I pulled into Mount Vernon for a rest stop. Mazda lady pulled into the McDonald's parking lot right behind me and headed inside in a hurry.

I lost the Mazda after that but overtook the Buick going through Everett. I caught my last glance of the U-Haul five minutes before I exited I-5 at the Edmonds off-ramp.

THE ASTORIA'S DESK clerk needed a shave. He was a skinny old Mexican wearing a maroon-coloured beret, a soiled Che Guevara T-shirt and Dayglo suspenders. I couldn't see below the counter but imagined blue jeans sagging at the crotch and greasy carpet slippers. I asked for Ray Smith. The clerk said, "Room 21." As I headed for the stairs, the clerk remembered something and called me back. "Your name Seaweed?"

I nodded.

"Ray's out of town for a couple of days. He left something for you." The clerk reached into a pigeon hole, then handed me a piece of notepaper folded into a square.

The note said, "MR. SEAWEED, I CHANGED MY MIND ON THAT MARCIA DEAL AND POINT MATLOCK. GOOD LUCK, RAY."

The desk clerk had picked up the sports section and was studying the day's racing form. I rapped a knuckle on the counter to get his attention. His attention span expanded when I laid a five-dollar bill on the counter and smoothed it with my fingers.

I said, "Half a sawbuck ain't much, but if you put it on Sunny Lady at Santa 'nita tomorrow, something wonderful might happen."

"Sunny Lady?" the clerk said, contemplating the banknote as if it contained the answer to the meaning of life. "Never heard of her."

"When's the last time you saw Ray?"

The clerk scratched his chin bristles with nicotine-stained fingers. He said, "There's 56 full-time residents live in this building. Coming and going day and night. How do I know when I seen Ray last? Sometimes he stops by the desk, shoots the breeze for a minute. I think the last time I seen him was two days ago, when he left your letter."

One or two or three resident old-timers were sitting in the lobby, watching soaps on a black-and-white TV. Empathizing with the romantic problems of wealthy society matrons and youthful surgeons. Nobody was interested in me or my problems.

I went upstairs and along a dark, windowless corridor that reminded me of a jail. The only light came from a single naked light bulb; it was a strain to read room numbers. I found 21 and hammered on the door. Nobody answered so I beat another tattoo. That annoyed Ray Smith's neighbour, a woman in a silk wrapper and hair curlers.

She opened her door the length of a security chain, said, "Noisy asshole! Get back to the reservation," and backed into her lair.

A soft chuckle sounded behind me and a deep voice said, "Hey, pal. You got a light?"

It was a big guy in a dark business suit. My brain was just registering the nylon stocking covering his face and the heavy elongated leather teardrop dangling from his wrist when my arms were grabbed by a second man who materialized out of nowhere. The first man's arm went back and the blackjack came swinging at my head in a big arc hard enough to kill a mule. I lunged forward. The blackjack glanced off my shoulders and maybe it clipped the guy holding me, because his grip relaxed. I lunged forward and upward and drove my head into the first man's chest. His head snapped forward. My momentum was too much for him. I kicked his shins and he fell backward with a choking cry, but the other mugger had picked up the blackjack. This time the swing was accurate. It was a numbing blow to my head, just behind my right ear. I fell on top of the first mugger's body. Lights came on in the corridor, lights were flashing inside my head, a woman was screaming. Then the roof fell onto my head and I passed out.

When I came to I was lying on a bed. I felt nauseated and dizzy — it was as if I were enclosed in a slowly rotating cylinder. The woman in silk wrapper and curlers was sitting on the bed beside me, holding an ice pack to my head. The desk clerk was checking my billfold.

I groaned and waved a weak arm. Weak, but strong enough to impress the desk clerk. He dropped my billfold onto the bedside table and said, "We ain't took nothing, mister. We was just checking to see who you was is all." He licked his lips and added, "I didn't know you was no cop; you should of said."

I tried to get up from the bed. Silk-wrapper woman put a hand on my chest. "It's okay, mister," she said. "Whatever you want, it'll keep. Take it easy."

I had a bad headache, but the vertigo was diminishing. When I closed my eyes it returned. I opened them again and focussed on a window sill. After a while my internal gyro kicked in and I sat up.

The desk clerk backed away from me. "This hotel ain't responsible for no damages, mister," he whined. "We got a sign on the desk that says so. It's established policy." He went out.

The woman said, "Pay him no mind. Manuel's a little prick, scared he'll lose his job is all."

She was about 60, a sallow, gaunt-faced woman as cute and shapely as a brick chimney. She had muddy eyes and a rasping voice and chronic obstructive pulmonary disease, but right then she looked and sounded like an angel to me. The room's furniture included a black-and-white TV. It was muted, tuned to the same soap opera I had seen downstairs. I realized that only a few minutes had elapsed since I had first set foot in the hotel.

I said, "Thanks ma'am. When you opened your door and screamed you probably saved my life."

She said, "I didn't do nothing. Your Crazy Horse act was more than them goons could handle. The one guy had to carry his partner downstairs."

I checked my billfold. Nothing was missing. I took out $100 in $20 bills and pushed them under a pillow.

I said, "Those muggers. Was one of them a red-haired guy, looks kind of Irish?"

She went across to a window and looked out, moving slowly as if her feet hurt her. "I think so," she said. "Hard to tell in the dark."

"Tell me about Ray Smith."

"Can't tell you nothing. I only been here a few days, just blew in from San Berdoo. Ray seems an okay guy to me. Pretty quiet."

I tried to cross the room and made it to the door at the first go. When I opened it, the woman said, "Say, mister. What's your name?"

"Silas Seaweed."

"I'm Mavis. Drop in, anytime." A sound like a buzz saw came out of her mouth but maybe she was just laughing. "I'm sorry what I said to you earlier. You know. Calling you Injun."

"That's what I am."

That buzz saw sound followed me into the corridor. The desk clerk was out there waiting. He lowered his eyes and backed up to the opposite wall. A bunch of keys dangled from his belt. I said, "Use your pass key, friend, and open Ray Smith's door for me."

He shook his head and started another hostelry-etiquette lecture. Fed up, I grabbed him by the throat and shook him. When I let him go he opened the door to Room 21 and stepped aside. He didn't follow me in. I don't blame him. Ray's was another sad little cubicle. The only difference between this one and Mavis's was the odour of liniment instead of cheap cologne. Ray Smith's clarinet case stood in a corner. It looked lonely.

I went downstairs. The clerk vanished into some lair behind the desk. The TV watchers were still glued to their set, except for one gaunt, thick-shouldered old guy reading a newspaper by the window.

As I crossed to the door the old guy looked up from his newspaper and grinned at me. "Seen your buddies leavin' just now," he said with a chuckle. "You gave the one of 'em a shitkicking, hey?"

I stopped in my tracks. "You saw them leave?"

"Yeah. The one guy was nursing his *cojones* with both hands." The old man fished a cigarette from his shirt pocket and put it in his mouth.

"Did you happen to notice their car?"

"Sure," he said, the unlit cigarette moving up and down in his mouth as he spoke. "It was parked down the block."

"Let me guess. How about a dusty Buick with tinted windows?"

The old guy nodded.

I had been outsmarted. A team using two cars and cellphones had trailed me all the way to Seattle. The other car had probably been a Mazda Miata.

I self-medicated with 440 mg of Walgreen's Aspirin and walked the downtown streets for half an hour until my aches settled down and my head cleared.

The Astoria Hotel was near the waters of Puget Sound. I could smell ocean when I walked back to my Chev. I threaded my way up Seattle's steep streets to Interstate 5, flipped my sun visor down and headed south, thinking about black Buicks, Mazda convertibles and a woman driver who might easily be a gorgeous blonde wearing a grey wig and a silk neck scarf to disguise her tender years.

POINT MATLOCK LIGHTHOUSE was a white tower painted red above the keeper's railing. It stood at the edge of cliffs above a drift-log–strewn beach, where flocks of small birds ran along the tide line pecking at delicacies left by receding waves.

I turned my back on the lighthouse. From what I remembered of Ray Smith's description, Marcia Hunt's former house should have been within a few feet of where I was standing now. But there was nothing. Not even old foundations or scattered bricks. Nothing except nodding wild flowers and coarse grasses. Smudges of smoke on the far horizon drew my eyes to a couple of freighters. No trace of the old military fort remained.

Half a mile away was the village of old Point Matlock — a weathered Texaco station, some wood-frame houses, a café that had survived since the military occupation. I drove to the Texaco station and pulled up at the pumps. A kid fixing tires in the service bay glanced up and shouted, "Be right there!" in a cheery voice. It cost me $30 to top up my tank. I sauntered into the service bay and said, "I owe you 30 bucks."

"Be right with you, mister."

"I also need information. I'm trying to get a lead on a woman who lived here once."

"How long ago?" Compressed air hissed as the kid inflated the tire from a hose.

"More than 20 years."

"Hey, man. You're talking, like, Stone Age." He checked the tire pressure with a gauge, nodded, and then was ready to give me his full attention. He pointed across the road to the Matlock Café and said, "Grab a cup of coffee and ask Mrs. Teller. She's been here longer'n God."

THE MATLOCK CAFÉ might have been designed by the man who did Mom's Café. It had the same furniture — a counter, booths, a Wurlitzer. The customers looked interchangeable. Only the waitress was different. She was an elderly woman, skinny as a rail, wearing rhinestone-covered eyeglasses. She had snow-white dentures a size larger than needed. Every time she spoke, or grinned, her teeth went roaming until she sucked in her cheeks to reposition them.

I sat at the counter. Without being asked, she slapped a mug of coffee in front of me and said, "Stranger, we got world-famous pies here: apple, cherry, raisin and banana cream. Which one you gonna have?"

I said, "Make it apple." Anticipating her next question, I added, "Better make that à la mode."

"That's what I like," she said, sucking in her cheeks. "Man who knows what he wants."

The pie was good, but I didn't see why it was world famous. The waitress sat on a stool and watched me eat. Smoke curled up from a cigarette in an ashtray on the counter next to her elbow. She picked up the cigarette, tapped the ash off and stuck it into the exact centre of her mouth.

I said, "Weren't there some old military houses near the lighthouse at one time?"

"Yep. Houses and barracks. Them that hadn't fallen down was torn down. This whole area is a state park now. 'Cept for my café." The cigarette jigged up and down as she spoke.

"I was afraid you were going to say that."

"You a family tracer?"

The question startled me. I said, "I'm making inquiries about a family that lived here once."

"That's what I figured. Most strangers what come visiting Point Matlock is historians. You'd be one of them generalists."

She meant a genealogist and probably thought I was tracing my family tree.

I said, "I'm looking for a woman called Marcia Hunt who lived close to the lighthouse."

"I don't remember no Marcia Hunt."

"She might have used the name Harkness."

She refilled my coffee mug, stubbed out her butt, lit another and folded her arms. Her brow furrowed with concentration. "Marcia Hunt, eh? She wasn't living here lately or I'd remember."

"Marcia was a Canadian. Played piano in a band sometimes. I'm told that she gave birth to a baby girl while she lived here."

Hearing the word "baby" made the woman's eyes light up. "There *was* a woman with a baby squatting in one of them old military houses. Near the lighthouse it was, but I don't know if she was Canadian. She could have been anything. But that house, if it *was* her house, it burned down long ago." She shook her head, remembering. "Landsakes. There were lots of girls squatting and carrying on in them days. Maybe some of 'em played in bands and maybe some of 'em played at something else. The ones that I remember all wore long dresses and played guitars. Carried their babies slung on their backs in sheets like I seen your squaws do in John Wayne movies." She sighed heavily and added, "Well, I can't help you, Jack."

Old-timers drinking coffee at the scattered tables had been listening to our conversation. Without encouragement they contributed their reminiscences. Nobody remembered Marcia.

I thanked everybody and had my hand on the doorknob, ready to leave, when the waitress said, "Pity you ain't a military buff, Jack. If you was, I could steer you somewhere interesting."

I moved a step closer. She said, "We get lots of folks poking around the site. People looking for army souvenirs — badges and belt buckles. They come out here with electric gold-finder outfits, checking the ground for buried treasure. You should see what they dig up. Bullets, handguns, even some old cannons that the military dug under and forgot. If you was interested, you could go talk to Colonel Porter, used to live here. He runs the Porter Museum at Snake River. Knows everything. Got books with dates in 'em and suchlike."

SNAKE RIVER WAS another 25 miles down Interstate 5. The Porter Museum was a retired gas station painted to simulate a frontier fort. Doors and windows had been bricked in, dummy gun towers guarded each corner. Two muzzle-loading cannons stood on either side of the entrance. Somebody had gone to a lot of trouble to make the exterior resemble log construction, but the illusion only lasted until you were within 100 yards. Closer than that, the building looked like a painted gas station.

Colonel Porter was a tall, easygoing man of about 75, who looked

ready to go square dancing. He had on a string necktie with a miniature longhorn clasp, a blue-checkered shirt, jeans and cowboy boots.
The inside of his museum was filled with military hardware, war books,
old battle pictures and a collection of American flags. There were no
customers.

I said, "I'm from Victoria, B.C., looking for a woman who went missing a long time ago." I told him my name and explained my visit to the
Matlock Café.

"That would be Mrs. Teller you were speaking to. I see her regularly."
He grinned. "I hope this isn't a wasted journey for you."

"The woman I'm looking for is called Marcia Hunt, but she might
also have used the name Harkness."

The colonel tucked both hands under his arms and looked at his
feet, frowning as he tried to conjure names. "Sorry, Mr. Seaweed. Don't
recall any such name."

"Think nothing of it. Coming here to see you was a long shot at best."

"At least I can give you a cup of decent coffee," the colonel said and
went behind his counter where an aluminum percolator bubbled. "As you
can see, I'm not exactly bursting at the seams with customers." He took
the coffee pot off the hotplate and poured two cups.

He said, "When I got out of the service after the war I married Milly
and we moved to Point Matlock. I've always been interested in military
history and I ended up with this collection of antiquated junk. My wife
had been an army nurse and she shared my interest. When Milly died a
few years back, Point Matlock contained too many disturbing memories.
I kept seeing things that reminded me of Milly so I moved here."

We settled into rocking chairs on either side of an old campaign
chest. He said, "Tell me about this woman."

I told him as much about Marcia as he needed to know and said, "If
my information is correct, Marcia was at Point Matlock about 1981, living
in an abandoned military house close to the lighthouse."

"That's very possible. The fort at Point Matlock was decommissioned
in 1950. For a while there was a caretaker, but the place was pretty much
rundown when the installation was abandoned. As an economy the caretaker was paid off and the government just washed its hands of the place.
The inevitable happened. Vandals set fires and broke glass. Some small

houses were occupied by squatters and stayed more or less habitable as late as the early '90s. In 1997 the land became a state park."

"Mrs. Teller said that you have records of the old fort."

"That's right. I've got rosters and copies of orderly sheets from the fort's earliest days, but my information only concerns the military occupation."

I sipped coffee and said, "It's strange how quickly tracks get covered up. We're talking about a woman who, if she's still alive, is only in her 40s. When she was in Point Matlock she had friends, neighbours. There might have been other little girls there too, who played with the woman's baby daughter. But she left no mark on the place, might never have existed."

"You say the woman had a baby?"

"That's right. It was born right there. Born in a house near the lighthouse, in fact."

"Why, that might make all the difference," said the colonel. "My wife was a registered nurse. For years she was the only nurse in the area. And Milly delivered lots of babies. We had no full-time doctor in Point Matlock, and people used to call on her in emergencies."

The colonel went into private quarters behind a dangling bead curtain and returned with a cardboard file box. He riffled through it until he came out with a bundle of well-fingered notebooks tied together with red ribbon. "These are Milly's diaries. She started keeping them in high school and kept at it all her life," the colonel said as he untied the ribbon. "When was this baby born?"

"Marcia was two or three months pregnant when she sent a postcard to a friend in Victoria. The baby was probably born in late 1982 or early 1983."

Colonel Porter picked out the proper journal, thumbed through it and found the page he was looking for. He ran his finger down the page, moving his lips as he encountered interesting passages.

He handed me the book, his finger marking the place he'd been looking for. And there it was:

> December 28, 1982. Snow nearly all washed away by today's
> rain. Wrote a letter to Edith, thanked her for recipes.
>
> Called at noon to see Marcia in the white house. Poor girl
> suffering badly with pains. Her first child. Another woman living

in the old Todd House helping. Marcia's live-in (a black-haired Russian who seemed drunk or stoned) interfering and getting in my way. I scolded Marcia for smoking cigarettes then felt bad because she started to cry, poor thing.

Marcia's friend, or husband, I don't know which, fetched me at eight tonight, panicked, of course, as they always are, but not necessary. Marcia delivered a baby girl, mother and child well. Wanted to name the child after me — another! But I demurred. Instead, they'll call the infant Alison Harkness Hunt.

After another search in the diaries, the colonel found one more significant entry, for June 12, 1983:

Saw Marcia and Alison today at the Texaco station. They were leaving for Reno. Marcia looking tired and peaky, but the baby seemed healthy enough. Maybe the desert air will help. I asked about her husband-companion, but Marcia evasive. I think he is in legal trouble.

The way some people live!

The colonel looked at me expectantly.

I said, "Frank Harkness married Marcia Hunt in 1982. He had a bad reputation. When Marcia's parents found out about the wedding they went nuts. They thought she was marrying beneath them and figured that Harkness was only interested in their money — the Hunts were well-off. Marcia was a minor and had married without permission. Her parents tried to have it annulled. The whole affair was mishandled. After a big argument, Marcia ran away. Apart from a single postcard, nothing has been heard of her since."

The colonel had stiffened. He said stonily, "What kind of folks are these? Have an argument and never speak to each other again?! Too proud to apologize and make up? They must be insane."

"It's a sad story. Lives wasted, and for what? It beats me."

"Folks like that hardly seem worth helping. But what's your next step, Mr. Seaweed?"

I thought it over and said, "I might as well call on the local authorities. Your wife's journal suggests that Harkness was in trouble with the law. I didn't mention it earlier, but Harkness was a U.S. citizen. He skipped north to evade justice."

"Tell you what," said the colonel. "There isn't much going on in the museum today. If you like, I'll close up early. I've got a bit of influence with the local law. The sheriff is an ex-military man, a friend of mine."

SHERIFF OMAR FIRKINS was dozing with his feet on the desk when the colonel and I walked in on him. At the sound of his office door opening, the lawman poked a lazy finger under the brim of his hat and eased it back until he could see who his visitors were.

"Damn, Colonel," said the sheriff, yawning and recrossing his legs. "Don't matter how much I try, I can't get a wink of sleep on this job."

The colonel grinned at him. "What's the matter, Omar, you been checking the all-night taverns again?"

"Nope." The sheriff gave another giant yawn. "Been over to the high school lecturing kids on traffic safety, but all they want to talk about is crystal meth and crack cocaine. They call it jib now. Jib! Don't ask me why."

Sheriff Firkins grinned amiably, got to his feet and shook hands with both of us. The sheriff's movements were slow, but his blue eyes were bright and observant.

The colonel made introductions. I said, "I'm looking for leads on a case involving Frank Harkness. That name is an alias. Frank Harkness's birth name was Frank Turko."

Firkins' light grey eyes clouded noticeably. He sat down at his desk again and punched a button on his office intercom. Leaning back he said, "Mind showing me some ID, Mr. Seaweed?"

I showed him my police badge and my B.C. driver's licence. The sheriff examined them closely and said, "Frank Turko? I remember him, all right. Frank made quite a wave around here. The way I understood it, the Mounties up in Canada made life too hot so he came back stateside." A secretary appeared at the sheriff's door and leaned through the opening. The sheriff said, "Myrtle, dig out the file on Frank Turko, a.k.a. Frank Harkness."

The secretary went out.

Firkins said, "We busted Frank Turko in the '80s. The reason I remember it, we don't handle many extraditions in this office. Our typical crime is fishing without a licence or stealing firewood. We get a big case, it sticks in our minds."

The secretary came back with a file and put it on the desk. Sheriff Firkins studied it in silence, raising his eyes to study me once or twice, then said, "I arrested Frank Turko in the Snohomish Hotel on June 11, 1983. Somebody tipped us off, an anonymous phone call. We figured it was one of Turko's connections, somebody who wanted to horn in on his drug business. Anyway, Turko was in the Snohomish, enjoying breakfast with a tourist. Some guy on a fishing holiday. The two of them were in the dining room having a nice conversation about steelhead trout, and I had to interrupt. Turko made no fuss at all. He came quiet as a lamb. The State of California had an outstanding warrant on him. He'd been charged with manslaughter after a killing in Oakland years earlier. He made bail and took off. Later, the charge against Turko was raised to homicide, but by then Turko had skipped."

The sheriff absently drummed the table with his fingertips. "We arrested Turko and held him here until formalities were completed between the sovereign states of Washington and California. Later, somebody told us that Turko was tried, convicted and sentenced to life."

"There you go," Colonel Porter said, interrupting my musings. "Chances are, Turko has kept in touch with Marcia."

"Do you know where Turko's incarcerated, Sheriff?"

"I might know, Mr. Seaweed, but I ain't telling. That'd be an infringement of the prisoner's rights," Firkins said, grinning and keeping me in suspense. "But hell, Frank Turko ain't going no place. Why don't you speak to your people in Victoria? Have them wire an official request to California Corrections. I expect they'd co-operate."

The colonel and Sheriff Firkins wanted to continue socializing. I thanked them for their help and took my leave.

As an afterthought, standing by the office door, I said, "Just one more thing, Sheriff. That tourist, the fisherman having breakfast with Turko when he was arrested. Do you happen to recall his name?"

The sheriff rustled through his papers again. "Yep, it's right here. That fisherman's name was Tommy Alfred."

I GOT BACK INTO MY CHEV. After writing a few notes I headed back to Interstate 5.

Finding Harkness had been just too easy. I didn't like it. It was difficult for me to believe that Patrick Coulton hadn't been able to dig out this information long, long ago. But Coulton was dead. I wondered if Coulton's widow was still alive, and I decided to check it out as soon as I got back to Victoria.

But first I had to pass through Seattle.

I was seriously in lust with Barb and really didn't know what to do about it. I asked myself what Barb wanted. A long-distance relationship with a serial womanizer? Possibly not. I drove to the Banjo Club and after sitting in my car for five minutes decided to go in. The place was nearly empty. I recognized the waitress behind the bar and said, "Hi, Jean. I was hoping to run into Barb."

Jean smiled at me and said, "You're Silas, right?"

"Right."

"Yeah. Barb told me about you." Jean's smile faded. "The reason I'm here is because Barb's down in California." She lowered her voice. "Her old man is sick."

The implication struck me like a blow. For a second I had doubts about Barb. I said slowly, "Her old man?"

Jean grinned and said, "Don't worry, I'm talking about Barb's father. He's got a bad heart. It sounds serious."

I tried to analyze my complicated feelings, but I hadn't progressed very far before Jean said, "You want a drink, Silas? Cuba Libre, isn't it?"

"No, thanks. Tell Barb I dropped by, will you?"

A customer came in, sat at a table and raised one finger. Jean went over to him. I went out.

It was a long lonely drive back to Canada.

CHAPTER EIGHT

My office appeared to have changed little in the 48 hours since I had seen it last. I used my key to let myself in and switched on the answering machine. Standing by the window while the tape rewound, I caught glimpses of the people passing to and fro outside. Nearly everybody looked pale and preoccupied and tense.

My voice-mail clicked in. Several messages were from a person named Norbert, who wanted to buy Constable Halvorsen's dinner. I found Norbert's unctuous tones annoying. In my imagination I saw the beautiful constable gazing adoringly at this unknown admirer across fine crystal and silver and a linen tablecloth. Who did she think she was? The upstart constable was now using my office as her personal answering service.

I thought: I better put a stop to this. Then I thought: Wait a minute. Think this over first.

Then some real messages came on. The street jiver's messages were becoming specific. Called me a chicken-fat turkey. Warned me of the harm that would befall a man who stood between the speaker and his rightful goods. Seaweed could make amends by putting $4,000 in a bag and giving it to a certain party in Waddington Alley. Otherwise, pretty soon Seaweed was gonna get gutted alive. Maybe worse.

Somebody left a garbled message about missing lottery tickets.

A friend of mine, Pete Sharp, had mailed a postcard from Brazil, hinting at fabulous opportunities and inviting me to meet him in Manaus. To divert my mind I made junk-mail paper airplanes and sailed them across the office. My wastebasket was Puerto Barrios, Guatemala. The top of a filing cabinet was Devil's Island. Burma, almost inaccessible these days, was my coat rack. Just for the hell of it I wondered how much a trip to Brazil would set me back. I built one more glider and launched it across the room. It climbed over the Andes, banked east, crossed the Falkland Islands and nosedived into Liverpool. I wondered how Sarah Williams was getting on without me. Shit. I was daydreaming instead of taking care of business.

I phoned Vancouver PD and got Mrs. Coulton's telephone number. Paddy Coulton's widow had retired to a seniors' complex in White Rock. I phoned the complex and after some palaver was routed through to a registered nurse named Elizabeth Dickins.

I told Mrs. Dickins what I wanted. She said, "I'm sorry to tell you that Mrs. Coulton has had a little setback. She fell yesterday and we believe she's had another mild stroke. Right now she's in Surrey Memorial Hospital. I doubt if she'd be much use to the police at the moment."

I went out to the washroom, poured myself a glass of water and carried it back to my desk.

I couldn't stop agonizing about Barb. What should I do next, send her a condolence card, flowers? Maybe I should phone one of those radio advisors. Gracious dispensers of free advice to a nation's crackpots, and worth every penny.

The phone rang. It was Charles Service, sounding affable. He was coming downtown on business. We agreed to meet at Lou's Café in 15 minutes.

LOU'S LATEST WORRY was the Saanich arsonist. He delivered coffee and said, "I know how to fix that firebug."

"What?" I said absently. I was thinking about my trip to Point Matlock and I wanted Lou to go away.

"That arsonist, pal, the guy setting fires all over Saanich." Lou puffed out his cheeks.

I said, "Okay, Lou. How would you handle him?"

"I'd do what we did in the old days. Put a car tire around the guy's neck and set fire to it."

"You kidding?"

"Hell no. I'd make a public spectacle of the bastard."

"Jesus, Lou. Is that how they do things in Europe?"

"You bet. You want old buildings, you gotta take care of them. Why you think they still got all them ancient cathedrals? They got them because they know how to deal with punks. Try running around Europe with a can of gasoline and a box of matches, see where it gets you." He wandered off, angrily flicking a dishrag at table crumbs before going behind his counter to brood.

I was nursing my third cup of coffee, thinking about Fred Eade, when Charles Service arrived arm-in-arm with Sarah Williams. Sarah looked very pretty in a navy-blue dress. Service was wearing another expensively cut suit from British Importers. They looked good together, although, in my opinion, Service's attempt to bridge the generation gap was slightly absurd. Sarah was hardly 40. Service was at least 65. But I had to concede — Service was in great shape. Probably played tennis every day, eschewed cholesterol. Treated women like shit and never gave it a thought. Lived the stress-free life of an uncaring asshole.

Lived very much like me, in fact.

Sarah Williams held out her hand. I touched her cool fingers. She gave me a full-eye-contact smile that made me wonder what was going on inside that pretty head. It occurred to me that she might refer to our recent encounter. I was somehow relieved that she didn't.

I signalled Lou and ordered more coffee. Sarah surveyed the diner and said, "So this is Lou's? Isn't it just *too* cute."

Was I being patronized? Before I could decide one way or the other, Service said, "Didn't you know? This is one of Piggy's buildings."

Sarah gave the lawyer a long look. "Oh, really?" she said, "Chalk up another triumph for the Piggy-wig."

I was seeing another round in an endless, secret game. The lawyer turned to look at me but didn't say anything. I said, "Have you given any more thought to the matter we spoke about last time?"

"You're referring to the reward money?"

I nodded.

He said, "Yes, I've thought it over. Go ahead, pay whatever it takes. We've got to follow every lead." He reached into his breast pocket and brought out a chequebook. "Five thousand, was it?"

I nodded.

"To whom should I make it payable?"

"To me," I said. "If it's made out to me personally, I might be able to save you a few bucks, negotiate a better deal."

The lawyer gave me a long stare.

Sarah leaned toward me and said, teasingly, "Charles doesn't trust you, Silas. He's afraid you'll take the money and spend it in Hawaii."

Service was annoyed. He said abruptly, "You're talking nonsense. I prefer to keep things businesslike. It's not a matter of trust."

"Actually," I said, kidding, "that kind of money is very tempting. A guy I know has a business proposition in Brazil. It would be fun to go down there and check it out. A few thousand would just about do it."

"Five thousand wouldn't go very far, would it?" asked Sarah, round-eyed. "Friends of mine did one of those Amazon adventure tours. Visited that opera house in Manaus and so on. They were only gone a couple of weeks and I'm sure it cost them $20,000 apiece."

Service, whose frown indicated that he didn't approve of this banter, slid a blank cheque across the table. It was made out to me.

Service said, "All right. Now, Silas. How about a progress report?"

"I've learned a few things, we're making headway," I said.

I had their full attention. Service didn't shift his eyes from my face. I looked right back at him and said, "When Frank Harkness married Marcia Hunt, he was a U.S. citizen. A fugitive from American justice."

Service said, guardedly, "That's certainly news to me."

I said, "After that showdown at the mental hospital, Marcia moved to Seattle. Harkness either accompanied Marcia or followed her soon afterward. They lived as a couple in Point Matlock."

"Yes?" said the lawyer, leaning forward. "Go on."

"Marcia and Frank weren't together long. It must have been a very rough time for her. Harkness was arrested by Washington State police in 1983. After formalities he was returned to California to face a homicide rap."

Sarah gave a sharp intake of breath. Service reached out to give her hand a squeeze.

I said, "Harkness was tried, convicted and sentenced to life. We're making inquiries. When we find out where he's incarcerated, somebody will have to go and interview him."

Service nibbled his lip abstractedly. "Well, that will make things a lot easier. You should be able to wrap this mystery up now."

"Life in a prison!" Sarah said mournfully. "How sad. What a waste."

"Right," said Service. "But Harkness wasted other lives besides his own, including your cousin's."

Sarah said, "But how can you know that? She loved him well enough to chuck away a fortune. Marcia must have had *some* happiness from the relationship."

"'Tell you what she did get from Harkness," I said. "She got a baby."

That remark struck the lawyer like a thunderbolt. He jerked bolt upright in his seat.

I waited a moment. Service was twisting his gold signet ring around on his finger. He snapped impatiently, "Come on, Seaweed. What else do you know?"

I said, "Marcia gave birth to a daughter on December 28, 1982."

Service had been listening with a rapt expression, his eyes narrowed. "Are you certain of these facts, or making educated guesses?"

"I'm practically certain of my facts. The information is from reliable sources."

"But this is remarkable, Silas," Sarah said, shaking her head in wonder. "It's amazing. You must be a very clever detective." She sighed and looked wistful. "God, when I think of Marcia, finding out that the man she loved was a murderer."

"Apparently she had a baby to contend with as well," said Service. "That must have made things even worse."

Sarah was aghast. "Charles! What a thing to say!" she said. "Only a *man* would think that. Can't you understand? That little baby gave Marcia strength, it made her strong!"

Service was dubious. "If you say so," he remarked grudgingly.

I said, "Marcia and the baby left Point Matlock for parts unknown. That's all I have to report for the moment."

Sarah Williams let out a long sigh. "Congratulations, Silas. You've performed a miracle." She appealed to the lawyer. "Hasn't he, Charles?"

He tipped his head. "Good work, Seaweed."

She said, "That other detective, the one you hired before. What was his name?"

"Patrick Coulton."

"Exactly, Coulton. Why didn't he dig all this up years ago?"

Service pushed his chair back and stood up. "I don't know." His voice had changed. Service was either lying or withholding the truth. He touched Sarah's shoulder and said, "Sarah, it's time. We have another appointment, remember?"

"Damn the appointment. Must we go so soon?" Sarah said, pouting. "I haven't finished my coffee, and I want to ask Silas about Brazil."

Impatience rose in Service's voice. "You know we're in a hurry, Sarah."

Sarah wrinkled her nose to signify disappointment but stood up dutifully, saying, "Well, keep up the good work, Silas. I'm looking forward to seeing Marcia again, and meeting my little niece."

The lawyer snapped, "*If* she exists, she isn't your niece. And she won't be little, either. She'll be in her 20s."

Sarah gave a mocking laugh. "Men! You're all so *practical!*" She turned her smile on me. One amused eye closed in a tiny wink. She said, "Mr. Seaweed's different from you, Charles. He's a dreamer, a romantic."

I looked from one to the other and said, "How do you think Mr. Hunt will react to news that he's a grandfather?"

"I haven't the least idea," said the lawyer. "Right now it's all hypothetical, so I prefer we keep this stuff to ourselves. We don't want to raise false hopes. Dr. Cunliffe is concerned about Mr. Hunt's heart. The whole thing's going to be … " He broke off, then added, "Better we wait a while and see where things go from here." Service's tone showed that he would not brook further discussion on this point.

Sarah looked at me. "Call me anytime. We'll have a private talk." Our eyes locked.

Service's stony frown deepened. He coughed unnecessarily and she turned away. Lou opened the door and bowed them out.

That Lou, I thought. Bloodthirsty, but polite.

CAPTAIN BLOGGS WAS in his tiny office, staring out across Fisherman's Wharf. Nothing seemed changed. The big Atlantic fishing trawler was in its usual berth on the outside float. Bloggs gave me a friendly grin.

I pointed to the rusty ship and said, "That trawler's still here, I notice."

"Be here forever," he snorted. "There's problems with the engine and I doubt if they've got a proper engineer in the crew. They're nuts if they think they'll sail that thing past Cape Beale, never mind Guatemala." He sighed and changed the subject. "What brings you down here?"

"I'm looking for Fred Eade. He told me he lived on one of these houseboats."

"Fred ain't got a *house*boat. What he's got is a worn-out fishboat with the guts torn out of it. Lives like an animal, him and his woman. I had all kinds of complaints about them two this morning. Seems that Fred had a drinking party. The ruckus kept his neighbours awake all night." Sighing, Bloggs pointed me toward the *Ocean Reaper*, a big, black-hulled craft that had once been a west-coast seiner.

I meandered across the floats to find Fred Eade, but my mind was elsewhere. I was thinking about Effie Yokwats and wolves when a white Mark v Jaguar cruised slowly past the parking lot, did a California stop and turned right onto Superior Street. It was too distant for me to see who the driver was.

I boarded the *Ocean Reaper* and banged on the pilothouse door. Somewhere within the boat a radio was playing soft rock — electronic guitars and drumbeats were barely audible above the sound of lapping water and creaking timbers.

A voice from behind me said, "You'll need to bang louder'n that to wake Fred. The bastard was hooting and hollering and carrying on like a maniac all night. Kept the whole dock awake. Now I reckon he's sleeping it off."

The speaker was a wharf rat — an ancient, weathered, bearded man about five feet tall who resembled an angry gnome. He was standing on the deck of his floating hovel, moored immediately astern. It was in fact a junk Airstream trailer, perched atop a raft of waterlogged timbers. Without another word the man vanished inside his Airstream and slammed the door.

I rattled the *Ocean Reaper*'s pilothouse door again. It was locked. I walked the decks, looking for a way inside, stepping over piles of care-lessly coiled rope, rusty buckets, bits of used construction lumber full of projecting nails. I found an unlocked deckhouse and went inside. It was dark, airless. Curtains covered all the portholes; the smell of rotten fish was strong. There was a rusty old drill press mounted on a workbench, rusting tools scattered everywhere. A ladder poked up through an open hatch. I peered below, into blackness, and called Eade's name. Nobody answered. I swung my legs over the hatch coaming and started down the ladder.

At the bottom I waited until my eyes became accustomed to the dark. Vague shapes materialized. Iron stanchions supported the deck. Between the stanchions the hold was partitioned into cargo spaces with lengths of two-by-eight timbers. Forward, a deeper blackness marked the presence of a watertight door set in a bulkhead. The floor was wet and slippery, oily water slapped beneath deck plates. Cautiously, groping like a blind man, I went through the door and moved forward. When I paused to listen and heard faint scraping noises, my nape hairs stiffened. Something or somebody had moved down there. I said, "Fred! Fred Eade?"

My words sounded unnaturally loud in that confined space. Nobody answered. I moved forward gingerly and felt one foot losing purchase as it reached a hole in the floor. I withdrew my foot and stooped down, feeling with my fingers. I had located the cavity where the engine had once been housed.

The place stank. It was hot and humid. Sweat ran down my cheeks. I heard that scraping sound again. This time I had no doubt — *somebody* was in the dark there with me. I froze. Less than 10 feet away, something was alive, breathing. I groped on the floor until my hand encountered a short piece of two-by-four. I advanced again, feeling with my feet to skirt that hole. I was flailing with the lumber, swinging it in an arc. Whoosh. Whoosh.

The timber struck a solid object and sent a bone-jarring shock up my arms. The lumber fell with a clatter. The darkness was broken when another door opened. A grey-brown shape passed through it. The door banged shut and left me in total darkness again. From beyond the door, above the muffled sound of footsteps, came another sound — somebody was muttering indistinctly. I heard an animal noise. My heart skipped. Something was moaning, pleading. It was a high whining, like a dog in pain. Or a wolf. Hairs stiffened on the back of my neck. I crawled now, fearing the unknown horrors that pressed all around and half afraid of plunging down a hole in that dark menacing space. The floorboards were wet, greasy. Oily water splashed my hands and soaked my pants, but at last I reached the next bulkhead and dragged its door open.

Filtered light streamed down a stairwell. A shadowy figure stood 10 feet away. Something heavy smashed into my shoulder. The shock drove me backward and the thing that had struck me clattered to the floor. There came that same moaning cry and the sounds of heavy feet, running. As I floundered through a cabin between a pair of bunk beds, my hand brushed against something soft and warm and wet. Feet raced across the deck above as I climbed stairs to reach the pilothouse. The pilothouse door was now wide open. Fifty yards away, a fat man was fleeing across the floats, so I reached toward the ship's rail unthinkingly, intending to vault ashore. Pain radiated from my injured shoulder.

I clambered over the rail and ran in pursuit, but my quarry had disappeared. Ashore, in the parking lot outside Mom's Café, a car engine started. Then a green Toyota Corolla sped out of the lot and raced away.

I was watching the Toyota disappear along Superior Street when a woman came around the corner of the float, leading a small child by the hand. When she saw me she stiffened and swept the child into her arms. I looked down at myself. My left hand and the sleeve of my jacket were red with blood; my pants were soaked with oily water.

I remembered the thing I had touched inside the *Ocean Reaper's* cabin. The thing that had been wet and warm and soft.

The old wharf rat was sitting in the doorway of his floating Airstream, reading a newspaper. I said, "Did you happen to recognize the man who ran away from Fred's boat just now?"

"I didn't hear nothing and I didn't see nothing!" the old fellow shouted angrily. "Ain't I gonna get no peace today?" He spat into the water and went inside. I went back aboard Fred's boat.

The *Ocean Reaper's* pilothouse was an untidy clutter of unwashed coffee cups, old newspapers, decaying paperbacks and rumpled wet-weather clothing. An empty beer bottle was balanced atop the ship's compass. A soiled brassiere dangled from a steering-wheel spoke. A steep stairwell led down to the accommodations. I put a hand on the railing. Looking down I saw part of a red-sleeved arm protruding from a bunk. As I descended, the whole of a bloodstained T-shirt appeared. Then I was looking at a familiar bearded face. His eyes stared sightlessly into space. It was Fred Eade. He had been shot.

My cellphone didn't work properly down below. I went up on deck and called Ribblesdale. A woman with a voice I didn't recognize answered the phone by saying, "Calvert Hunt residence, Georgiana speaking."

I said, "This is Sergeant Seaweed, Victoria PD. May I speak to Sarah Williams?"

"I'm sorry, Miss Williams is not at home."

"Mr. Service then."

"Excuse me, I'll check to see if he's in."

A minute dragged by. Georgiana came back on and said, "Mr. Service doesn't appear to be at home either. Is there any way I can help?"

"Yes," I said. "Georgiana, would you mind having a look to see if the white Jaguar is on the property?"

"I beg your pardon. What did you say?"

"The white Jaguar. I want to know if it's on the grounds or in the garage."

Another minute passed before Georgiana said, "I've just had a quick look. The Jaguar is parked in the garage."

I said, "Sorry, Georgiana, but this is very important. Are you quite sure that neither Mr. Service nor Miss Williams are on the property at this moment?"

"Quite sure. I've just said so, haven't I?" she said testily. "I'm far too busy for this. If you don't believe the things I say, come and see for yourself."

Georgiana slammed the phone down.

BERNIE TAPP ARRIVED promptly. Men in blue uniforms roped the whole area off and the serious crimes squad began its investigation. Bernie waited on the float with me, delaying his questions while a first-aid man examined my bruised shoulder and recommended ice packs.

Bernie had a newish corncob. He reamed it out and filled it from a leather pouch while I described how I'd found Fred Eade's body. I told him about the green Toyota Corolla and gave him its licence number.

I said, "I'm pretty sure the driver is a guy called Sidney Banks."

Bernie took out a spiral-bound notepad and started writing. I told him about meeting Eade in Mom's Café.

"One more thing," I said. "Remember Frank Harkness?"

Bernie thought for a moment. "The drug kingpin who went down in a plane crash? Sure, I remember him."

"Frank Harkness was married to Marcia Hunt."

Bernie's eyes widened.

I said, "I have proof that Frank Harkness was alive years after his plane went down. He was arrested by Washington State police in 1983."

"Arrested for what?"

"Homicide."

Bernie nodded. "That figures."

A technician appeared on the *Ocean Reaper*'s deck and beckoned Bernie aboard.

I said, "Right now, my guess is Harkness is doing a lifer somewhere in California. I'll be checking into it."

Bernie's pipe had gone out. He sucked a few times and then pulled out his matches. Instead of striking the match he put everything back into his pockets, shook his head and went aboard the *Ocean Reaper* without a word.

I went home.

I WAS IN MY COTTAGE, holding an ice pack to my bruises, when my house phone rang. A woman said, "This is me."

Her voice was nervous, low-pitched. I heard background voices and music. I guessed she was calling from a bar. I said, "Hello."

The woman said, "You don't know who I am, do you?"

"Should I?"

"I'm Fred Eade's woman. You've seen me once at least."

A picture of the cheerful, raffish blonde that I had seen with Fred Eade in Mom's Café came into my mind. I said, "You're Patty Nolan. Where are you calling from?"

"Never mind that." She was nervous and irritable. "I got a message for you. Information."

"I'm listening."

"It ain't that easy. I got all the trouble I need and don't need no more. How do I know I can trust you?"

"Does this have to do with Fred's murder?"

"Yes and no," she wailed hysterically. "Maybe it has, I dunno. It must have." She wept softly for a moment. "I need money," she sobbed. "I've got nothing to live on, not a cent. I know you and Fred were working on a money deal. You were gonna pay Fred for information about Marcia?"

"That's right. What do you know about it?"

"Fred was my guy, I know everything he knew, we worked together." She choked back more tears. "I need that reward money bad, mister. Are you talking cash?"

"Yes. We can make a deal immediately, in my office."

"Where's your office?"

"It's the neighbourhood cop shop, across from Swans pub. You know where that is?"

"Sure," said the woman.

"Will you come?"

"This ain't a set-up? I had nothing to do with Fred's killing."

"It's not a set-up."

"All right, I'll be there in a few minutes. If I smell a rat, I'll be outta there, understand?"

She hung up. It was nearly seven o'clock.

Fifteen minutes later I was in my office, listening to footsteps approaching along the corridor. The door opened and Constable Halvorsen walked in. She had on a strapless green dress that fitted her like a second skin, alligator shoes and a matching leather handbag.

"On your way to dinner?" I said.

Her eyes narrowed suspiciously.

I said, "I listened to your telephone message. Your boyfriend Norbert wants to take you out and I thought … "

"Norbert's not my boyfriend!" she snapped. "I don't have a *boy*friend."

I was pleased to hear it. I didn't say anything. I'd been screwing up all of my male-female relationships lately and I didn't want to screw up with her.

She sat on the edge of my desk, swinging one shapely leg and looking like something out of *Vogue*. "I didn't expect to find you in here, but since you are, I have something to tell you."

I raised my eyebrows.

"Well," she said, getting up from the desk and crossing to the door, "I complained about your methods, but that's before I knew you properly. I've been finding out that you have a lot of friends on the street, that's all."

"Thanks, Halvorsen," I said to her retreating back. She went out, closed the door, opened it again, poked her head through the opening and said, "*Denise*. Call me Denise. And by the way, I don't have a *man*friend, either. If Norbert calls again, tell him I'm busy."

PATTY NOLAN WAS LATE. Over an hour had passed since our telephone conversation.

Chantal was outside on the street, walking her strut, signalling johns. From her hips downward, all she had on were black net stockings and high heels. The johns were middle-aged men driving family sedans, young men driving old Volkswagens. They drove around and around — down Pandora, left at Wharf Street, up Fort to Government Street, then another left until they reached Pandora again — driving the hooker circuit, checking talent. Prostitution has been going on here for a century and a half. Hookers arrived in Victoria right after the gold miners, in 1858. Back then, johns walked or rode in horse-drawn carriages. Prostitutes stood under street lamps lit with whale oil. Every few years, Victoria's chief magistrate goes on a morality crusade. Under pressure from the top, futile police activity ensues. Hookers go underground and bide their time. When the pressure eases — as it always does — johns come out to play again and hookers go back to work again.

Chantal noticed me standing at my window and waved. I was watching something on the roof of the building across the street.

When Chantal heard the gun go off, she thought it was a firecracker. Then she saw that my office window had smashed into a thousand pieces. She saw me fall.

Chantal began to scream, but I didn't hear her.

CHAPTER NINE

I had been hit by a burst from an AK-47 assault rifle. One bullet grazed my temple. Another passed through the flesh of my right shoulder and clipped the collarbone. Technicians from the Serious Crimes Unit found empty shell cases on the roof of the building across the street, and they dug 17 rounds of 5.45 mm ammunition out of my office's drywall. I was lucky; Kalashnikov's pretty little gun is lethal at 1,350 metres.

After a screaming ambulance ride to the Royal Jubilee Hospital and a session in Emergency, I was removed to Intensive Care and guarded round the clock by uniform-branch constables.

Alex Cal and Jiggs Murphy had alibis. Bernie Tapp arrested them anyway and gave them a tough grilling until their lawyer showed up.

A manhunt failed to turn up Fred Eade's former companions — Patty Nolan and Sidney Banks. Sidney Banks was a petty crook with a rap sheet a mile long who had done a couple of stretches in Wilkinson Road. Once for B and E, another for a convenience-store robbery.

This all bypassed me. When I regained consciousness a pair of white-coated interns were beside my bed, speculating about possible retrograde amnesias, concussions, potentially disastrous post-traumatic neuroses and a lot of other things that I didn't understand. One thing I knew. My injuries couldn't be serious because I felt no pain. I opened my eyes and raised a hand to touch the bandages around my scalp. A series of explosions occurred between my ears. I passed out again.

The next time I woke up, my room was in near-darkness. I thought I'd gone blind until a shadowy outline moved in a corner. When I croaked, somebody pushed a button on the wall and crossed to my bed. I concentrated. Bernie Tapp's ugly mug swam into view.

"How am I doing?"

"You been shot up pretty good, pal. But like I told the medics here, you're too mean to die before you collect your pension." He grinned down at me. "I just rang for a nurse. You need anything?"

"An Aspirin. Maybe two."

DR. CUNLIFFE DROPPED by and checked my charts. He said, "I spoke to the specialists. They expect your headaches to disappear in a few days, don't anticipate any long-term ill effects. Your collarbone seems to be healing nicely. How does your head feel?"

"I think the surgeon sewed a couple of riveters inside there. Two angry men with hammers."

"That bad, eh?"

"Worse. When do I get out?"

"Three or four days if you like. You'll need in-home care for a while."

Nursing staff kept my visitors to a minimum, but investigators from Serious Crimes came by a few times. Charles Service snuck in with Sarah Williams for one brief visit. Sarah brought flowers. Service delivered grave nods and sad shakes of his distinguished white head. Denise Halvorsen sent flowers and a huge get-well card signed by 100 street bums.

Meanwhile, I didn't know which was worse: residual headaches or my sister's nagging.

Linda stood by my hospital bed, arms folded across her chest, tapping the floor with one foot and saying angrily, "I suppose you're satisfied now. Here you are in a sickbed, you could be dead, and you probably don't even have term insurance! Don't you know that if your skull was normal flesh and bone instead of solid wood you'd be history? Do you know it's a miracle you weren't blinded permanently? And what do you think about that, smart guy?"

"Nothing."

The tempo of Linda's breathing increased and her eyebrows nearly vanished into her hairline as she added, "And who are all these cards and flowers from? Are they from people who'd take you home and nurse you from death's door like I have to?"

"Why don't you read them and find out?"

"I suppose I must, you being too sick to move a muscle," she said, getting angrier with every word. "You big dumb animal. Well, there's a card from Chantal somebody. Another from Sarah somebody. A stupid note from Denise somebody. And here's a nice note from a Mr. Service. When are you going to settle down with one woman? Then I wouldn't have to run around picking up the pieces of your life, blood being thicker than water! All these women are probably no better than common street-walkers. I've seen some of the women you hang out with. You make me so mad, you big galoot! Who's Mr. Service anyhow? And Denise? Who's she supposed to be? Why don't you meet some decent girl for a change and settle down and get married instead of running all over, chasing women and carrying on?"

Linda's husband, Dick, was behind her, shrugging his shoulders and winking sympathetically until Linda wheeled around and saw him.

She said, "So, smart guy. Why don't you finish packing Silas's things so we can take him home?"

"Sure, honey," Dick said.

Spinning on her heels to stare at me again, Linda said, "I suppose you know how stupid you look, one side of your head shaved bare where the doctor had to patch that big dumb brain box of yours, two black eyes. And your shoulder all smashed up."

"I know," I said. "I'm sorry, Sis."

Linda sniffed and started to cry.

LINDA AND DICK'S house overlooks Colby Island on the opposite side of the Warrior reservation from mine. I moved into their spare room and tried to be invisible. The fishing season had closed, so Dick had taken a contract to repaint suites in a James Bay retirement complex to keep busy. Every day Linda made breakfast for the three of us. After breakfast Dick drove off in his pickup truck, while Linda went across to her clerical job in the band office.

Chief Mallory, Victoria's top policeman, dropped by to see me, kitted out in his full-dress regalia. As usual he spent half an hour retelling stories about the great times that he and my father had enjoyed when they were young together a million years ago, killing grizzlies and trophy bighorns and 200-pound Tyee salmon.

When the chief ran out of exaggerations and I could get a word in edgewise, I asked if anybody else was pursuing the Marcia Hunt inquiry. Apart from absently twirling his moustache, he acted as if he hadn't heard. Then he coughed and said, "For financial and other reasons, Victoria is rethinking the entire neighbourhood policing experiment."

This was serious. I said, "What, permanently?"

"Ah, well, my boy," he said evasively. "That's not *entirely* my decision. Victoria's police budget is set by others and isn't bottomless. But to be frank, Silas, we've had the odd complaint about your methods … "

I tried to interrupt. Chief Mallory raised his hand to shut me up. "But you're an invalid and mustn't trouble yourself about these things. Concentrate on getting well. We'll talk again." He gave me a wink and trundled off in his chauffeured limo.

The next visitor was Bernie Tapp. I was sitting in Linda's yard, studying a book on Canada's western birds, when Bernie showed up. The Eade murder was still a big mystery. Bernie had found out that the green Toyota Corolla had been stolen from a West Vancouver shopping mall.

Bernie said, "I'm just a bit curious, pal. Why did somebody shoot you?"

"I don't know. Alex Cal and Jiggs Murphy are the obvious suspects. But maybe it was the guy who bumped off Fred Eade."

"Fine, same question. Why would the guy who rubbed out Fred Eade want to do the same to you?"

"I still don't know."

Bernie said, "Somehow, there's got to be a tie-in between Harry Cunliffe's killing, Marcia Millions and Fred Eade."

"I think so too, but if there *is* a tie-in, I haven't yet found it."

"But you're looking. Maybe Frank Harkness is a key link?"

I nodded.

Bernie said, "While you were out of action I took it upon myself to call California Corrections. Asked them about Frank Harkness.

For some undetermined reason they haven't been too co-operative. Some cockamamie bullshit about prisoner's rights. So we took it up the ladder. Still nothing."

I didn't respond immediately, and for some reason Bernie thought I was holding something back. His frustrations began to show. Abruptly he said, "What's that book you're reading?"

"Nothing."

"Looks like a bird book."

"That's what it is. I picked it up at Munro's."

"So it's not nothing," he exploded. "It's a bird book! Are you ashamed of having a bird book? All kinds of people have bird books."

"Well, at least now I know the difference between a hawk and an eagle."

"How about vultures? You got pictures of vultures in there?"

"What kind?" I asked, turning to the index.

"The kind that hangs around back alleys and bars."

His own unwavering glare reminded me of eagles. I said, "What's up?"

"I'm talking about that Ruger Blackhawk you *found* in Waddington Alley. Ballistics did a good job on it. A bullet from that gun was extracted from the dead body of an Edmonton street hustler three months ago."

"What? Pimps battling for turf?"

Bernie nodded.

"So," I said, "what next?"

"What I did, I brought Jiggs Murphy in and asked him where he was when the Edmonton pimp got shot. Murphy told me he was in Calgary at the time. I couldn't shake him."

IT WAS TIME for me to get back on the horse. Charles Service wanted to see me and I had questions for Dr. Cunliffe.

Service asked me to meet him in the Ross Bay cemetery. I idled in the bushes near the Fairfield gate and watched him arrive in the Lincoln town car. I limped behind, keeping an eye on him as he strolled along tree-shaded avenues to our designated meeting place. He paused several times to shake his head at vandalized statuary and gravestones. After he'd seated himself on a park bench overlooking the sea, I joined him.

Two full-rigged barques were racing up Juan de Fuca Strait. One was the Russian sail-training vessel *Pallada*. The other ship was the *Cuauhtémoc*, from Mexico. The massive barques were accompanied by a flotilla of smaller square-riggers and schooners, all of which were headed home following visits to Victoria's sea festival.

Service said, "One of my ancestors immigrated to Canada on a ship like that, in 1850. He was a carpenter. Hired by the Hudson's Bay Company in London. Some of the shops he helped build are still standing on Government Street, including the general store once owned by Richard Carr." Service looked at me and said, "You know who Richard Carr was, I suppose?"

I did know, but I shook my head because Service was enjoying his talk.

"Richard Carr was Emily Carr's dad," Service said and pointed. "That's Emily's grave, over there. The Service family plot is about 20 yards away from it."

I expected Service to segue into a familiar yarn — the one about how, if one's Victoria forbears had only been sagacious enough, they could have snapped up Emily Carr's paintings for $5 each, those then unsellable paintings now being worth hundreds of thousands each. Mercifully, Service refrained.

There was worse to come, though. After a rambling discourse about the weather, the latest from Iraq and the wonders of medical science, Service cleared his throat and said, "Mr. Hunt wants me to tell you, Silas, how grateful he is for your heroic efforts." Struggling to get the proper ring of sincerity into his utterance, he added, "It's a shame, but Calvert Hunt's medical condition is deteriorating rapidly. Physically, he is now quite feeble, his mental condition is fading. He is forgetful and incoherent. Dr. Cunliffe doesn't think he has Alzheimer's, precisely, but Mr. Hunt's senility is fairly advanced."

The lawyer stopped speaking and stared at the grass.

I said quietly, "In other words, you want me to call off the search for Marcia Hunt?"

Service looked relieved. "It's nothing personal," he said. "We're impressed with your work. But the fact is, we've had quite a lengthy discussion ... that is, me, Sarah and Sarah's mother, Phyllis Williams ...

After taking everything into consideration, we're all agreed that Marcia is certainly dead. We won't try to influence matters further. We all think this would be Mr. Hunt's decision also, were he capable of making rational judgments."

I said abruptly, "How old is Dr. Cunliffe?"

Service seemed taken aback. He frowned and said, "I think Harry's close to 80."

"And still practising medicine. He doesn't look 80."

"Perhaps not. But I know for a fact that Harry's about the same age as Calvert Hunt. Why?"

"It strikes me as a bit curious. If Dr. Cunliffe is about 80, he must have been at least 55 when his son was born."

"Harry's first wife died childless. He was about 50-odd when he got a woman called Evelyn Boothroyd pregnant and married her. I say 'woman.' Evelyn was scarcely more than a high-school girl. The marriage was a complete disaster. Evelyn stayed around long enough to give birth to Harry Jr.. Then she ran off to join a commune."

"Does Dr. Cunliffe keep in touch with her?"

"Dunno. Why don't you ask him?"

"Perhaps I will. It's not too important."

Service moved on the bench and said, "Don't be a stranger, Silas. As soon as you're fully recovered we want you to visit us at Ribblesdale. Sarah and I will be giving a pool party. You must come."

"I don't think so. Ribblesdale's a dangerous place for Indians."

Service's smile vanished. Flushed and indignant he got to his feet, and for a moment I thought he was going to storm off without speaking. But he calmed himself with an effort, shook my hand and said with an attempt at levity, "You enjoy cemeteries, Seaweed?"

"Love 'em," I said. "Cemeteries give me the long view."

I'D ARRANGED TO MEET Dr. Cunliffe for lunch at the Oak Bay Marina Restaurant. I got there early so that I could stretch my atrophied hamstrings with a stroll along the waterfront.

Pensioners were throwing day-old bread at the ducks. Tourists were posing for photographs near the plastic killer-whale sculpture. A 100-foot sailboat was putting out from the marina. A helmsman and a bikini-clad woman seemed to be the ship's entire crew. I was wondering how one couple could possibly handle the large ship by themselves when the helmsman touched a button on his steering console. Electric motors whirred and the huge mainsail unfurled itself from the boom and climbed the mast unaided. On the shore by the boat shop a man was painting a rowboat. I watched him until a kingfisher flashed across my sight. The bird swooped into the water and re-emerged with a wriggling sliver of silver in its mouth.

Dr. Cunliffe arrived.

I knew the marina's maitre d' and he gave us the best table in the house. I ordered halibut steak. The doctor ordered green salad. He drank herbal tea. I sipped Foster's lager, thinking that the doctor, skinnier and greyer than ever, would benefit from steaks and ale himself.

Outside, a man was standing on the wharf, dangling herrings by the tail. Every once in a while a big seal's snout appeared from the water and snatched the herrings from his hands.

I said, "Did you know that they want me to drop the Marcia Hunt inquiry?"

"Yes. How do you feel about that?" The doctor's voice creaked like an old door opening.

"What Charles Service wants is irrelevant. I was too polite to tell him that, of course, but I won't quit any job half done."

"Won't?"

"The genie's out of the bottle." I grinned and added lightly, "Besides, I'm relentless."

"Why? Professional pride? Or is it because you want to nail the man who shot you?"

"Or the woman," I said.

The doctor blinked. "That thought never occurred to me."

I said, "Your son loved boats. I met a man at Fisherman's Wharf who knew Harry well. Captain Bloggs."

Some pleasant memory stirred the doctor and he smiled.

I said, "In my business it's easy to jump to conclusions. But I was making progress on the Marcia Hunt deal. And something else. I was learning things about your son. There are a couple of threads that connect Marcia Hunt and your son with the late Fred Eade."

He stared at me for a moment until realization dawned. "That's the man murdered at Fisherman's Wharf?"

I nodded.

Dr. Cunliffe was electrified. "Eade knew Harry?"

"Almost certainly. Eade was a fixture around the wharf when Harry worked on fishboats."

"Yes. I suppose so. Harry worked a couple of summers for a man called Taffy Jones." Dr. Cunliffe's voice had grown stronger. "How did you get on to Fred Eade?"

"He replied to a personal ad that I put in the *Times Colonist*." I changed the subject. "Charles Service told me that Calvert Hunt isn't well."

Dr. Cunliffe's eyes were guarded. "Calvert Hunt is neither better nor worse than when you saw him last."

I signalled for another Foster's and devoured the last traces of my lunch. "I know that your son spent a lot of time at Calvert Hunt's estate. Apparently he had full run of the facilities there. How did that come about?"

"The Hunts and the Cunliffes have been family friends for years. We had a regular bridge foursome every week till my first wife died. It's not always a good idea to be pally with one's physician, but it seemed to work all right for Calvert and me. When Marcia Hunt was a young girl, she spent a lot of time with my first wife. Calvert liked my son and always made him welcome."

"Was your son's nature anything like Marcia's?"

The doctor looked at me through half-closed eyes. "How do you mean?"

"Was Harry moody, temperamental?"

"Possibly. Like a lot of energetic boys, he could be trying at times. But generally, I'd describe Harry as a happy kid. He had an independent nature. Just before he died, Harry backpacked across the States and Mexico. Thumbing rides and doing his thing, as they say."

I said, "I must have been misinformed. I thought that Harry spent his last vacation working on Taffy Jones' boat."

"He *did* work with Taffy, but only for a couple of weeks. The fishing season closed early that year. Harry spent the rest of his vacation hitch-hiking." The doctor smiled. "He'd send me postcards of his travels. I'd trace his route on an atlas. He hitchhiked as far south as Cabo San Lucas on the Baja Peninsula, then took the ferry from La Paz to Mazatlan. He went across to San Miguel and Mexico City, then winkled his way back north through Nogales into Arizona. His last postcard to me was mailed from Reno, Nevada."

I said, "Did your son keep a log of his travels?"

"Why yes. I believe he did. I'll look for it."

"If you find it, would you mind passing it along to me? You'll get it back."

"Any special reason?"

"No. Nothing special. It's just a hunch."

The doctor glanced at his watch, then reached for the check. He said, "Sorry, Seaweed. Enjoyed our chat but I've got to run. Patients waiting."

We shook hands and I watched him go, a thin, frail, stooping old man.

That big sailboat was nearly out of sight now, heading up Juan de Fuca Strait toward the Pacific. I watched it until a flash of reflected sunlight drew my eye to a single-engine plane approaching Victoria city from the northeast.

I was reminded of another aircraft. The one piloted by Frank Harkness that fell into the sea a long time ago. Where was Marcia Hunt? I had plenty of questions. The leads that I'd worked so hard to find had dried up, one by one. Patrick Coulton was dead. With his secrets. Fred Eade was dead, with his secrets. Frank Harkness's were locked away with him in a California prison.

What next? The trail to Marcia Hunt had ended when she and her baby left Point Matlock for Reno, Nevada ...

Reno?

CHAPTER TEN

After my lunch with Dr. Cunliffe I permitted myself a recuperative afternoon nap, got up at 3:30, and went out to my little private garden. It was a glorious late summer's day. I didn't feel particularly fit, but I had felt a lot worse the day before.

My laurel hedges needed trimming, my lawn was an inch longer than I like it. Instead of getting out my hand mower and grass shears, I sat in a garden chair and watched a wren perched atop a distant totem pole. Wrens like Indian poles — northern wrens favour mortuary poles in particular. The wren winged off into a stand of oaks. Moments later an albino squirrel ascended the pole and sat quietly on top of it. I was working on a can of Foster's lager when somebody approached my cabin. I didn't necessarily want company, so instead of answering the knock on my door, I peered through a gap in my hedge to see who it was. It was Sarah Williams, looking radiant. I felt a little surge of optimism and opened my garden gate.

"Here," I said. "You may use the tradesman's entrance."

I extended my hand, but instead of taking it, Sarah put both hands on my upper arms and presented her cheek. I kissed her lightly and said, "I like your perfume. What is it?"

"*Nuit d'amour.*"

"Perfect," I said. "Come into my night-scented garden."

Sarah was wearing a high-necked white silk shirt, a short purple skirt and white low-heeled pumps — simple clothes probably worth more money than my car. She had a small purple-and-white leather bag tucked underneath her arm and a nice smile on her face. Her long, tanned, lovely legs were bare. She seemed happy to see me. I told her what I was drinking and asked her if she'd like to have one as well. She nodded and sat down on my other chair. I went in to the fridge, took out a couple of cold cans, got a glass and carried it all out to my garden. I was feeling better all the time.

The white squirrel was still enjoying its high perch. I poured Sarah's drink, handed it to her and pointed to the pole. I said, "White squirrels are rare. When a Coast Salish sees something unusual, he generally thinks that something bad will happen."

Sarah seemed amused. "Such as?"

"Such as a bad winter. Or that someone will die soon."

"Someone is bound to die soon, but that's not necessarily bad. It's equally likely that somebody will be born soon," she said.

I turned my chair around to face hers. "I'm very glad to see you."

"Likewise." She examined her fingernails. "Did Charles Service telephone you today?"

"No. Your fiancé did not call me today."

"My what?" she said, bursting into laughter. "You don't really think that I'm planning to marry Charlie?"

"What else? That huge diamond perched on the fourth finger of your left hand indicates that you're engaged to somebody."

"This bauble is an oft-convenient subterfuge." She slipped the ring off and dropped it into her bag.

I said, "What's this about Charles Service phoning me?"

"We're having an electric security gate put up at Ribblesdale. Finally. Complete strangers come up the drive in their bloody cars, want to know if they can have a house tour. Usually it's no bother, the gardener or somebody else sees them off." Sarah paused. "Yesterday was a bit different. Iris Naylor scared off another prowler. He was creeping around in the bushes, middle of the afternoon. Frightened the daylights out of the poor cow."

"Did she phone the police?"

"No. She told Charles instead. He ordered her to keep the police out of it." Sarah looked at me inquisitively.

I said, "There's more. You're not telling me everything."

Sarah nodded and said, "That prowler. He was a Native man."

"A skinny man wearing a headband?"

Sarah's eyes widened. "So Charles *did* phone you after all?"

I shook my head. "No, he didn't call."

"Funny," she said, without elaboration.

I said, "Iris Naylor, she's a queer fish."

Sarah frowned and said, "She's a professional victim. Naylor comes from a world where people waste entire lives waiting for something to turn up." She put her empty glass down and said, "Not me, though. Right now, for example, I'd like to see your house."

"In a minute," I said, smiling. "That Jag outside. Is it yours?"

"No. It belongs to Calvert. I take it out occasionally, if it's not raining. Just to keep the old girl running."

"I noticed a Jaguar just like it a few days ago, in James Bay. It looked like yours but I couldn't see who the driver was."

"Probably me. I don't think there's another car like it in these parts."

We went inside the house. My tape player was on: Charlie Musselwhite was wailing away at "Cristo Redentor." I was going to switch it off when she said, "Please leave it on. I love Musselwhite's harmonica playing. I have the same piece at home. Mine's a CD."

She turned to examine the carved and painted wooden spirit masks hanging on my walls. She paused before a Thunderbird and said, "It's very beautiful, I suppose, but I'm not sure I'd want it in my house."

"Why?"

"There's something a bit spooky about it. Like you, sometimes."

She had been looking at me as she spoke. Now her gaze shifted back to the window. She stood irresolutely for a moment and said irritably, "Oh, for Chrissake, Silas! What are you waiting for?"

The next thing I knew, she'd stood on her toes and put her open mouth on my mouth. Adrenaline, testosterone and other beneficial hormones waved a magic wand across my aches and pains. I forgot about my sore arm and picked her up.

When I awoke it was dark. I put on a bathrobe and lit a dozen candles. A fishboat entered the harbour and sailed past the reservation. Its passing wake crashed against the shore in a series of diminishing sound waves. Stretching and yawning prettily, Sarah got up off my bed, blew me a kiss and carried a candle outside to my one-holer. Afterward I watched her wander about my house, naked, humming to herself, picking things up, looking at them and putting them down again in new places. She was still naked when we banqueted on Kraft Dinner and grapes and drank Chardonnay. Then, tired of food, she leaned across the table and put her tongue in my mouth. Then I was out of my chair and pulling her toward me again.

IT WAS SEPTEMBER 22. Downtown Victoria was still jammed with tourists. Outside Gottlieb's Trading Post a unicyclist was juggling cardboard boxes and sponge-rubber balls for a large, enthusiastic crowd. The juggler's svelte assistant, nude-looking in a flesh-coloured body stocking, circulated with a hat. The aroma of coffee wafting from a nearby shop proved irresistible, so I went inside and found a seat. Glass-fronted coolers displayed pastries, fruit pies, sandwiches. Women in pale blue uniforms attended gleaming espresso machines. The unaccustomed heft of the .40 Glock revolver I was packing in a shoulder holster was uncomfortable. I reached to adjust its weight, but a slight muscular tenderness reminded me of still-healing wounds.

Suddenly, everybody in the shop turned to watch a commotion outside. Pedestrians were scrambling because somebody had just driven a shiny black Viper onto the crowded sidewalk. The car was parked half on, half off the street. I was admiring the driver's audacity until I saw that he was Jiggs Murphy.

Murphy stayed in the driver's seat. Cal got out of the passenger side, slowly unfolded himself to his full impressive height and stood outside the coffee shop for a few seconds, ignoring the frowns of passersby.

Cal was a walking cliché. Today the pimp was kitted out like a bad-ass rapper and was all in red — red sharkskin shirt, red cotton shorts and red-leather sandals that looked as if they'd been freshly soaked in blood. Chunky gold nuggets hung from red silk cords around his neck.

A moment earlier I had been enjoying life and now I was consumed by a hatred so intense it took my breath away. I straightened my back and reached for my gun and for a few seconds seriously considered killing him on the spot to rid Victoria of the man directly responsible for half its cocaine and crystal-meth fatalities. But I wasn't ready to spend 25 years in jail. I promised myself that Cal's day of reckoning was coming.

He ambled into the coffee shop, taking his time about it and swinging a pair of sunglasses. He barely glanced at the customers because he was reserving his glances for a waitress behind the counter.

The girl was as skinny as a stick beetle, with thin arms and legs and an unformed, immature figure. Fluffy blonde hair framed a pretty, catlike face. She had huge, darkly painted eyes and a pouting mouth with full, moist, red lips. The girl was chattering happily to a colleague until she noticed the pimp. Panicked, she backed away until her outstretched arm touched a wall. Then she turned and ran through a doorway.

A middle-aged woman came forward and nervously took Cal's order. While waiting, Cal turned his back on the counter and looked around until he saw me.

"My, my. Look what we got us here," muttered Cal thickly. "I do believe it's that wagon burner."

Instead of killing him, I grinned at him.

"I was you, Indian, I wouldn't feel safe walking the streets."

It took a lot of work, but I managed to widen my grin. "Why is that, big guy?"

The pimp's lips tightened. He put on his sunglasses. "Because, a man like you, all kinds of mischief might befall him," he said, speaking in fake Louisiana-swamp accents. "Drops down open manholes, suchlike disasters. Maybe even get shot, a broken bone or two."

I said, "You got me worried, pal, shaking in my boots. Only, I'm not scared in the same way as that little girl just now. I'm worried that you're gonna get scared and leave town before I get around to dealing with you personally."

The pimp wasn't impressed. He shot me a look of genuine amusement and said, "You gonna stand still, give me another chance to shoot you?" With a soft chuckle he added. "Say, I got a handle on you now. I been thinking you was maybe just a jive-turkey, a naïf, taking my gold. But I see you stupid. A dumb-ass hero. You a man with a mission."

"I'm a man with a mission. You're a man who needs elocution lessons."

The waitress arrived with Cal's order — two coffees to go and a bag of pastries.

I said, "Tell you one thing, Alex. If nobody else, the parking patrols will be sorry to see you leave this town."

A white-bearded commissionaire was ticketing the Viper. Jiggs Murphy stamped about the sidewalk, waving his arms and shouting. The commissionaire's hide was bulletproof. With stolid indifference he closed his notebook with a snap, turned his back on Jiggs and marched off.

Cal picked up his order. Leaving the coffee shop, he said, "I'll be catching up with you, bigmouth. Somebody around here gonna get closed up, only it won't be me."

As the Viper pulled away, a harried-looking man came over to my table. He was new here; I'd never seen him before. "Excuse me, sir," he said, wringing his hands nervously. "I'm the manager. That big guy, the one who just left … ?"

"You mean Alex Cal."

The manager licked his lips. "He's a friend of yours?"

"Alex Cal has no friends."

"I'm not surprised, the way he carries on. He disturbs the customers and frightens my staff. Some of the girls who work here are just teenagers — he's old enough to be their father. But he asks them for dates, follows them home."

"Call the police. You pay taxes, you're entitled to protection."

"I've telephoned the police. By the time they arrive he's gone. Nothing gets done."

"That's the way it is. We have to operate within the law."

"We? Are you a policeman?"

"I am, but my mandate is a bit different than most. I'm a neighbourhood cop, an intermediary between the law and potential jailbirds."

"So why didn't you do something just now?"

"Do what? I can't arrest a man because he tries to pick up girls in restaurants. You've probably done it yourself."

"Maybe, but I haven't made a practice of chasing girls young enough to be my daughter. I don't tell them how much money they can make as prostitutes." The manager shook his head and said bitterly, "I've heard stories about him. They say he's a drug dealer."

"He's the cocaine king of Victoria. Cal is smart, cagey. The narcotics squad has shaken him down a hundred times, but it's hard to nail him because he never carries. Others do his transactions, take all the risks." I reached into my pocket, drew out a business card and gave it to the manager. "The next time Alex Cal bothers you, call this number."

IT WAS MY first visit to the office after being shot. It had a musty, cooped-up smell. Maintenance had patched several holes where bullets had penetrated the gyproc and repainted them with splashes of latex that did not quite match the original faded beige.

A mountain of junk mail lay under the letter slot. I dumped it on my desk. Irresolute, I raised the blinds and stood at the window, eyeing the spot on the building opposite where the sniper had stationed himself. Cal had boasted about being the triggerman, but perhaps that's all it was: a boast.

Had Patty Nolan set me up? How? And what did she have to gain? I thought about Fred Eade's murder.

Bernie Tapp's theory was that either Patty Nolan or her fat friend Sidney Banks had killed the old biker during one of their wild parties. I imagined the scene — Fred Eade and the fat man, drinking heavily in the *Ocean Reaper*'s cabin. Kidding each other and showing off in front of Patty Nolan. Maybe Fred had pulled his commando dagger, waved it threateningly. Banks, overreacting, had drawn a gun …

Well, I didn't know who'd shot *me*, but I knew, or was beginning to think I knew, who had murdered Harry Cunliffe. It seemed likely that the same person had murdered Fred Eade.

For something to do I checked the junk mail. There were a couple of gas-discount coupons from Esso — Payless Gas was increasing its market share and Standard Oil was trembling in its boots. The Bay's fall fashions were on parade. I could have a Christian Dior camel-hair jacket for less than a thousand dollars. If that didn't attract women irresistibly, I could drench my body in Fendi Uomo, a fragrance for men of extraordinary passion at 80 bucks a splash.

My phone rang. Lou said, "I saw you going in, Silas. It's been a while. How you been? They got all those bullets dug out of you?"

"I'm fine. I'll be doing 10 rounds in Moran's gym before long."

"Your boxing days are over, who you kidding? Say, I got a spaghetti special going today. You want any?"

"Send some over, along with apple pie and coffee."

"You got it, pal. Keep away from that window 'cause I hate to lose my paying customers."

I sat down, put my feet on the desk, leaned back and looked at Queen Victoria, frowning at me from her picture frame. What a woman. Today, though, her gaze seemed distinctly chilly.

I thought: Yeah, I'm over the hill. Lou had spelled it out — my boxing days were over. I was 40 and a failure. My neighbourhood policing dream was on the verge of being cancelled. Charles Service thought I was a lightweight.

The phone rang again. I picked it up and said, "Silas Seaweed."

Nobody answered, but I could hear the caller's heavy breathing and street noises. I waited 10 seconds and said, "Is anybody there?"

A man said, "Who ... who is that?"

"Silas Seaweed."

The caller said, "Hang on a minute," and put his hand over the mouthpiece. The hand was removed and the caller said, "You the cop, the guy was shot?"

"That's me."

"Just wait," the caller said.

He was speaking for somebody else, probably somebody sharing a phone booth. The pause dragged on. I did not recognize the voice. It was male, slightly slurred. He sounded like somebody nursing a toothache. The caller said, "Somebody wants to give you a message."

"Fine, go ahead," I said patiently.

"You gonna be around there for a while?"

"I'll be here as long as you want."

The phone went dead.

I began to brood about Sarah Williams and pillow talk, but all that did was prompt stirrings of sexual desire. I picked up the phone and called Sarah's mother.

A girl with a French accent answered and said, "Mrs. Phyllis Williams' residence."

I told her who I was and asked to speak to Mrs. Williams.

The girl asked me to wait. After a longish interval she came back and said, "I'm sorry, sir. Mrs. Williams is not at home."

The phone went dead. Well, that was that.

Calvert Hunt was not interested in me anymore. Phyllis Williams never had been interested in me, apparently. Maybe she'd heard that her expensively educated daughter was running around with lowly Aboriginals?

I brooded about this until the sound of approaching footsteps brought my reverie to an end. I reached for my Glock, clicked off the safety catch and held the gun below my desk. The Glock had one round in its chamber and 15 hollow-points in its magazine. If I ever shot anyone with it, the bullets would expand on impact and make one helluva mess of a human body.

A shadow appeared in the door's frosted glass. The door opened. Lou came in carrying a tray covered with a tea towel. He saw me return the gun to its holster and gave me a long sideways look. "Expecting trouble?"

"No, Lou. I'm just an old scaredy-cat."

Lou put the tray on my desk and said, "Gotta run, pal. Drop by later, have a chat. I got a plan for catching the guys who done you. Used it a couple of times during the war."

"Right, Lou," I said as he went out.

Lou made his own spaghetti sauce, using lots of onions, mushrooms, a touch of olive, a little garlic. I was enjoying the food when my mystery caller phoned again. I heard the same nasal breathing, the same background traffic noise. He said, "You there?"

"I'm trying to eat my lunch. Make it snappy."

"I got a message for you."

"Let me have it."

"She didn't do it."

"Who didn't do it? Do what? What are you talking about?"

"She had nothing to do with the shooting, that's all."

"Listen. I'm not clear on this. Which shooting are you talking about? Mine? Fred Eade's?"

"Never mind," the man said crossly. "I don't answer no questions. I give you the message straight, that's all. Things is all stirred up."

The guy hung up. I picked up my fork and toyed with Lou's spaghetti, but my appetite had gone. I pushed the plate away and sagged in my chair. A cobweb was under construction between coat rack and wall. Dust motes danced in the sunlight falling through my window. I looked at the queen. No help there.

Options? I could talk to Gregarious George. I could look for Jimmy Scow. I could go to headquarters and try to see Chief Mallory. Request permission for a quick trip to Reno. But in my heart I knew Mallory would nix it.

Nobody could tell me what to do on my *own* time, though. If I twisted his arm, Dr. Cunliffe was sure to approve a few more weeks of paid disability leave.

I phoned Denise Halvorsen's pager. Denise sounded less than overjoyed when she responded.

I said, "What are you doing for the next hour?"

"I'm busy."

"I'll be interviewing a woman and I need a female PC along. Meet me in my office in 10 minutes."

I hung up.

EFFIE YOKWATS LIVED in a small townhouse in Vic West. Denise Halvorsen drove me over there. When I banged on Effie's door, nobody answered. I put my eyes to the letter slot and saw a tiny hall and the foot of a flight of stairs. Shadows moved where window blinds fluttered in a breeze.

I said, "Denise, you stay here. I'm going round back."

I reached the back door just in time to catch Jimmy Scow. He was trying to decamp, barefoot and naked except for Jockey shorts, with the rest of his clothing bundled under his arm. I frogmarched Jimmy back inside, unlocked the front door and asked Denise to go upstairs and fetch Effie.

Jimmy was cursing police officers everywhere eloquently and imaginatively. He could scarcely look at me, and when he did it was with unutterable loathing. I hardened my heart and told him to get dressed. Effie came downstairs wearing a bathrobe. She was embarrassed and wouldn't look at me either.

I said, "Effie, I want to know. Why did you quit working for Mr. Hunt?"

Effie muttered indistinctly.

I said, "Effie, you won't tell me so I'll tell you. You're the one who put that rush effigy in Calvert Hunt's room."

Effie put her hands over her ears and shook her head from side to side.

I nodded toward Jimmy and said, "You asked Effie to do it. You made the effigy and asked her to put it there. And you're the one's been prancing around Ribblesdale in a wolf mask, scaring the bejesus out of Iris Naylor."

"You don't know what you're talking about," Jimmy said. "You're a disgrace to the Salish Nation and you don't know a fucking thing. What you are is a stooge for the White establishment."

"Thanks for your vote of confidence, Jimmy. Thanks for being so upfront about things you know fuck all about." I smiled sweetly and added, "It's natural to be upset about the shit that's been coming your way. I understand that. But all you've accomplished so far is losing Effie her job and putting yourself on another hit list."

"What do you mean? What hit list?"

"You know what I mean. The hazard that put you into the big house still exists. It lives on Foul Bay Road."

Jimmy told me to fuck off again. It was pathetic.

I said, "Effie. Please. Look at me."

Effie raised her face, but her gaze was fixed on my shirt.

I said gently, "Effie. This is what happened: Sarah Williams told me that she'd discovered you and Jimmy were having an affair on Mr. Hunt's premises. Jimmy's a convicted criminal, and Miss Williams overreacted. The upshot was, you quit. Everybody is extremely sorry about it. You've been much missed by everyone, by Mr. Hunt in particular. Mr. Hunt likes you, he liked having you around."

"That's a crock," Jimmy said. "You don't know what's been going down."

"Of course I know what's been going down," I said patiently. "You're putting your head in a noose, that's what's going down."

"I ain't scared. I'd rather be dead than a coward. And she's not going back there to that goddam house," Jimmy said angrily. But instead of appearing tough he seemed helpless, like an animal chewing its leg off to get out of a trap.

Effie's eyes glistened with tears.

I said, "Jimmy, I want to know who taught you Ghostfinder ritual."

The question caught him like a blow. "I'm into T'sumqalaks. I'm into Wolf ritual and Wolf Song," Jimmy said evasively.

"You're into Ghostfinder ritual as well," I said. "People have been talking. Where did you practise it, Canoe Cove way?"

Jimmy Scow folded his arms. After a few seconds he nodded.

I said, "Keep your head down. The pair of you. For the time being you'll both stay away from Ribblesdale. I mean it. Trust me, things will work out."

"Nobody tells me what to do," Jimmy shouted. "You sold out to the White establishment but I got a plan. I got reasons for doing what I been doing."

"What's wrong with you two?" I said to Effie. "You want Jimmy back in jail?"

Effie began to weep hopelessly. With tears and snot coursing down her face she ran upstairs. Jimmy told me to go to hell and ran upstairs after her.

Denise said uncertainly, "Now what?"

"Now nothing," I said. "He might die, but there's nothing else I can do."

DENISE DROVE US back over the Bay Street bridge. We travelled about four blocks before curiosity overcame her. She pulled in to the curb, switched off the motor and said, "All right. You win. I know you're not going to tell me anything till I come right out and ask. Why might Jimmy Scow die?"

"Two men have been killed already. Harry Cunliffe and Fred Eade. Jimmy's likely to be the next."

"You seem pretty sure of yourself."

I didn't say anything. Denise tapped my knee and said, "If you're so sure, why not place him in protective custody?"

"Any more jail would kill him. Jimmy's barely making it as it is. If he didn't have Effie's lifeline to hang onto, he'd be drowning now."

"Will you tell me about this ritual, magic, whatever it is?"

"Certain ritual is getting rare. Jimmy's reached way back into history for T'sumqalaks. There's a good reason why it's rare. It's an ordeal few people are willing to tolerate."

I was beginning to sound preachy and grinned to lower the tension. Denise said grimly, "Talk, you bastard."

I said, "What's that thing called when you run out of air? Just before you lose consciousness, you start to see things. Visions. White lights at ends of tunnels?"

"Anoxia," Denise said.

"Right. Anoxia. Shortage of oxygen."

I slouched down in my seat until I was sitting on my spine, my knees jammed against the dashboard. I said, "Ritual is all about power. If a shaman found a young boy with the necessary aptitude, he'd take him under his wing sometimes. Teach him how to get great tamahnous."

"Yes, tamahnous, I keep hearing about that."

"Tamahnous is spirit. In the present context I'm talking about ghost spirit," I said, speaking slowly. "That shaman would take his student up to a big bluff above the sea. Make the boy hold a heavy rock in his hands and have him jump into deep water. Tell him to go right down to the bottom and hang on.

"Underwater spirit is called Keysalt. My great-granddad knew an old Puget Sound shaman called Duke Kehalic. Duke Kehalic wanted a certain boy to get Keysalt tamahnous so he kept sending that boy down into the water. For a long time nothing happened. Then after a while the Duke's boy went down and found a big underwater house. A spirit in the underwater house asked the boy if he came from good family. Well, the boy did come from good family so he answered, 'Yes.' The spirit told the boy to open the door and come in.

"The boy went into the underwater house and saw a lot of women and slaves at the other end of the house. The spirit said, 'Do you see the women and slaves?' The boy said, 'I see them.'

"'Fine,' the spirit said. 'That's yours. I'll give you all those people.'"

"That's a neat trick," Denise said thoughtfully.

I said, "That boy I was telling you about. After his adventure he woke up lying at the foot of the bluff. He went back home and his people asked him, 'Have you got Keysalt tamahnous?' The boy told them he had it.

"Pretty soon the word went out. That young boy had Keysalt tamahnous. Big time. They had the boy gambling, they bet priceless copper plates and slaves against him. Canoes, blankets, women. That boy just wins and wins."

"That sounds very nice. A nice little story."

"But what I didn't tell you, Denise. When that young boy was underwater, the spirit said, 'You're going to have to pay for this tamahnous. I want your first wife. You've got to send your first wife to me.'"

I straightened up in my seat. "That young man — he was a man now — he fell in love and got married. It was wonderful. He had a big house and plenty of money, slaves, canoes. He was with his wife one night when Keysalt came to him and said, 'Remember what you've promised? You've got to give your first wife to Keysalt spirit.'

"That young man loved his wife, didn't want to part with her. So he got one of his slaves, dressed her up in fancy clothes, and he took her to the bluff. When he got there he shoved her in the water, but she wouldn't sink. He kept pushing her down and she kept floating back up. Keysalt spirit knew she wasn't the first wife. You can't fool him. Keysalt knows everything.

"Just about then, the young man's people came up in canoes to take him home. He got in the canoe and covered himself with a goat-hair blanket. When they got back home the young man's people said, 'We're home now.' But the young man doesn't move. The people took the blanket off him, but he wasn't there. Keysalt spirit had taken him instead of his first wife."

"And this happened a long time ago, did it?"

"Yes, Denise. It happened a long time ago."

"Could it happen again, do you think?"

"Good question. If it happens again it would cost Jimmy. Big time."

CHAPTER ELEVEN

It took me two days to drive to Reno. My Chevy ran well, but the old beater lacked air conditioning and it was 118 degrees in the shade in Alturas, where I stopped to load up on iced drinks and gas. The late sun was yellow on Nevada's arid mountain slopes when I left the hot lonely desert behind and crossed the Truckee River in downtown Reno. I checked into a hotel on the Strip and spent the next 15 minutes cooling off under a shower.

THE CASINO'S GAMING ROOM was a space-age fantasy, large as a football field. A place of flashing lights, jingling bells, inescapable Muzak. Loudspeakers announced winning keno numbers. Hordes of brightly dressed people swept between gambling stations like schools of jellyfish. Glittering shoals of one-armed bandits, working 24 hours a day, seven days a week, nibbled at the purses of women in stretch pants and sequined blouses and tinted eyeglasses. Men slumped over blackjack tables, drinks at elbows, their bald heads reflecting the glow of immense chandeliers. Stone-faced dealers in white shirts and black pants showed their teeth when winners tipped them and looked neutral the rest of the time.

After three hours at a $25 poker table I was up nearly a thousand. The other winner was a skinny oilman from Oklahoma. His eyes were shadowed by a tipped-forward 10-gallon hat. The tip of his bony chin and hooked nose seemed to touch as he chomped an unlit cigar. He had on a pale blue shirt, with little chromium tabs weighting down his collar, and a narrow black-ribbon necktie. The oilman picked his hole cards up slowly with a bony, liver-spotted hand, looked at them once, then left them face-down on the green-felt table. When he won he flipped his hole cards one at a time, dragging out the action deliberately in a manner that irritated some of the other players. The losers were a succession of impulse gamblers who sat in when a seat became vacant, dropped a few hundred, then folded.

Unlike the blackjack dealers, the poker dealers were a jovial crew, rotated every 40 minutes. They were Marvin, Terry and Gayle. Marvin and Terry looked like Sonny and Cher. Gayle looked like Dolly Parton on crack, but she was full of fun and earned plenty of tips.

Beauty queens circulated with trays of free drinks. I sipped rye and water. I was looking at a $400 pot. I held a pair of kings and had one more card to come. The player to my right had just bet the limit. I had watched him lose steadily. When he frowned he had at least three of a kind. He was frowning. I folded my hand and got up, leaving my stake on the table to hold the seat. I pushed through the crowds to a washroom and splashed water on my face. A white-jacketed attendant handed me a towel and whisked a brush across my shoulders. I tipped him a Canadian dollar. The attendant stared at the foreign currency morosely and was still staring at it when I went out. Instead of returning to the game I sat at a bar with my back to the poker tables.

Despite the crowds, I felt the room's desperate loneliness. I knew that if I continued to play I would lose my stake. One of the pit bosses came over and sat on the next stool. He was a darkly handsome man with thick wavy hair, about 30. He smiled amiably and said, "You're doing all right. Where did you learn to play poker?"

"Victoria, B.C."

"They got any heavy action up there?"

"There's a couple of clubs. If you know where to look you can find big weekend games on construction sites, logging camps."

"Yeah, that's the way it's done. A hustler shows up with a canvas carryall, holes in his socks, straw between his teeth. Cleans the suckers out on pay night."

"That's right. Arrives on a bus, leaves in a private plane."

"Here in Reno, it's the other way round," said the pit boss, laughing. Then he added, "Enjoying yourself here, people treating you right?"

"I've got no complaints."

"I guess not. You're up, what, about a grand?"

I nodded. The pit boss didn't miss much. A waiter came over and the pit boss insisted on buying me a drink. He said, "If you're interested, there's a spot on a no-limit table upstairs. Guy plays like you, he could make a bundle."

"Or drop one."

The pit boss shook his head. "I've been watching. You're playing a good game, not trying to win every hand."

"This is my first night in town, I'm just enjoying myself, fooling around. Tomorrow I go to work."

"What kind of business you in?"

"I'm a cop," I said and gave him my card. "I'm looking for a woman."

"Ain't we all," said the pit boss, studying the card.

"This one's been missing over 20 years."

"If she had the bucks, she could have spent the whole 20 years right here, in this casino. We've got shops, restaurants, a hairdresser, tanning salon, spa, swimming pool. Two shows a night. A guy with your luck, you might run into her."

"I wouldn't recognize her if I did. She's probably changed her name as well as her appearance. I don't have much to go on."

"Well, if I can do anything for you, give me a shout." He gave me his own card. The man's name was Dean Costello and his title was senior floor captain.

"You have a musical director in the hotel, Mr. Costello? Somebody who arranges music for the acts?"

"We've got a house band. A guy who stands in front and waves his arms. I guess he's the musical director."

"The woman I'm looking for was a piano player. Small-town professional. She worked with a little group in Seattle, long time ago. Had a nice voice. If she came to Reno and stayed, she probably worked the clubs."

"You've got your work cut out then. She'd be one of the herd, pal. Every warbler in the country heads here. We've got the largest transient population in the United States. I'm an old-timer in Reno, been here three years." He tugged at his chin, thinking. "Our band leader is also new, arrived a few weeks ago from the Big Apple. But you might talk to Barney Bevis. He's featured in the Kitten Lounge, downtown. B.B. arrived when they had horse troughs on the main drag. If the lady ever played professional piano in Reno, Barney would know." Costello got off his bar stool. "You doing any more gambling while you're in town?"

"Probably. I'm staying in this hotel. You guys make it hard to go anywhere without passing the slots and the tables."

"Psychology at work, Mr. Seaweed. But good luck."

We shook hands. I played another half-hour and lost $100 in the process. My timing had gone, I felt stale, the cigarette smoke in the room was beginning to bother me, so I cashed out. When I went to collect my room key at the front desk the clerk said, "Your things have been moved out of Room 463, sir, to a view room on the eleventh floor."

I raised my eyebrows.

"Compliments of Dean Costello."

Costello had comped me to a suite. A basket of fruit stood on a coffee table next to a bottle of Canadian Club and polished crystal glasses. There were flowers everywhere.

The city was spread out below me. Restless gamblers walked the Strip under the whirling lariat of a 10-storey neon cowboy. Electric showgirls with immense peacock-feather hats kicked their heels on a distant rooftop. The 10,000 lamps of the Circus Circus sign banished the night. Ribbons of moving automobile lights spread from the brilliance like spider webs. Beyond the golden bowl of the city, where scuttling money spiders wove their traps, darkness claimed the desert and it rolled on, black and mysterious, toward the distant Sierras. Jet planes glided noiselessly in and out of Reno airport, red and green lamps winking.

Somebody had hung my clothes exactly as I had left them in the other room. Satin sheets were turned back invitingly on my bed. I stripped, showered. After flossing dutifully, I cleaned my teeth, then crashed.

TO REACH THE restaurant for breakfast I had to pass through the gambling areas. It was only 7:30, but the place was crowded. In the poker pit the oilman was sitting behind a big pile of chips. Three rappers had replaced Sonny and Cher and Dolly Parton.

After breakfast I strolled Sierra Street to the Truckee River. Like every other visitor to this quickie-marriage, quickie-divorce capital, I stopped on the bridge and stared down into the shallow water where, according to legend, jubilant divorcees hurl old wedding rings. The early sun glinted on tiny wavelets rippling across the pebbled bottom. I saw no golden rings — only beer bottles and plastic bags and a rusting shopping cart. To my surprise, nervous pan-sized trout darted in and out of the shade.

Although it was still early I was sweating by the time I reached the downtown precinct office. A uniformed Reno cop stood in the entrance hall with his arms folded, staring impassively at a sobbing woman. She was crouched in a corner, clutching her drawn-up knees, hiding her face between her arms. Mascara tears dripped onto her legs and traced little black tracks along her white thighs. A man wearing blue jeans and a tartan shirt knelt beside her with one hand touching her shoulder. Nobody spoke.

Inside the building, three plainclothes men were at a water cooler, laughing. Behind an inquiry desk a clerk with a huge beehive hairdo that almost concealed her tiny face was speaking into a telephone. When she hung up, I said "I'm a policeman from Victoria, B.C. Maybe I could talk to somebody, one of the detectives here."

"You're a what?" She stared at me as if I were a Martian.

"I'm a cop."

Her eyes shifted to a point behind me and she shouted. "Hey, Ben. You got a minute?"

A broad-shouldered man detached himself from his friends at the water cooler and strolled across. He gave me an appraising glance and said, "What can I do for you?" He had an easy, assured manner, not quite friendly.

"I'm a cop from Victoria. I'd appreciate it if you could spare me some of your time."

"The only Victoria I know in these United States is in Texas, but you don't look like no Plains Indian. You from up north?"

"Right. I'm Silas Seaweed."

"Detective-Sergeant Conklin." He extended his paw and I shook it. "I just finished my shift, Mr. Seaweed, but I can give you a minute. Come on."

He led me into a small, solid-walled cubicle furnished with a bare table and two chairs. A feather boa dangled from a coat hook — the only touch of colour in that white-painted space.

Conklin sighed as he eased himself into the chair behind the desk and brushed a hand across his eyelids. There were dark crescents beneath his eyes and black stubble on his chin.

I said, "Busy night, Sergeant?"

He shrugged. "Call me Ben. The night was about normal."

"You mean it was tiring, frustrating and largely a waste of time?"

Conklin grinned. "Am I listening to the voice of experience?"

"I pounded a beat for a while."

"Way I feel this morning, I should quit before I develop my first ulcer. Trouble is, what would I do? There's too many private dicks in this town, you can't make a dime."

"Just so we're clear. Right now I'm on sick leave because somebody took potshots at me."

Conklin's dark eyes narrowed but he smiled and said, "They gonna give you a medal?"

I grinned at him and said, "I'm looking for a woman called Marcia Hunt. She's a Canadian citizen, been missing a long time."

"Does she have a record?"

"No. She was married briefly to a convicted felon named Frank Harkness, a.k.a Frank Turko."

"What exactly do you want?"

"A big favour. I want to know whether you have sheets on these people."

"Tell me about them."

I told him.

Conklin examined his fingers. "Suppose I find that these people have local records. So what? How would that help?"

I shook my head. "I don't know, I'm clutching at straws. The trail is cold, dead. I haven't got a lead."

"I won't promise anything. This is irregular, as you know." Conklin stifled a yawn with the back of a hand. "Mostly, when outside police come here they bring introductions."

"I have a personal stake in this thing. I'm working on my own time."

"If I find something, where can I reach you?"

I gave him the name of my hotel and got up. "I'm standing between a man and his bed."

"I wish you were, Silas, but you're standing between me and a shopping cart. My wife works shifts too, at a casino in Sparks. It's my turn to buy groceries and do the housecleaning."

I WAS SOON GRATEFUL that I had comfortable walking shoes and a thick skin. I checked the talent agencies first, without success, and then the legwork began. I combed Reno's taverns, bars and clubs, starting at the big casinos on Sierra Street and working outward, asking polite questions of impatient people who had troubles of their own and were not particularly interested in mine. This town was full of dangerous strangers. People hid inside velvet-lined cages and lived lonely, insulated lives. I spoke to musicians and bootblacks and concierges and waitresses. I spoke to men who had been playing piano so long they could hold complex conversations while performing lounge-bar standards and never miss a note. I chased down numerous false trails and came to a dead end every time. I bought drinks for lonely people sitting on bar stools at seven in the morning, questioning them before they were too smashed to remember what day it was.

I dosed my residual aches and pains with over-the-counter Tylenol and worked my way through the Nevada Bell directory. It took a long time, but I slowly eliminated most of the Hunts, Harknesses and Turkos in the state. I checked old city directories. I went to Carson City and combed the state archives, trying to find out whether Marcia Hunt had ever bought property in Nevada, registered a child into the school system, applied for social assistance, a driver's licence, a fishing licence.

A job printer made me 1,000 cards with my phone number on them and the message:

MARCIA HUNT, WHERE ARE YOU?

REWARD OFFERED FOR INFORMATION.

And I managed to give most of the cards away.

Back at my hotel after every fruitless day I checked for messages. Ben Conklin did not call, nobody called. My greatest discovery was a joint where the barman had a 10-word vocabulary and the patrons were all serious drinkers. The place had a sawdust floor and no jukebox. It was a place where people could destroy themselves without interference from any earthly authority provided they paid cash and kept quiet about it. Some nights I went in for an hour or two, watching winos fall off their stools, crawl outside, throw up, then return to continue their slow suicide. These were people who had examined the game and didn't like the rules. The ante had got too high, they'd folded their cards. Sometimes I thought they were onto something.

TAFF'S KEYBOARDS WAS an old-fashioned music store located on a street near the railroad tracks. A faded, sun-cracked wooden sign over the shop door announced that pianos were for sale, trade or rent. I pushed the door and a bell chime jingled me inside. Racks of sheet music filled every space not occupied by instruments. There were pianos, organs, and electric keyboards. Somewhere out of sight, a piano was being tuned. A silver-plated bell push was screwed to the countertop. I hit the button with the palm of my hand and the tuning ceased. Thick red curtains swung apart and an elderly man shuffled in. He wore black patent-leather shoes, black pants with a silk stripe down the legs, and a white, collarless shirt. He had black sleeve protectors on, and dirty hands. "You're too danged early," he said. "I'm not finished and when I am I'll let you know."

I said, "I'm not who you think I am."

The old man frowned. "You're not from the movers?"

"No, I'm a cop."

"Goldanged movers are always buggin' me about something. They called this morning, supposed to pick up that Steinway in the back, but it isn't ready."

"I heard you tuning it."

"A cop, eh? Well, you're not going to buy a piano so what *do* you want?"

"I'm making inquiries about a missing woman. I hope you can help."

"How much is this gonna cost me?"

"A few minutes of your time."

"Good. Sumbitch came in here last week packing a gun. Asked for money, but he didn't get none." The shopkeeper cackled at the memory.

I said, "Twenty years ago, more or less, somebody called Marcia Hunt, also known as Harkness, might have come into this store and bought a piano."

"Smart woman if she did. I've got the best deals in town, don't let anybody tell you different." He scratched his ear with a finger, then stared at his dirty hands. He said, "See that? Dust everywhere. Wait a minute."

With that he turned on his heels and pushed his way through the red curtains. I heard water running. The shopkeeper returned, wiping his hands on a dirty towel. "I'm going to have a cup of coffee. Let the movers wait," he said and busied himself with a jar of instant behind the counter. "Okay, mister," he said. "Talk."

The shopkeeper listened intently while I told my well-rehearsed tale, then he excused himself and went out back again, returning immediately with a kettle of boiling water. He poured the water into two mugs. "Here," he said, "help yourself. There's only decaf. I hope you're not one of these coffee purists."

"Thanks," I said, looking at the murky green-grey concoction before me.

"That's me," he said complacently, lighting a cigarette. "Rather spend my time bullshittin' and drinking coffee than taking care of business." He inhaled deeply, then coughed until his face turned purple and veins protruded from his temples. When the coughing fit subsided he put the cigarette in an overflowing ashtray. Blue tobacco smoke spiralled upward and hung over his head like an inversion as he poked around in drawers. He said, "I've got records going back to 1943. Book for piano sales, other book for rentals and repairs. The sales book is kinda skimpy. Best times I had were in the '50s. There was money around them days. Mothers still wanted their kids to learn *real* music. Sometimes I'd sell two pianos a month. Now mothers buy their kids DVD players and iPods. I'm lucky to sell six pianos a year. Kids that do take up music are into saxophones and guitars, but I won't touch 'em."

He put on a pair of glasses and browsed his records. After less than a minute he pointed a long nicotine-stained finger. "Here it is," he said. "Marcia Hunt, 1379 Pitchpine Road. I sold her a Heintzman upright for $600 on August 6, 1985." He laughed. "What do you know! We hit pay dirt or not?"

I chewed my lip. Marcia was no ghost. Twenty years ago she had been here, in this room. She had walked through the same door. To judge by the age of his stock, she might have gazed at the same pianos. I thanked him and said, "Did Marcia pay cash or use a credit card?"

"Cheque. I've got a copy of the invoice." He handed it across for me to look at and asked, "What difference does it make whether she paid cash or not?"

"I think she only used her real name when she had no other option. It's made her hard to trace."

The invoice was as the dealer had said — Marcia had paid by cheque. There, in a neat signature written with a fountain pen, she had acknowledged that the piano had been delivered to her residence in good condition. This was the same hand and the same pen that had written a thank-you note to Dr. Cunliffe. The reason she continued to use the name Hunt, instead of Harkness, remained a mystery.

PITCHPINE ROAD WAS a rutted desert trail branching off Highway 395, 10 miles south of town. The road had been built to service a long-abandoned silver mine. What remained of an ancient prospector's dream was a collection of vandalized corrugated-iron sheds and rusty narrow-gauge rail spurs. Beyond the mine, the road had been fenced in places where optimists had tried to develop hobby ranches. Side roads snaked off toward a range of humpbacked hills. Hovels with sagging porches and cracked windows baked in the heat. Scrawny chickens scratched among weeds. House dogs, snoozing in the shade, came to life and barked as I drove past in my Chevrolet.

Real-estate signs advertised lots for sale, but the signs were ancient. Some lay flat on the sun-baked earth, overgrown by cactus and creosote shrubs. I kept going past tumbledown barns and sun-drunk horses till a fingerpost marked 1379 pointed me toward yet another side trail.

This trail, washboarded and barely wide enough for a single vehicle, wound down an ancient water-carved draw between wind-eroded sandstone cliffs. Brown hawks rode on thermals high above. More hawks perched motionless on fence posts and utility poles. I bridged a rise and stopped the car. Stretched before me was a dun-coloured valley, locked in on every side by low hills. Beyond, shimmering in the heat haze, the Sierras rose beneath a blue cloudless sky.

According to Reno's city directory, 1379 Pitchpine Road was rented to Mrs. Joan Alfred. A grove of trees surrounded a tall, wind-driven water pump. Nearby was a neat red-painted house and a large barn, enclosed by white picket fence. I got back in the Chev, drove on and parked near the barn.

The house was a square, box-like bungalow with a pyramid roof pierced by a brick chimney. It was surrounded by a wide, screened veranda. Three steps led up to the veranda. I climbed the steps, crossed the veranda and knocked on the door.

A painter's easel with an unfinished canvas was set up in the veranda's shade. Nobody answered the door so I looked at the canvas. It showed a wrinkled, grey-haired ranch hand holding a chestnut horse by its bridle. The horse was unfinished, as was some background detail. The work, expertly done, was signed "Allie."

I knocked again, waited a minute and went back down the steps. Standing with my back to the house, I noticed somebody lying in a hammock suspended between two lemon trees near the water tank. I went across. The man depicted in the unfinished oil painting was asleep in the shade. He had on an open-necked cotton plaid shirt, blue jeans and cowboy boots. An empty glass and an empty bottle of Jack Daniels sat on a table within reach of his hand.

I cleared my throat noisily and said, "Sorry to disturb you, sir."

The sleeper did not answer. Except for the slight movement of his chest when he inhaled, he might have been dead. He was either drunk or pretending to be. I left him to it.

Two German shepherds appeared along the valley, followed by a rider on horseback. When the dogs noticed my Chevrolet they began to bark and pelted toward it until a call from the rider brought them back. The rider was a black-haired woman mounted on a chestnut mare. I strolled across the yard and opened the gate for her. The woman raised a hand to shade her eyes, looking at me without expression as she rode through the gate and into the barn, followed by her dogs.

The woman permitted the chestnut a small drink from a water

trough. She then removed her heavy western saddle and threw it across a trestle with practised ease. She glanced at me once or twice, with little apparent curiosity, as she tended her mount. The dogs, lying quietly with their bushy tails brushing the ground like twin brooms, watched her lead the chestnut into a stall.

She was tall. Skinny rather than slim and heavily tanned. Her cheeks and neck were as wrinkled as a dried apple. She had dark, deeply set eyes, black eyebrows, a large nose and a wide mouth. With her high cheekbones, firm chin and youthful carriage she must once have been a beauty, before the sun ruined things. I guessed she was about 50, but her face, neck and hands were 10 years older.

After forking some hay into a manger and watching the chestnut eat for a minute, she turned to me and said curtly, "Mister, I hope you're not a pain-in-the-ass salesman, a government assessor or a lost prospector, because I want a cold shower and you are in the way of it."

I turned on my best bogus charm. "I'm not lost. I probably hate salesmen as much as you do."

She let out a breath and made a small, angry, impatient noise. "Who are you then, and what do you want?" Her diction, unlike the usual desert drawl, was clipped and precise.

"I'm a cop, my name is Silas Seaweed. I'd like to ask you a few questions, if I may."

"You're not local, I know that."

"True."

"I'm Joan Alfred," she said, looking at me through half-closed lids. "You can wait for me on the veranda. Don't set foot inside the house unless invited or I won't answer for the dogs."

Fifteen minutes later, Joan Alfred had on slacks, a green silk shirt and beaded Navajo moccasins. Her long black hair, still damp from the shower, showed a few grey strands. She had painted her mouth with dark red lipstick, and it was again obvious that before too much sun she had been very beautiful. She invited me into the living room. The two dogs followed us and flopped down by a brick fireplace. The room had a polished wooden floor and was furnished traditionally with leather chairs, heavy Mexican chests, Navajo rugs. She said something to the dogs, stood with her back to the fireplace and lit a cigarette.

"I'm from Victoria, B.C.," I said. "I'm making inquiries about a woman named Marcia Harkness."

Joan Alfred's expression did not change. "How does that affect me?"

"Marcia was a pianist, a good one. In 1985 she bought a piano from a shop in Reno and had it delivered to this address."

"I wouldn't know, but so what? I've only lived here 15 years or so."

"Does the name Marcia Harkness mean anything to you? Or Marcia Hunt?"

"No."

I said, "Before you came, I was admiring a painting on the veranda. Is it your work?"

"No, my niece is working on it," she said impatiently. "Allie's away at art college right now."

"It's very good."

Her nostrils flared. "Mr. Seaweed, are you here to talk about paintings, or what?"

I stood there looking at her, wondering how to play this. I said carefully, "The city directory lists you as the tenant here, ma'am. Would you mind telling me who your landlord is?"

She turned things over in her mind and shrugged. "I don't know whether I should. Maybe the owner doesn't want people to know."

"No offence, Mrs. Alfred, but it probably wouldn't hurt to tell me. The owner's name will be registered in Carson City. It would save me a little trouble, that's all."

"Why should I save you a little trouble?" she said sharply.

Immediately, she relented. "I'm sorry," she said, sounding as if she meant it. "That was stupid. I've had a long hot ride and perhaps my mood isn't the best. Would you like some cold lemonade?"

"Thanks. I'd like that very much."

She threw her half-smoked cigarette into the fireplace and went through a bead-curtained doorway. I crossed to the fireplace and took a closer look at the picture hanging above the mantelpiece. It wasn't a painting, as I'd first imagined — it was a faded brass rubbing showing a round-faced king. The king wore a crown and was holding an orb and a sceptre.

The door to an adjacent room was open. An arrangement of photographs in silver frames stood atop an upright piano in a corner.

Joan Alfred returned with a jug of iced lemonade and two glasses and set them on a coffee table. She poured two glasses of lemonade, handed one to me and motioned me to a chair.

She sat opposite, smiled and said, "I'm sorry. This house is owned by a Mrs. Fantelli. Mrs. Agnes Fantelli. She lives in New York. The place has probably been in the Fantelli family's hands for more than a century. They were the original owners of the Pitchpine silver mine."

The old house creaked.

Joan Alfred smiled again and said, "This place comes alive twice a day. In the morning when the sun expands the wooden boards, and at night when they shrink." She lit another cigarette.

I stood up. The dogs raised their heads. "Do you mind if I pet them? I like dogs."

"It's all right. They're used to you now."

I dropped slowly to my heels, showed them the back of one hand, then gently stroked their heads. They lay docile, unresponsive, watching me with big yellow eyes. I looked at the brass rubbing and said, "Are you English, Mrs. Alfred?"

She was sitting with her legs crossed. My abrupt question unsettled her. One moccasin came free from a heel. To give herself time to think she leaned forward and pulled the moccasin on again. She said, "Me, English? Why do you ask?"

"That rubbing reminds me of some that I've seen before. They were done in English churches."

She stared at the rubbing, lips pursed. "My husband was English," she said and got up. "It belonged to him. That's supposed to be King Alfred. After Tommy had had a few drinks he used to boast that King Alfred was his ancestor."

"And was he?"

"Not as far as I know. But then, I never met any of Tommy's family." She smiled and moved closer. "Tommy was a sailor. He jumped ship in Oakland. To me, Tommy seemed exotic, larger than life, but then, I was young. I didn't know much about men. He was a lot more exciting than the boys I'd met in California. So I married him, like a sap."

"Why were you a sap?"

She shrugged. "Tommy never loved me. I was his way to getting a green card." She spoke self-deprecatingly. "But Tommy made me laugh. How he made me laugh."

A strand of hair had fallen across her left eye. She brushed it away with the back of a hand.

"So. You married an Englishman. Doesn't that make you English too?"

She shook her head. "I'm a Russian out of Oakland, California. My father's family was from the Ukraine. Mother was Lithuanian."

"That's what I thought," I said softly. Her smile faded. Before she could speak I added, "I want to show you something, Mrs. Alfred." She followed me into the next room and we looked at the upright piano together. I said, "That's Marcia Harkness's Heintzman. The one she bought in Reno."

"Heintzman, that's a pretty common name for a piano, isn't it?" she said, avoiding my eyes.

I said, "You told me you were Russian. I think that your name before you married Tommy Alfred was Turko. Your brother was Frank Turko. Frank changed his name to Harkness when he went to Canada."

But I'd overplayed my hand. She strode to the front door, flung it open and pointed outside. "Clear off. Get the hell out before I set the dogs on you!"

The dogs were growling and their hackles had risen.

I was tired. The trail to Pitchpine Road had been long. I said impatiently, "Mrs. Alfred, neither you nor Marcia has anything to fear from me."

"You've got that right, mister," she said caustically. "Especially Marcia. You can find her at 2500 Stateline Road. She won't mind if you look her up, believe me."

"'Cept for one thing," a voice said. That ranch hand was standing on the veranda, holding a shotgun. He wagged the shotgun at me and said, "Listen up good, mister. You and me are going across to the trees together. You first. Put your hands in the air and keep them there. Try anything foolish and I'll blow you away. Now *move*."

CHAPTER TWELVE

The ranch hand was a tall, angular-faced man with a tight mouth and dark, pebble-hard eyes. He had thick shoulders and arms, a heavily muscled body, and — in spite of his 50-plus years — he moved as lightly as a dancer. Short-cropped hair covered his head like frosted wire wool. He had the look and manner of one who had spent many long dreary years pumping iron in prison exercise yards. This was Frank Harkness, I had no doubts about it.

He was about as expressive as a Caterpillar tractor, but I had him figured. This shotgun-toting incident had been spur of the moment, a senseless attention-grabbing device, the sort of drama that had probably served him well in jail, but was a recipe for disaster in the real world. Now he'd backed himself into a corner and didn't know what to do next. I kept these thoughts to myself while he checked the contents of my pockets and then wordlessly locked me inside a concrete-block pumphouse that stood adjacent to the water tank.

The pumphouse's metal door clanged shut, leaving me in the dark. I felt around for a light switch and turned it on. A twin-tube fluorescent fixture flared into light and added its electric buzz to the intermittent noise of a water pump mounted on a small surge tank. I leaned wearily against the tank. Frank Harkness represented the unknown, upon whom so many people had projected their terrors, real and imagined. That minute I felt useless, marginalized.

The pumphouse's sloping roof consisted of asphalted plywood sheets supported on two-by-six joists. The sturdy steel door hung on industrial hinges. After examining them I saw there was no way, short of using a drill or explosives, that I could remove the door's hinge pins.

A malicious impulse prompted me to switch the power to the pump off. The next time somebody flushed a toilet or ran a bath over at the house, they'd run out of water. After thinking about it, I switched the pump back on again. Harkness might get mad, come back and blast me with his shotgun. This wasn't Canada. I was in NRA country. U.S. courts dealt leniently with gun-toting citizens defending — or claiming to defend — their homes from intruders.

Several hand tools dangled from wall hooks — a crescent wrench; a selection of screwdrivers, pliers and the like; and a ball-peen hammer. I picked up the hammer and hefted it. It would make a dandy weapon.

Time passed rather slowly, giving me ample time to think, and remember.

Tommy Alfred was the name of the man eating breakfast with Frank Harkness when the latter was arrested by Sheriff Firkins back in the '80s. Ergo, Joan Alfred was Frank's sister. That made her Marcia Harkness's sister-in-law.

I selected the largest screwdriver, climbed atop the surge tank and went to work. In 10 minutes I had separated a four-foot section of plywood roof from its joists. Nails creaked loose and laminated wood ripped noisily as the pieces came apart. I put my eyes to the opening. After watching for a few minutes, I saw Joan Alfred come out of the house and go across to the barn. A few minutes later she returned to the house and went indoors. There was no sign of the ranch hand.

I started levering again. It took me less than 15 minutes to create an opening wide enough to climb through. I got out, dropped to the ground — nothing the worse for my experience but for a ripped pant leg — and ran back to my car. I had the Chevy started and moving before Frank Harkness came charging out of the house. He gave me both barrels but it was a futile gesture. I was too distant. I honked my horn at him and kept going.

TWENTY-FIVE HUNDRED STATELINE ROAD was a cemetery. A marble stone over Marcia Hunt-Harkness's grave told me that she had died on February 18, 1987. Her grave marker was exactly like hundreds of others on that well-tended hillside. A vase of wilted roses, with a slight fragrance still clinging to them, stood before the slab.

The cemetery's custodian was a small portly man named Mr. Motherlake, wearing a Pirates baseball cap and well-tailored khaki coveralls. His office, in a miniature Parthenon, overlooked inescapable evidence of man's mortality. Being surrounded by death seemed to buoy Motherlake up rather than otherwise. When I entered his office, his grin of sunny optimism widened. He pointed to a seat opposite his desk and said, "You found her then?"

"Exactly where you said she would be."

Motherlake clasped his hands across his wide stomach and said comfortably, "Never known 'em to move, once they get settled."

I hesitated. I wanted to know Marcia Harkness's exact cause of death and that information was probably contained in Motherlake's filing cabinets. I said, "Mr. Motherlake, I need advice."

"You certainly are a curious man," Motherlake teased. "All you do is ask questions."

"It's important for me to find out who signed Mrs. Harkness's death certificate."

"Another young man in a hurry. I meet a lot of them here," Motherlake said, his chin moving up and down. He exhaled a long sigh and added, "It's those gravestones out there. They remind people that time is running out and it makes 'em impatient."

"I could go to Carson City, request the information through official channels, but weeks might pass before those bureaucrats moved."

"True, Mr. Seaweed, and the chances are that even then those bureaucrats wouldn't tell you. They take death certificates very seriously in Carson City."

"Here's the truth," I said. "I'm a cop on the skids, working on a case in my own free time."

Motherlake looked me in the eye. Everything I said was being filtered through his bullshit detector so I gave it to him straight. I said, "There's a kid back home who was railroaded into jail. Got five years for a crime he didn't commit. I'm trying to straighten it out, make amends."

"I don't get it. This kid. Is he supposed to have killed Marcia Harkness?"

"No. It's complicated. Marcia's death is the key to solving some old mysteries." I slapped my hand on his desk and added, "The hell of it is, Mr. Motherlake I'll swear on a stack of tombstones there's a copy of Marcia's death certificate in this very office."

The brilliance of Motherlake's smile diminished by a particle. "Ah," he said. "But my records are confidential."

We sat facing each other with a desk between us.

A two-wheel vehicle the size of a golf cart was towing a utility trailer loaded with gardening tools through the cemetery. Motherlake watched it for a while; then, without a word, he lumbered out of his seat and went across to the filing cabinets. Soon a photocopy of Marcia Hunt-Harkness's death certificate was in my hands. A glance at the certificate told me that Marcia's physician had been Dr. Robert Danwell of Reno.

I said, "You seem like a happy man, Mr. Motherlake."

"I got the world's best job," he said, pointing outside. "Never had a single argument with the folks who pay my wages."

THE HEAT OF THE DAY was not waning with the sun, and I had not eaten since breakfast, but I drove past a hundred air-conditioned restaurants because I wanted to make one last call before the business day closed. I entered one of Reno's older high-rise office towers just after 6 P.M.

I got out at the sixth floor and entered an empty waiting room. "Dr. Danwell just left," the nurse-receptionist said. "You just missed him."

She had a gentle voice and sounded genuinely sorry. I took a closer look at her. She was a middle-aged woman dressed in white, wearing an old-fashioned nurse's cap of starched and folded linen. A name tag pinned to her breast said she was Ethel Walters, RN.

Next door, in Dr. Danwell's consulting room, a chair creaked. Some-body whistled a few bars from *Aida*.

Ms. Walters blushed and said, "I'm sorry, sir. Dr. Danwell's appoint-ments are over for the day. Perhaps I can book you in tomorrow ... "

The door opened and Dr. Danwell came in. He took in the situation at a glance and said, "It's fine, Ethel, my golf game doesn't start for an hour. I'll see the gentleman now."

We went into his office. Dr. Danwell sat in his leather chair, staring across Nevada's parched desert as I gave him an edited version of my search for Marcia Hunt/Harkness. When I stopped speaking he sat in silence for a full minute. Then he rang for Nurse Walters. When she answered, he said, "Please dig out Marcia Harkness's file and bring it here."

He turned to me. "I'm always happy to co-operate with the police, but you'll forgive me, Mr. Seaweed, if I try to keep this brief."

The doctor leaned back, collected his thoughts and said, "Marcia was my patient for about two years. She was a generally healthy woman with a good constitution. I saw her just a few times. As I say, she was healthy, but she was unlucky enough to get shot by a rustler."

The doctor stopped speaking to see how this news affected me, but I was wearing my Indian stone face. He went on, "Marcia owned a small ranch. A few head of cattle, some sheep, horses. This is a big country. It's practically impossible to control range theft. As I recall, there'd been some rustling in Marcia's area and the local sheriff wasn't able to do much more than send a man out in a patrol car once a month."

The nurse entered with Marcia's file. Dr. Danwell glanced at it briefly before setting it on the desk. "As I was saying. Marcia and her neighbours organized a vigilante group. She and some others were out patrolling the area one night and came across some men butchering sheep. Things turned nasty. There was a shootout and Marcia was hit in the chest by a bullet."

"Killed?"

"Not outright. One of the vigilantes was an army vet with combat experience. They did all the right things and got Marcia to a hospital. She was operated on right away and lingered for a few days before dying."

"What was the official cause of death?"

He consulted the file and said, "Marcia's death resulted from pneumonia and secondary infections following massive gunshot trauma."

"And presumably the rustlers got away and were never seen again?"

He smiled, but the smile did not touch his eyes. "Wrong. Those rustlers were captured within a few days because the police had a good description of both them and their truck. The killers were ranchers themselves. There was a big to-do about it when the facts came out."

"Do you remember, Doctor, whether your patient was tattooed?"

The doctor frowned. "Not that I recall." Another thought seized him and he sat up straighter. "What are you getting at?"

"Marcia Harkness had a rose tattooed on her right shoulder."

The doctor shook his head. "Well, it's possible." He opened the file and browsed for a moment, then glanced at his watch, moved impatiently on his chair and pointedly closed the file. He said politely, "Now, sir, if you'll forgive me, I have to leave."

He stood up and switched on a quick professional smile.

"Just one more thing before I go. Is Alison Harkness your patient also?"

He smiled. "Allie? Oh, yes. I believe she's doing well at Pearson Art College. Winning prizes, getting her name in the newspapers."

Dr. Danwell folded his arms and looked thoughtful.

I said, "Something wrong, Doctor?"

"No. Just thinking about the Harknesses. Strong-minded women, the pair of 'em."

AFTER THREE HOURS of poker I was down $550. I lost a big pot with a jacks over eights to a woman holding four fives, then I watched the same player win with a straight flush, another four of a kind, and several three-of-a-kind hands when everybody else was holding two pair. I cashed out and sat at the bar. My heart wasn't in the game. I was thinking about Allie Harkness instead of cards. Would Allie be like Joan Alfred and refuse to co-operate? And just exactly what was Joan afraid of?

THE NEXT DAY, after a fine breakfast at the House of Pancakes, I drove out to Alison's art college. Its campus was situated on what, until recently, had been raw desert. Saguaro cactus stood like sentinels on the surrounding hills. Within the campus walls, irrigation sprinklers watered grassy lawns. Hundreds of transplanted deciduous trees provided welcome shade. A parking-lot attendant directed me to the administration building. A clerk in the registrar's office obligingly checked Alison's schedule and told me how to find her. I crossed a green, tree-shaded quadrangle to the arts building, found Room 201 and waited in an air-conditioned corridor until Alison's art history lecture ended. I watched the class through a window. Alison sat in the small room with seven other students — I picked her out easily. Four of the students were male, two of the female students were natural blondes. Alison had long black hair, like her aunt, tied in a ponytail, and I saw a likeness between her and Calvert Hunt.

After the lecture, Alison chatted with her instructor as fellow students filed out of the classroom. The instructor looked up when I entered and gave me a nod of polite acknowledgment but continued his conversation for a minute. Alison looked incuriously at me.

She was as tall as her aunt, possibly six feet, and, like Joan Alfred, deeply tanned from the Nevada sun. She had heavy eyebrows, huge dark eyes and a straight nose, too large for real beauty. But she was an attractive woman with a good figure, wearing faded Levis and a yellow T-shirt.

Her conversation with the instructor ended and they both came across. I smiled and said, "Excuse me, Miss Harkness. I'd like a word, if I may." The instructor went off.

Alison was holding school books against her chest. She said, "You're the man who visited the house yesterday?"

"That's me, Silas Seaweed."

"I heard. You were asking questions about my mother."

"Can we talk? I've got a lot to tell you."

"Not now," she said. "I have classes and I need to sort a few things out first."

That was the wrong thing to say to me. I made a prune mouth at her. The investigation was going sideways. Alison's cool reaction was irritating, to say the least.

I gave Alison my card and said sweetly, "Fine, you've got things to sort out. Life's all about choices, isn't it? I'm returning to Victoria. If you rearrange your priorities and decide to chat, you can catch me at this number for another couple of hours. Then I'm gone. Goodbye."

I turned on my heel and strolled away.

I'D TRADED MY HOTEL SUITE for an $18-a-day efficiency apartment near Taff's piano shop. I was packing my bags when somebody knocked on my door. Looking through the peephole, I saw Alison's distorted image. I opened the door and glanced along the corridor. She was alone.

"May I come in?" she said.

"Sure, come in."

She moved in a step, glancing around the sparsely furnished apartment, seeing the depressing beige colours, the '70s kitchen with its stainless steel sink and twin faucets. The air in the room stank of yesterday's hamburgers and fries. Two suitcases lay open on the bed. My loose pocket change, keys, maps and a briefcase were strewn across the dinette table.

I took my remaining shirts from their hangers in a closet, lay them on the bed and began to fold them, one at a time. I said, "My ex-wife taught me how to fold shirts. It's a skill I've never forgotten."

She said timidly, "Have you forgotten your wife?"

"Not yet."

The noise of vehicles passing along the road outside came in rhythmic waves because of a traffic signal. A fly buzzed in the window.

"Do you and your ex-wife both live in Victoria?"

"Yes."

"I'm tired of secrets," she blurted at last. "I've never understood it, any of it, and I don't think that Joan does either." She glanced at her wristwatch. "This couldn't have come at a worse moment. I have exams coming up and it's only an hour until my next lecture."

I shrugged and resumed my packing.

She stamped her foot and said angrily, "You know something? I hate this fucking room."

"How do you think I feel? I've had to live here."

"Let's go outside and sit beside the motel pool," she said. "I need air."

I closed the lid of my suitcase, put a knee on it to compress the contents and snapped the catches.

I said, "That's it. Let's get out of here." I lugged my things out to the parking lot and locked them in the Chevy.

Alison seemed on the verge of tears.

I said, "All right, let's quit playing games, okay ?"

"Okay. I'm … I'm sorry. I guess I was rude earlier."

"Yes, you were. The question is, why?"

She didn't answer, but the thought foremost in my mind was: like mother, like daughter.

We found a bench in the shade across from the pool, its surface liberally sprinkled with fallen leaves. Alison threw her arm across the back of the bench. "Please," she said. "Please tell me about Victoria."

I took a deep breath and said, "You haven't been there?"

"I've never been anywhere except Nevada and California. But I run into people from Victoria all the time." After a pause she added, "It sounds very nice."

"Did Joan tell you what happened between me and your father yesterday?"

Alison covered her face with her hands and groaned. Shaking her head, she said, "Oh, God! Had he been drinking? He's crazy when he gets drinking."

She was flushed to the roots of her hair now.

I gave a speech. "Victoria is a small coastal city on the edge of rain forest," I said. "It was established by the Hudson's Bay Company back in the mid 1800s. It's British Columbia's capital city. If you like tree-lined streets and parks and heritage buildings you'll probably like it. I have a feeling you'll be seeing Victoria before long; then you can decide for yourself."

The girl's eyes lit up at this, but she said nothing.

"It's a long story, Alison. Your mother was born in Victoria, in the house where your grandfather still lives."

She gave me a startled look. "I have a grandfather? He's still alive!" she exclaimed, sitting bolt upright.

"In Victoria you have a grandfather, a great-aunt and your mother's first cousin."

"I knew it!" she cried. "I just knew it!" Then her face clouded. "But there's something horrible too, isn't there? Terrible things happened that nobody talks about."

"It should be talked about. Too many years have been wasted."

Alison's hand still rested on the back of the bench. I resisted an urge to reach out and touch it reassuringly. Instead I said, "Does any of this frighten you?"

"A bit." She nibbled the inside of her lower lip with her teeth, and the crease between her eyes deepened. "But I have to know, no matter how awful. Not knowing is the worst thing in the world." She touched my knee with her long fingers. "Tell me why my mother left home and never went back."

"Shouldn't you be asking your folks instead of me?"

"Do you think I haven't? They *never* talk about it, not a word. Daddy hates Canada, Victoria especially." Alison's face got a little harder. Her chin jutted like the prow of a battleship.

I said, "You probably know that your mother left home because of a disagreement with her folks."

Alison was frowning at her left thumb.

I said, "Anyway, there was a clash."

"Don't apologize, just tell me what you know."

"I know that when your mother was younger than you are now, she met your father. A man your grandparents disapproved of."

Alison nodded. "I knew that much. Daddy was wild, a merchant sailor. He spent years at sea, even after I was born. I hardly saw him until he showed up after Mother died."

She had a faraway smile and was mentally reviewing a childhood fantasy. No doubt it was a fantasy suggested by a protective mother to explain the missing father. It stopped me for a minute, but now Alison was an adult. It was time for the truth.

"Your father wasn't away at sea, Alison. He was a … " I paused, unsure how to phrase my next words.

She moved her body impatiently. "Oh, don't stop now, please! Not just when I was going to learn something. I told you. Not knowing is terrible. Nothing could be worse than what I've imagined, believe me."

"You might be wrong. Before he changed it, your father's name was Frank Turko. He was born in Oakland, California. As a young man he was involved with a motorcycle club. Something happened, there was a fight. A man died and the courts ruled your father responsible."

My crude description dropped into a vast silence. Alison stared at the grass below the bench and opened her mouth, but no words came.

Finally she raised her head, and eyes met mine. "Please go on. I don't care how awful it is, really. It can't be as bad as things I'll imagine."

How to explain a senseless tragedy? Hardly a tragedy, a melodrama. I plunged ahead and said, "Years before you were born, your father was arrested in California and charged with causing wrongful death. He was released on bail. Instead of waiting for the trial he went to Canada, changed his name and started a new life. He met your mother and they got married."

"I know that part's wrong," she said, her voice coarsened by deep emotion. "My mother and father were unmarried, nobody ever made any secret of it."

I shook my head. "Your parents *were* married."

She looked at me in a confused way. "But if they were married, why would Joan tell me otherwise?"

"Joan's probably only heard part of the story. What I told you is true. Your parents were married before your birth, but your mother's parents tried to have the marriage annulled."

"So that's it. That's why Daddy hated them," she said in a smaller voice. Eyes narrowed, she continued, "But if Father wasn't a sailor, maybe he didn't kill that man in California, either?"

"I'm sorry, Alison. Be that as it may, your dad spent those missing years in jail … "

She leaned toward me. "What happened to him?"

I took a deep breath and said calmly, "Your parents left Canada for good, many years ago. Your mother went first, to a seaside place near Seattle, where you were born. Because of that trouble in California, your father was a wanted fugitive in this country. But he followed."

Her face relaxed and she murmured, "Daddy must have loved her very much to leave Canada, where he was safe."

"It cost him his freedom."

Her shoulders dropped. I couldn't see her eyes anymore, but I had to tell her everything now, get it all out, the good and the bad. Without looking up she said, "I've got this memory. Sometimes I think it's a dream but it probably isn't. It was when Mummy died. We drove over this big bridge, then Aunt Joan came back here to live with me."

"One of the San Francisco Bay bridges probably, near Oakland."

"Right. Then about six years ago, Daddy showed up."

"Is that the first time you'd met him?"

"Yes. The seafaring story, it never really made sense. But I accepted it." She nodded, thinking aloud. "To spare my feelings, Daddy and Joan concocted this story and stuck to it. They didn't want me to know that my father was a criminal."

She stared at the pool. "My grandfather, the other people in Victoria. Do they know all of this?"

"They know very little of it. Yet."

Pent-up emotion flared into anger. "They don't know that their meddling caused my father's ruin?"

"It's complicated. There's two sides to this story. There always is."

"I don't care, the hell with them!" Her voice had risen. A cleaning woman wielding a broom on the opposite side of the pool turned to stare.

Alison got up from the bench and had taken an angry stride before I caught her. "Wait," I said roughly. "Don't you think this idiocy has lasted long enough? Don't you think somebody in that stubborn clan of yours should act sensibly for once?"

Tears filled her eyes and she sobbed. I didn't try to stop her.

JOAN ALFRED MET ALISON and me at the door. Joan was looking thoughtful and withdrawn. There were dark half-crescents beneath her eyes, a glass of whisky in one hand and a bottle of Jack Daniel's in the other. She pecked Alison's cheek and said, "Come in, Mr. Seaweed. I'm sorry about yesterday."

She manoeuvred uncertainly to a chair and sat down in it. "I've been up all night," she said.

Alison went into the kitchen. Joan's eyes closed, but when she heard Alison returning she jerked awake. Alison had fresh lemonade with her. She poured three glasses and said, "It's a new day. Let's celebrate."

I said, "Where's Frank?"

Joan was still nursing half a glass of whisky. "The hell with Frank," she said. "I told him to clear off until he got his head straight."

I said, "Just so we're clear. Let's not have any more bullshit about sailing ships and sealing wax and cabbages and kings."

Joan laughed and said, "Whatever. I'm not completely ready to face a new day, and I'm sure as hell not celebrating anything with lemonade."

Outside, the two dogs and the family cat were lying companionably in the shade.

Joan said, "It's hard, hanging out the family's dirty laundry. Frank crashed and burned, but when I was little he was my hero. That's the way I like to remember him."

That was okay with me.

Joan drank what was left of the whisky in her glass, lit a cigarette and said apologetically, "When you came here yesterday, I took you for an ex-con. Maybe somebody from San Quentin who knew that Frank was my brother. Frank was a big wheel in his day. There's a notion that some old drug money is sloshing around out there somewhere. This isn't the first time strangers have come banging on our door."

Joan turned to Alison and said, "I'm sorry, Allie. We didn't want you to know about Frank's past. We just couldn't … " Her words trailed off. Alison flew from her seat. The two women hugged each other and burst into tears.

I left the room and stood on the veranda. A slow anticlimactic hour passed before Joan invited me to rejoin them. I told them a few things about Victoria. I discovered that Frank had left Joan Alfred completely in the dark about his activities in British Columbia. She knew virtually nothing about Marcia's family.

Joan fetched a photo album from her room. Over sandwiches we browsed through many old pictures and I tried to fill more of Alison's historical blanks. Among the pictures was one of Marcia, as a baby, in a carriage being pushed by a young girl. The caption read: "Marcia, on an outing with Effie."

This was a different Effie — Effie Yokwats's mom.

They agreed to lend me some of their precious photographs. I borrowed several, including one of Alison at a student art exhibition. It showed Alison posed with a bearded young man in front of a painting. When I asked Alison about it, she explained that this was a casual stranger who had stopped to admire the work. Alison had been talking to him when a classmate strolled by and snapped the picture.

IT WAS LATE when I left Reno in my old Chev. I enjoyed driving Nevada's long lonely roads, watching the colours change from pale sages and golds and pinks to the deep-scented purple of the desert night. The air was fresh and clear. Away from civilization's electric luminescence, stars came out and filled the sky. At midnight I paused at a rest stop for 10 minutes and watched the moon rise above Mount Shasta. I remembered a half-forgotten dinner party from long ago where one guest, a witch-like woman with long, white hair wearing a black velvet gown, spoke of mysterious happenings on Shasta at the time of the full moon. Maybe. Shasta's mysteries I would leave for others to elucidate. All I knew for sure was that Alison was Marcia Hunt's daughter. I was also quite sure that I had seen Marcia's grave. Whoever Fred Eade had found, it wasn't Marcia. I was certain that Dr. Robert Danwell had been Marcia Hunt's physician. I was still sure when I drove through Eugene and Portland.

Certitude accompanied me to Barb's house in Seattle. It was mid-night. She heard my knock on the door and answered at last. Half asleep, she slipped the lock and watched me from behind the chain lock. Interior candles outlined her naked shoulder and thigh, transforming her long hair into a silvery halo and her face into a dark mystery. "Silas," she said in her soft voice. "Silas Seaweed."

The door closed while Barbara slipped open the chain, and then I was through with a rush and we fell into that universe where nothing is impossible.

Almost nothing.

CHAPTER THIRTEEN

Back in Victoria I called by my office, where I was glared at by my answering machine's angry red eye. I switched it on and checked junk snail-mail while the cassette tape rewound. Bernie Tapp had called several times. There were two cryptic messages from the cagey mystery man who spoke out of the side of his mouth. Iris Naylor wanted to talk to me. Most of my calls came from Sammy Lofthouse.

Lofthouse was a small, cocky, cigar-smoking lawyer with a permanently blue chin who looked as if he slept in his suits. The kind of man who left his cellphone on in theatres, shouted at waitresses and dropped damp cigar butts into coffee cups. Before I could decide who to call first, the phone rang.

Bernie Tapp said, "Listen, pally. We need to talk, pronto. Some guy told Chief Bulloch you were nosing about in Reno. He is very ticked."

"There's no law against me playing cards in Reno."

I heard Bernie's rapid intake of breath. "Cut the malarkey. You were work-ing on the Calvert Hunt deal. You know it, I know it. Bulloch knows it."

"Is that the whole lecture?"

"No. There's more. I want you here in five minutes. I want to watch you squirm. We've arrested Fred Eade's girlfriend, Patty Nolan. She won't speak to anybody except you or that sleazebag Sammy Lofthouse."

"Sammy is acting for Patty Nolan?"

"In a manner of speaking. She's retained his services. The only advice he's given her so far is to keep her trap shut."

"That's not bad advice, but she didn't need a lawyer who charges Lofthouse's fees to tell her that."

"The trouble she's in, she needs more than a lawyer. She needs a miracle."

"What's she charged with?"

"Conspiracy to traffic in stolen automobiles, but that's just for openers. She's also a material witness to Fred Eade's killing."

"Where is Patty being held?"

"Wilkinson Road jail. You willing to talk to her?"

"Sure."

"Meet me at headquarters in an hour."

"Make it two hours," I said. "I need a workout." Bernie slammed the phone down.

I yawned. My mouth was sour from too much coffee and too many hours cooped up in the Chevrolet. Still, things were moving along nicely.

MORAN'S GYM OCCUPIES the top floor of a rundown brick heritage warehouse near the Gorge waterway. I did 15 minutes with a skipping rope, pumped iron for a while and was whaling away at Moran's heavy punching bag when Gervais LaFleur sauntered in wearing a blue pinstripe suit, an open-necked white shirt with a button-down collar, and custom-made shoes that looked as if they'd just been dipped in black nail varnish.

Gervais, who had a black belt in Brazilian ju-jitsu, was a 50-year-old account executive with one of Victoria's brokerage firms. He waved at the pugs drinking coffee at Moran's lunch counter before disappearing into the change rooms. When Gervais came out five minutes later wearing a Speedo swimsuit and Nike Airs with bobble-top stockings, I was waiting for him. He looked as happy to see me as I was to see him.

"Silas, old chum," he said. "Where have you been hiding yourself?"

"I've been laid up and out of town."

"This place isn't the same without you. Moran has been in mourning. Is it true that baddies have been throwing knives and things at you?"

"Not quite, but forget that. I want to ask you about Charles Service."

Gervais frowned at his manicured fingernails.

I said, "Just between you and me, Gervais. How much money a month is Service sniffing up his nose?"

"I don't know. But whatever it is, Charlie can afford it, believe me."

"Who manages his money?"

"Not me, worse luck."

"Can you find out who does?"

"Can birds fly? It'll be the work of an instant, but first, Tony's impatiently waiting to rub aromatic oils on my body."

"One more thing, Gervais. Do you know Sarah Williams?"

"Of course I do. Doesn't everybody?"

"Is Sarah rich?"

"*Was* rich, Silas. *Was*. She and Mummy Williams plowed their all into one of those dot-com fiascos and lost their little embroidered nighties because of it."

"What, everything?"

"Every last *sou*."

"Both of them?"

"Well, Mummy Williams still has a little annuity I suppose," Gervais said thoughtfully. "She must have. Sarah has a ritzy condo. But if Charlie Service wasn't picking up all of Sarah's tabs, I don't know how the poor thing would manage."

"Gervais," I said enviously, "are you hiding a catcher's mitt inside that Speedo?"

Smiling complacently, Gervais threw his muscular bronzed body upon Tony's massage table.

Moran came across to me, chewing an unlit cigar, and said, "We've got a game on this coming Friday. Usual time. Some of the boys want to try Texas hold'em for a change — $20 ante, winner takes all."

"You and the boys have been watching too much TV. Texas hold'em is a shitty game, 90 percent luck. Gimme seven-card stud, or Omaha."

"Does that mean you won't come?"

"Well, no. I think I'm on a winning streak right now. Count me in."

I HAD A SHOWER and returned to my office. The phone rang. It was Sam Lofthouse. He said, "Hey, Seaweed. Let's talk about Patty Nolan. Know who I'm talking about?"

"Sure. Fred Eade's girlfriend."

"Yeah? Well if she's his friend, how come she shot him?"

I said, "Did she?"

"Probably, I don't know. Patty says no, but maybe she's lying. Somebody shot him. Patty had motive, opportunity."

"What was her motive?"

"Fred was beating her up," Lofthouse said. "Maybe Patty went downtown and some dyke advised her to shoot the fucker."

"Sammy, what do you want from me?"

"Reward money. I hear you offered Fred five grand for certain information."

"Do you have information worth five grand?"

"My client has. I'm acting for her."

"Goodbye, Sam," I said, ready to hang up.

"Just give me a minute," Sammy said urgently. "Let me sort some things out here."

I could imagine him, a cigar in his mouth, a telephone wedged between his neck and his shoulder, juggling a briefcase full of notes. "Okay," he said. "This is the deal. My client is smart enough to know that she needs the best lawyer in town, but I don't do pro bonos and Patty is broke."

"If that's the case, how come Patty's your client?"

"I'm getting to that. Either Patty has some information about a case you're involved with, or she's blowing smoke up my ass. She thinks she can get money from you."

"Patty gives me the information. You get the reward?"

"Right. You catch on quick."

"Okay. I'll think about it."

"Have we got a deal, Silas?"

"You don't have any deal with me. I'm not your client. I'll talk to Patty first, hear what she's got to say. Maybe I'll get back to you."

I pressed the disconnect and called Calvert Hunt's residence. Iris Naylor answered.

I said, "This is Silas Seaweed. Sorry I'm late returning your call, but I've been out of town."

Her reply was so long coming that I thought she'd gone. I said, "Hello, are you still there?"

"I'm sorry, Mr. Seaweed," she said apologetically. "If I tell you something, will you keep it confidential?"

"Possibly, but I'm not a newspaper reporter. Cops don't always protect their sources."

"What about police informers? They're used all the time."

"Good point. But just so you know. If you tell me something and I need you to repeat it in a court of law, I wouldn't hesitate to subpoena you."

"Well, I'm sorry, it was probably nothing."

"Does this have anything to do with Ribblesdale's prowlers?"

"Actually, it does."

"Then I want you to tell me about it. It could be very important."

Iris Naylor sighed and said, "I feel quite disloyal. This may sound silly. It's to do with Mr. Service's hairbrushes. Two silver-backed hairbrushes that went missing from this house a few days ago."

"Yes," I said eagerly. "Keep talking."

"That's it, really. We saw something on the grounds here one night. A prowler or a dog. Something. Mr. Service and I were both here at Ribblesdale. Together in the lounge, and whatever it was we both saw it through a window. It's not the first time, of course. But he asked me not to report it to the police."

"Did he say why?"

"No. But this is what's so strange," Iris Naylor said breathily. "The very next morning, Mr. Service couldn't find his hairbrushes."

"Please describe what you saw through the window."

"I can't describe it. It was a moving shape. Something solid. We could see it flittering or running across the grounds, but we couldn't decide what it was. It definitely wasn't a moving shadow because the thing travelled at least 100 yards across our line of sight before it vanished."

"How big was it?"

"Again, I'm not sure. It was quite dark and the thing was some distance away. I would say it was bigger than a full-grown golden retriever. Smaller than a donkey."

"Could it have been a man?"

"It certainly didn't look human to me."

"Were you frightened?"

"Yes, a little. I certainly wish I'd never seen it. Thinking about it has kept me awake nights."

"You're suggesting that this shape got into the house and stole a pair of hairbrushes?"

"You're not taking this very seriously, are you?" she said sullenly.

"On the contrary, I'm taking this extremely seriously," I said and then heard voices in the background when somebody entered Iris Naylor's space.

"Please describe the hairbrushes to me."

She said in a whisper, "I'm not free to talk at the moment."

"Is Mr. Service in the house?"

"Yes, I think so."

"In that case I'd like to speak to him."

"Of course. I'll connect you."

A minute elapsed before Charles Service came on. I found myself yawning uncontrollably.

"Hello, Seaweed. What can I do for you?" said Service in a cheerful voice.

"You can prepare Mr. Hunt for some interesting news."

"What might that be?"

"I know where his long-lost daughter is. I've located his granddaughter."

I heard Service's quick inhalation, but when he spoke his voice sounded dubious. "That's marvellous, of course, but are you certain?"

"Yes. Do you want to meet me and talk about it?"

"Sure. When can I see you?"

"In a couple of hours."

"Why not come immediately?"

"I'm afraid that you'll have to wait."

"Why do I have to wait, what for?"

"That's my business," I said coldly.

"All right, but come here to Foul Bay Road, quick as you can. Bring any proofs that you've collected." His voice changed and became conspiratorial as he added softly, "And Seaweed, I hope you've been discreet. You *do* appreciate that Mr. Hunt loathes headlines."

"Don't worry about it. So far, the only people in this town who know about these things are you and me."

We both heard the click on the line as somebody replaced a receiver.

Now somebody else knew. Iris Naylor? Sarah Williams? I hung up without commenting.

BLACK STORM CLOUDS were hovering above the Sooke Hills when I set out on a five-minute walk to police headquarters. Dew sparkled on the weeds growing in a vacant lot near the Johnson Street bridge. As I waited for a traffic light to change, a girl about 15 trudged ahead against the red light. She had a shaven head and enough body piercings to fill a scrapyard. The rear half of her midriff was a red Chinese dragon tattoo.

The traffic light turned green. Suddenly I felt weary. I had to force myself on. I stopped at a camera shop on Douglas Street and ordered quick copies of the photographs I'd brought from Reno.

"YOU'VE BEEN A BAD BOY," Bernie said.

"Tell me about it."

Watery sunlight fell through Bernie's windows, yellowing his head and shoulders. The window had been opened to help ventilate the room. Victoria's police headquarters was new but had already acquired a faint institutional odour of human sweat overlaid with disinfectant. A pigeon alighted on the windowsill. Bernie got up, took a quart can of birdseed from a filing cabinet and scattered a handful on the ledge. The bird cocked its head and surveyed my friend with one tiny brilliant eye, ready for instant flight. It pecked a few seeds, then with another flutter of wings it was gone.

Bernie stayed facing the window, both hands in his pockets. He said, "Summer's going, Silas. It's clouding up. Did you bring your umbrella?"

"Umbrellas are for sissies," I said.

"Borrow that one in the corner," said Bernie, sitting down. "Otherwise you'll get soaked."

"That's very generous of you, Bernie."

"Don't thank me. Thank the guy who left it here."

"He won't mind?" I said, going along with Bernie's spiel.

"Not for a while. He's in the crowbar motel. After Bulloch is finished dealing with you, you might be able to deliver it in person."

I grinned. Bernie grinned too.

Bernie sat down and hitched one knee over the other.

I said, "Is Patty here?"

"Yeah, we brought her in from Wilkie jail. She's in the women's lock-up, biting her fingernails."

"I can understand she might be a little anxious."

"She ought to be. Patty's in big trouble."

"Who are you kidding? The only thing you can stick her with is possession of stolen property. To wit, one green Toyota Corolla. I'm sure she didn't kill Fred Eade."

"Who did?"

"Look. I'm half asleep, flailing around in the dark. I've got some answers and a lot of riddles. Let me talk to Patty before I keel over."

He said, "There's a tie-in between the Fred Eade killing, the guy who shot you, and Calvert Hunt. What is it?"

"I'm not quite certain."

A cold smile brushed his lips. "You're not certain, but you're pretty sure, right?"

"Fred Eade responded to an ad I put in the paper. But Fred's the kind of guy's been making enemies all his life. The town's full of people who would shank him for $5."

"The town's filling with people who would shank you for 50 cents."

"Maybe," I said. "But I'm not a politician. It's okay with me if every asshole in town hates me. Why should I care?"

"You don't care if people shoot at you, send you to hospital?" Bernie stood up abruptly. "Fine. You win. Let's go see Patty."

Bernie marched out of his office and I followed along the corridor. Printers hummed, footsteps echoed. The radio dispatcher's amplified voice could be heard over everything else. Uniformed cops sat at desks piled high with paper. We passed through a frosted-glass door into a public waiting room. A smiling policewoman was behind a desk, accepting a petition from six angry old ladies wearing identical felt hats, shapeless coats and sneakers.

Bernie frowned sourly at the grannies and growled, "This place is turning into a fucking madhouse."

We took an elevator to the top floor. A jail matron was waiting for us on the wrong side of a barred gate. The matron let us in. Bernie and I walked another long corridor to a small, high-ceilinged interview room. It was like the interview room in Reno; the only thing missing was the feather boa.

Patty Nolan was inside, pacing back and forth, wearing shapeless orange coveralls.

In a loud voice, Bernie told her to sit down at the table. I sat opposite. Bernie leaned in the corner with his arms folded, listening.

She said, "You must be Silas Seaweed."

"That's right. I saw you once, in Mom's Café. The day I met Fred Eade."

"Yeah, I seen you too, only I didn't really pay attention to you at the time. It was only later when I got talking to Fred about it that I tried to remember what you looked like."

Patty slouched in her chair, head forward, holding a half-empty Styrofoam coffee cup. The breezy sexuality that I remembered was gone.

I said, "You called me on the phone a couple of times, but never followed through. Why?"

When she spoke I could barely hear her words. She said, "I'm in a jam, mister. Has he got to be here?"

I looked at her. She drank the remaining coffee and began to poke the Styrofoam cup with long fingernails.

I turned to Bernie. "Give us a few minutes alone?"

Bernie pushed himself away from the wall and went out.

"Just so you know," I said, "the room's probably bugged."

"That figures," she said, with the toneless empty irony of a woman mistreated by men all her life. "I don't trust cops but I ain't afraid neither. They don't have nothing on me and they know it. That stolen car deal is a bum rap. If I had money, I'd be long gone."

"What do you want to see me about?"

She leaned forward and whispered, "I know where Marcia Hunt and her daughter are." She sat back to watch my reaction.

I had on my usual stone face. "You're interested in the reward money?"

She said, "I need money to get out of jail. Sammy Lofthouse will handle my case, but he don't do freebies. He wants $5,000 up front and I got nothing."

I gave it to her straight. "I've got bad news," I said. "The search for Marcia Hunt is over. We know where she is." Wearily, I stood up and said, "Sorry. I'll speak to somebody and … "

"Sure you will!" Patty yelled angrily. "You'll speak to some law student. He'll take me on as a practice case, play pretend lawyer, land me in worse trouble than I am already. To get out of this mess I need the best advice I can get. Don't you get it, mister? I could end up dead."

"You've been threatened?"

"Why do you think I ran away? The guy that killed Fred will kill me too, if he can. You're the last chance for me. For me *and* Sid."

"Sidney Banks?"

Hysteria made her voice veer up and down the scale. "Yeah, who else?"

"Sid was the man who spoke to me from a pay phone, has a funny voice?"

"Sid talks funny because half his teeth are missing."

I said, "I'm very sorry. If you'd reached me with the information earlier, it would have saved me a trip to the States. You might have had the reward. Now it's too late."

She stared at me with a curious expression. "What are you talking about?"

"I'm talking about finding Marcia Hunt's grave, in Nevada."

"Grave? Marcia Hunt's grave? What kind of deal are you handing me?" she said, obviously puzzled.

Something was out of kilter. I said, "I'm tired. Maybe I'm not thinking straight. Please make this quick. Tell me what you know about Marcia Hunt."

"Will I get the reward?"

"If you're entitled to anything, I promise you'll get it."

"All right. Here goes nothing. Marcia Hunt ain't dead. She and her daughter are living together on Hornby Island."

"You've got it wrong. Marcia Hunt is dead. I've seen her grave. She's buried in … "

"She's alive, I tell you! I talked to her less'n a month ago."

I tried to think. I assumed that the woman on Hornby Island was an imposter. Somebody that Fred Eade set up to cash in on the reward. But if that was so, why hadn't the imposter come forward herself?

Patty was still toying with her Styrofoam cup. Little bits of white plastic had fallen onto her lap. She had cut a row of crenellations with her fingernails. The cup resembled a miniature castle.

I said, "Let's have the rest of it."

"There is no rest. That's it. Marcia Hunt and her daughter live on Hornby Island."

"What's her daughter's name?"

"Hockey. It sounds dumb, but everybody calls her Hockey."

"What kind of name is that?"

Patty had the dull, stubborn look of someone who knows she is being disbelieved. "Don't ask me, mister. The whole deal is nuts. Marcia Hunt is a harmless airhead, a space cadet. Her daughter ain't much better. The pair of 'em live on social assistance, earn extra cash picking oysters."

"These women live openly on Hornby Island?"

"Sure. They've been there for years. Hockey was raised there, everybody knows 'em, they're kind of an island institution. Why don't you go to Hornby, check it out?"

I said, "Who put you on to them?"

"Fred Eade. Fred's known who they are for years."

"And Fred kept the secret until now?"

"Why not? As far as Fred knew, Frank Harkness's wife and daughter were just ordinary people. He had no idea they were related to Calvert Hunt."

"Just a minute. Are you telling me that Fred met this woman over there and recognized her?"

Patty shook her head. She had lost that scared look and was warming to her story. "No. See, Frank Harkness, the boss biker, had a double life. Most of the time Frank was hanging out in Wellington with the club. But he had this other life that was secret, personal. He didn't share it with nobody. So none of the bikers were ever introduced to his wife."

"Then how did Fred recognize her?"

"It's this way. The Wellington bike club used to buy pot on Hornby.

Even back then everybody was growing it. Fred was on Hornby Island one time and got talking to this crazy lady. She was admiring Fred's motorcycle and she told him that her husband had been a biker once. Fred said the lady was screwed up, but she had a photograph that she carried around in a purse. Sure enough, when Fred looked at it, it was a photo of Frank Harkness sitting on his Harley outside the Wellington club rooms. Fred was real surprised because he'd expected Frank's wife to be a beauty, you know, a class act. But this woman was a real mess. The story is, Frank's wife fried her brains on some bad acid."

Patty sounded convincing, and her story was filled with plausible details. I said, "I want to tie this down. This story you're telling me, it isn't second-hand?"

Impatiently she snapped, "What have I gotta do? I told you. I seen those women with my own eyes, I been in their house, I spent time with Hockey and Marcia."

I changed the topic. "You say that your life is in danger?"

Patty's sullen look returned. "The guy that killed Fred tried to kill me too. Me *and* Sid."

"What was his motive?"

"I dunno," she said, avoiding my eyes.

"You must have some idea."

"There's a lot of funny stuff going down. You don't know the half of it."

I said, "Has the court set your bail?"

"I was dragged up in front of some kangaroo judge, heard a lot of Mickey Mouse bullshit. The deal is, I don't get out of here without a lawyer."

"Are they treating you right?"

"Not bad. Wilkie Road isn't no Hyatt Regency, but I slept in worse places. The food is fair, and it makes a change from rocking around in Fred's boat."

"Are you prepared to tell me where I can find Sidney Banks?"

"No."

I stood up.

She said plaintively, "Will you talk to Sammy Lofthouse for me?"

"What I want to do first is go to Hornby Island. Speak to these two women. Lofthouse can wait."

I COLLECTED MY FINISHED prints from the camera shop, then started the short walk to the parking lot behind Swans pub. The heavens opened. Within seconds my hair and shoulders were soaked. I sheltered in a doorway and watched a pair of girls hurrying for a bus stop across the street. Rain gutters overflowed, the streets were flooded. A passing car sent sheets of water flying, splashing the girls from head to toe. Soaked, they shook their fists at the retreating driver, then, looking at each other, they dissolved into helpless laughter. Their bus arrived and hid them from view.

CHARLES SERVICE ANSWERED Calvert Hunt's front door himself. He greeted me with a smile and a handshake, then stood aside to let me enter. An inner door opened. Iris Naylor's face showed briefly. Service led the way to his office at the back of the house. I followed wearily, feeling half dead from fatigue, then sank into a chair. Outside, oak leaves littered the lawns, raindrops pocked the swimming pool. Hunt's Chinese gardener, dressed in a long yellow coat, was poking a stick into a drain near the three-car garage. Water dripped from a clogged gutter above a mullioned window and zigzagged down leaded-glass panes.

Service sat on the edge of his big desk, folded his arms and said, "Rotten sort of day, but the forecast is good."

"Next thing you know it'll be snowing."

"Snow in Victoria? That'll be the day!" retorted Service.

I took out some of the photographs I had brought from Reno and laid them on Service's desk without speaking. I showed them one at a time, like a card player. Service stared down at them without moving for a moment, then he picked them all up and examined them thoughtfully.

He put them down on his desk and tapped them with his finger. "All right. What are these all about?"

"The younger woman is Alison Harkness Hunt. She's Calvert Hunt's granddaughter. The other woman is Joan Alfred."

"Who is Joan Alfred?"

"Frank Harkness's sister."

A faint half-smile tugged at the corners of Service's mouth. "Oh yeah?"

"That's right."

"Why is there no recent picture of Marcia Hunt?"

"Marcia is dead. She was killed in a freak accident."

"Ah!" he said, getting up from the desk and crossing to the window to stare outside. During the silence a clock inside the house chimed the hour. The chime seemed to rouse the lawyer from his reverie. He turned and said, "Dead, eh? So that's why she never contacted the family."

"Obviously."

"Where did you find these pictures?"

"They were given to me by Alison, Calvert Hunt's granddaughter."

"But why are there no photographs of Marcia herself? After all, if you can ... "

I took out more pictures and handed them across. Service stared in fascination for almost a minute, then looked at them all again.

"Well," he said cheerfully, "that's Marcia, all right. No question. A little older than I remember her, of course. Her figure has filled out. But what's your proof that the other women are who you say they are?"

"There's plenty of proof. More than enough to convince Calvert Hunt."

"Maybe. But first you have to convince *me*. We're not disturbing the old man's final years unless the evidence is unassailable."

"I don't want to tell Mr. Hunt anything, not yet. There are some loose ends. I just wanted to prepare the way."

"Can I keep these photographs?"

"Yes, you can. But the question is whether you may." I grinned and added, "Please take good care of them."

Service shoved them into a desk drawer. "Right. This Alison woman. And Joan Alfred. Where are they now?"

"Nevada. They've been there most of Alison's life."

"Nevada? I'm surprised to hear it."

"Why?"

Service shrugged. "I don't know, really. Seems a bleak, hot sort of a place to me, not what Marcia was used to. Still, I expect she followed Frank Harkness, eh?"

"Not as far as I know."

"How did Marcia die?"

"She owned a little ranch. It's very odd. She was shot and killed by rustlers."

Service smiled fleetingly. "Well, it's an unusual end but perhaps not unfitting. Marcia was attracted to danger. Were the rustlers captured?"

"Captured and jailed."

"Her killers will be back on the streets again by now, killing other innocent people. Still, the U.S. Congress favours the death penalty. I wish our gutless Canadian government would do the same. Save the tax-payers' money."

"Maybe you're right. If they get the guy that killed Fred Eade and the guy that killed Harry Cunliffe, they could bring the hangman back, do a two-for-one special."

Service said, "Jimmy Scow killed Harry."

I didn't say anything.

"Well, Seaweed, apparently you've been busy. Perhaps we were too hasty, pulling you off the case."

"I had some lucky breaks."

"It took more than luck, but even so, I'm not completely convinced. So far all I've seen are some pictures."

The telephone on Service's desk began to ring. We both looked at it. Service picked it up reluctantly and listened for a moment without speaking. A spasm of annoyance narrowed his lips and his eyes. "All right," he snapped. "I'll be there immediately, dammit." Service slammed the telephone into its cradle and said tersely. "You'll have to excuse me. Wait here, will you?"

He went out. I went behind Service's desk, opened the top drawer and saw the pictures that Service had just put inside. I then closed the drawer and crossed to the windows. The mullions were partially concealed behind heavy brocade curtains with tapestry-cord swags. The windows were fastened by sturdy bronze catches. I looked for security strips on the glass — there weren't any.

Like most of the rooms in the house, this one had a handsome fireplace. There was a smoke detector on the beamed ceiling, but if there were motion detectors or other intruder alarms, I did not see them. I remembered seeing burglar alarms on some of the house's exterior doors.

Apart from a large banker's desk and four high-backed chairs, the room, or office, was sparsely furnished. One wall was filled with Service's law books. There were a couple of ordinary steel four-drawer filing cabinets, an old-fashioned floor safe and a large olive-green steel cabinet that at first sight looked like a table because it was draped with the same brocade as the window curtains. There were several hunting prints and four humorous lawyer cartoons in black frames.

The door opened and a thin elderly woman entered. She was wearing a plum-coloured woollen suit with a blue silk blouse ruffled to conceal her crepey-skinned neck. She had on blue stockings and low-heeled shoes matching the suit. Her figure was stooped and she walked with a silver-handled cane. Behind her came Charles Service, who cautioned me against speaking by holding a finger to his lips.

The woman surveyed me from head to toe and snapped, "So you're the Indian meddler I've been hearing about? I thought you were told to clear off."

"Now, Phyllis," said Service soothingly, helping the old woman to a seat. He smiled but was plainly ill at ease.

I remained standing.

"Well," she continued indignantly, "isn't that right, weren't you told to keep out?"

I nodded affably. "That's correct, Mrs. Williams."

"How did you know my name?" she said, surprised.

"Because he's a detective. It's his business to know things," Service said.

"You should never have been brought into this. Waste of time. Marcia has been dead and gone for ages." Mrs. Williams pulled her chin in and pursed her lips to show disapproval, then said to Service, "It was foolish of you to encourage Calvert."

"Did I encourage him?" Service smiled uneasily.

"Perhaps not," she said, then added, "But you didn't do all that you could to discourage him either. After all, you're his lawyer, he listens to you."

Service's grin slipped. "He listens to me when it suits him. When it doesn't, well … "

She was in one of Service's straight-backed chairs. When she tilted her head to look at me, she winced. Pain tightened her features. She stroked her neck. Heavy diamond rings sparkled on knobbly, arthritic fingers. She said to me, "Seaweed. What kind of name is that?"

"An old name," I said coldly.

"Well, Seaweed. You made no progress at all I suppose?"

I ignored Service's emphatic head-shaking and said, "I traced Marcia to Seattle. Somebody that I spoke to told me that she'd gone to Nevada."

"Oh? Well, now she's gone to hell I suppose. Marcia was a torment to her mother and to her father. I'll never understand why Calvert wanted to see that ungrateful baggage again. If Marcia were alive, she'd be here now, making his life miserable with her wickedness."

The high whine of ancient spite was unmistakable, uttered without regard for the feelings of those present.

"Now Phyllis, don't go upsetting yourself," said Service, shaking his head and speaking in a mock-serious voice. He turned to me and nodded pointedly toward the door.

I smiled, wished them good day and departed. Service followed me out into the passage and said, "These things we've been talking about. I hope you'll keep them under your hat. We don't want to set the cat among the pigeons unnecessarily, do we?"

I grinned to myself. Service was a creature of habit. Whenever he became anxious, he resorted to cliché.

CHAPTER FOURTEEN

I went to Dr. Cunliffe's house. He answered the door immediately and led me to his den.

The room was masculine, almost spartan, furnished with a couple of leather armchairs and a matching sofa. A carved Kwakiutl cedar chest sat beneath the window. Driftwood logs crackled in the fireplace. Dr. Cunliffe noticed my yawns. He said, "You look bushed."

"Probably. I drove almost non-stop from Reno, haven't slept properly for a couple of days."

"Why, for heaven's sake?"

"I intended to spend the night in Eugene, but when I got there I didn't feel tired, so I just kept going. Then I got to my office and one thing led to another. But pretty soon I'm heading for bed because tomorrow I'm driving to Hornby Island."

He gave me a clinical stare. "How old are you, 50?"

"Hell no, I'm just this side of 40. Do I look that old, Doc?"

"At the moment, yes, and if you make a habit of pushing your limits, you might not reach 50." The doctor pointed to one of the leather chairs and as we sat down he said, "All right, I know this isn't a social call. So what's up?"

"I'd like to ask you a couple of things about Marcia Hunt."

"Go ahead."

"How deeply was Marcia Hunt into the drug scene? I heard somewhere that a few people wrecked themselves with acid and wonder if she could have been one of them."

The doctor crossed his legs and thought about it before replying. "It's *possible*," he said broodingly. "Medical journals published some alarming reports during the hippie era. Pure LSD is safe in suitable dosages, but there were some nasty side effects because a lot of the stuff was made in kitchen laboratories. I knew of one tragic case. The lad involved didn't lose his memory, but he lost his sight and hearing."

"Permanently?"

"Yes. So to answer your question, it's possible. Marcia used drugs indiscriminately for a time."

"What was Marcia's drug of choice?"

"She used whatever she could get her hands on. Marijuana, heroin, speed. But I always thought that she'd come to her senses eventually and give it up."

"That might have been quite a trick, don't you think?"

"Why?"

"Well," I said, floundering in my response, "if she was hooked?"

The doctor shook his head. "She wasn't hooked when I knew her. And in my opinion Marcia did not have an addictive personality."

"You believe in a theory of addictive and non-addictive personalities?"

"It's the only theory that makes sense to me. Otherwise most of us would be hopeless drunks. Is the question very important?"

"It could be. There's a crazy woman on Hornby Island. Some people think she's Marcia Hunt."

My words made him blink. He peered beyond me, out toward the grey sea, as I told the story of my search for Marcia.

He said, "This Hornby woman. Do you think she's an imposter?"

"I don't know. By the way, did I mention that Marcia was still doing drugs when she gave birth?"

His face hardened. "That introduces another element. If Marcia had a child, it could be impaired."

I brought out my copies of the photographs. The first one he looked at showed an infant Marcia in her baby carriage.

He smiled. "The girl pushing the pram is Effie Charterhouse. She was the Hunts' housekeeper before Iris Naylor took the job."

"Is she related to the maid who quit recently?"

"Yes. They're mother and daughter."

The doctor resumed his scrutiny of the pictures. He gave a startled cry, leaped to his feet and hurried across to the window to examine one of them in stronger light. He lowered the photograph and gave me a bleak look. "What the hell's the meaning of this, Seaweed?"

Mystified, I went across to him.

The doctor shook a photograph under my nose and said angrily, "Don't you see who this is?"

It was the picture of Alison at the art show in Reno. She was standing next to the bearded young man. I said, "That's Alison with some stranger she met at an art show."

"The boy, damn it! Don't you recognize him?"

"No. Should I?"

"That's my son. It's Harry!"

It was five minutes before the doctor calmed down. He went out of the room and returned with a bottle of brandy and two glasses. He poured two stiff drinks and gave one to me.

I said, "I've never seen a photograph of your son in a beard. The boy I saw at the murder scene five years ago was clean-shaven."

The doctor nodded gloomily. "Harry used to grow a beard on his trips. He'd shave it off when he got home. I'm sorry, Seaweed, there's no way you could have known him. Bearded he looks quite different."

I put my half-empty glass on the table and sat on the sofa. My head ached. My eyes felt as if they had sand in them. I heard Dr. Cunliffe leave the room. The last thing I remember was feeling somebody spreading a blanket over me.

JIMMY SCOW WENT Canoe Cove way. To increase his power he stayed celibate four days, following which he indulged in sexual intercourse with Effie Yokwats to the point of exhaustion.

It was night. Scow was alone now. In the path of a thin slivered moon, wet pebbles shone like jewels. Arbutus trees thrust gnarled red arms at the blue-black sky. First Woman and her children drifted above the earth, blocking out stars intermittently. A sailboat, its anchor light faintly gleaming, floated on the cove, as mysterious as a mirage.

Naked except for a wooden wolf mask, Scow padded up and down along the high-tide line, collecting driftwood for a bonfire. When Scow lit his bonfire, blue smoke drifted out to sea. From his medicine bag, Jimmy Scow got the silver hairbrushes that he had taken from Charles Service's house and from them carefully harvested eight short hairs. Scow then took water that he had brought from Service's toilet bowl and dripped it onto four small pebbles. After the four pebbles were dry, Scow put them into the mouth of a snake, along with the eight short hairs from Charles Service's head. Scow shut the snake inside a bentwood box. If the snake ate the pebbles and the hairs, Charles Service would urinate blood; his head would ache unbearably.

Jimmy Scow ate some mushrooms. Shaking his spirit stick, singing Wolf Song, Jimmy Scow danced around his fire.

Along about midnight, Jimmy Scow lay down on a cedar-bark mat. The waters of the cove parted. Waves crashed against the beach. The lone sailboat rocked at its mooring.

Wolf and four of his wives waded out of the sea, bringing with them the acrid reek of rotting weed and dead starfishes and oysters left too long in the sun.

Wolf killed the snake and buried its meat in a secret place, because if Jimmy Scow saw the snake or the pebbles or the hairs again, he would lose his senses. Wolf then returned the dry skin of the snake to the bentwood box, saying, "Now your name is Killer-At-The-North-End-Of-The-World. Now you will kill with fire."

Jimmy Scow ate more mushrooms.

Jimmy Scow wrapped himself in the cedar-bark mat tied with a nettle-twine cord and threw himself into the sea, where he went to the bottom of deep water, anchored to a line supported by a cougar's bladder.

At daybreak the sailboat departed the cove. Later the same day, and on the third day thereafter, a Native crab fisherman came to check his pots. He saw but did not touch the cougar bladder.

For four days, nothing happened. When Effie Yokwats went looking for Jimmy Scow, she found him hanging head downward from a sandstone bluff, his ears and his mouth streaming blood. Small birds and stinging wasps swarmed around him.

Effie Yokwats put him in her car and drove him back to Vic West, where he came to and recovered. Because he had survived his ordeal, Jimmy Scow's people allowed him to keep his new name.

CHAPTER FIFTEEN

I phoned Nevada and spoke to Joan Alfred. I said, "Those photographs that I borrowed. One of them showed a young man talking to Alison at an art show. I believe he purchased one of her paintings. It turns out that their meeting was very significant."

"Was it?" she said incuriously.

"Yes. Alison told me that he was a casual stranger."

"That's not quite right. The man was a stranger, but the meeting wasn't exactly casual. I remember the way it happened, though, because it was one of Alison's first sales. What happened was, Reno newspapers ran feature articles to support an art show. The young fellow was only passing through town, but he happened to pick up a newspaper and noticed Alison's name. It interested him, but he didn't explain why."

THE LITTLE INTER-ISLAND ferry plowed across the narrow strait to Hornby Island. My Chevrolet was the only car on board. A few bicycle tourists had embarked with me, but they all trooped into the passenger saloon. I stood in the bows, wearing a heavy mackinaw jacket and thick wool pants. Ahead, Goose Cove emerged from the grey sea. Mount Geoffrey loomed in the distance. The Coast Range peaks, mantled with last year's snow, receded in diminishing shades of blue and white.

On the three-hour drive between Victoria and the ferry landing I had tried to sort out all the new information that I had obtained. There was one more person I would have liked to interview — Patrick Coulton, the old detective hired by Calvert Hunt many years earlier. But Coulton had been dead for years, had carried his secrets to the grave. Coulton's widow was ailing in a White Rock nursing home. I decided it was worth going to see her.

The ferry docked. I motored ashore, dawdling behind the bicycle tourists who disembarked first, weighted down with camping gear. I added my car to the lineup outside the Hornby Island pub. Inside, two loggers in tartan shirts, wool pants and cleated boots were shooting pool.

A barmaid appeared from a storeroom behind the counter. In khaki shorts and green pastel shirt, she could have posed for an L. L. Bean ad. I ordered a Foster's. When it came I said, "I'm visiting Hornby for a day or two. Anything interesting going on?"

"Sure," she said cheerfully, taking my money. She rang the sale and dropped my change on the bar. "Let's see. They've got a meat sale on at the Co-op. Everything in their freezer is half-price from now until the weekend. If that isn't exciting enough for you, they're showing a Jack Nicholson movie at the community hall tonight. On Friday there's a dance."

"These island dances," I kidded her. "They'll be formal affairs I suppose, tuxedos, long dresses, women in tiaras?"

Straight-faced, she replied, "The last time I saw a tiara was when Freddy the Freeloader showed up in here one night, pretending to be Princess Di."

"Was anybody taken in?"

"Only Freddy. The RCMP took him in to St. Joseph's hospital until he came down from whatever he was on."

The barmaid, about 25, ran a cloth over the already gleaming counter, then stood back, grinning. She had a face like Audrey Hepburn's in *Breakfast at Tiffany's*.

I said, "I'm hoping to run into somebody who lives here. Maybe you'd know her?"

"Maybe. Who is it?"

"A woman called Marcia Harkness. She has a daughter, Hockey."

"That her name, Marcia? We call Hockey's mom Mother Harkness. I went to school with Hockey. You'll probably find one or both of 'em hanging out around the Co-op. That's if they're not out oyster picking."

THE AREA SURROUNDING Hornby Island's Co-op store was laid out like a village green from a bygone age. The main building was a barn-like general store with half a dozen small cedar-and-glass shops clustered around it. Entrepreneurs in Birkenstocks and handwoven clothes sold locally made arts and crafts, books, ice cream. I noticed a bike-rental place and a café with outdoor seating. I bought an espresso and sat on a canvas-roofed patio to watch the action.

Ten yards away a young woman was hawking copper earrings. Periodically, people stopped to chat, addressing her by name. Nobody bought anything. The woman, smoking innumerable cigarettes, did not seem to mind whether she sold anything or not. She was thin. It was hard to guess her age because of her deeply weathered skin. She had ornate copper rings on every finger. But the rings, instead of gracing the fingers, drew attention to their calluses, broken nails, the black half-moons at the tips. These were the hands of an oyster picker. I was looking at Hockey Harkness. Rain began to beat on the canvas awning.

The earing seller was standing beside the road with her thumb out when I picked her up in my Chevrolet. She climbed in and I said, "Where to, Hockey?"

She smiled, revealing a missing front tooth. "Do I know you?" she said in a soft voice.

"No. But I came to the island because I'm looking for your mother. I heard people using your name. I was wondering how to introduce myself when it started to rain."

"Are you from the insurance?" she said, touching my sleeve shyly.

"No. Are you expecting somebody?"

"Ma doesn't get many visitors. If it's about the insurance you may as well talk to me."

"Well, I'm not from the insurance. My name is Silas Seaweed. I'm from Victoria."

"Well, you know my name, don't you?" she said, taking a tobacco pouch from a pocket and rolling a cigarette.

I said, "Just watch yourself if I have to stop the car suddenly. That seat you're sitting on moves forward sometimes."

She laughed and said, "This car's a limo compared to some of the heaps you see around Hornby."

As I drove I glanced at her from time to time, wondering if it were even remotely possible that the timid creature beside me could be descended from Calvert Harkness. It seemed unlikely.

Hockey pointed to a side road leading toward the sea at Tribune Bay. I turned off and we bounced along it in silence.

Set back in the trees were rustic shacks, apparently built of recycled materials. Hockey directed me to a tiny cabin in a clearing surrounded by Douglas fir and arbutus trees. As we pulled up, a woman who had been working in a vegetable garden scurried inside. She was a dumpy brown-coated figure in rubber ankle boots, wearing a scarf pulled tightly over her head and knotted beneath her double chin.

Hockey got out of the car and lit her cigarette with a box match. She did it like a practised outdoorsman, cupping her hands around the flame to shield it. I followed her inside the house. Hockey plunked her sample case in a corner, pointed to a wooden chair and asked me to wait. She went into another room.

The house stank of mildew, cats, ancient dirt and bathroom odours that no amount of airing could ever remove. Bits of clear plastic had been nailed over the sash windows' many broken panes. Dead insects shared the sills with empty jars and bottles. Heaps of newspapers lay everywhere, some neatly tied in bundles, others lying loose. There was a cracked teapot on the table, along with half an onion and several cloves of garlic. Rusty nails, bits of salvaged hardware and miscellaneous tools filled boxes and cans lying on the floor. The plasterboard walls had never been painted and were largely concealed by clothing dangling from nails. An unframed colour print of the Queen and Prince Philip was tacked up beside an airtight woodstove. Beside it was a big old sofa with stuffing protruding through holes. An assortment of wooden packing cases, spread with odd pieces of cloth, served as seats and tables. A black cat stalked in. Seeing me, the cat bolted, its tail straight up like a flag.

Hockey returned and stood in the doorway. "Ma says to ask what you want."

"I want to talk to her myself, please."

"Well, she's not used to visitors, Mr. Seaweed."

She showed me her gap-toothed smile again.

"I won't keep her long. We probably know some of the same people. I'm hoping your mother can help me find someone."

"What kind of work you do?"

"I'm a detective."

Disappointment made Hockey's mouth droop. "But I asked you if you were from the insurance company, and you said you weren't."

"I'm not from the insurance company."

Hockey came into the room and closed the door behind her. She leaned against the wall and said, "This is awkward."

I smiled at her and said, "Is your name Alison Harkness?"

Her shy smile reappeared. "Nobody calls me Alison now. When I was little, kids at school started calling me Harky — you know, from Harkness? Then it got sort of twisted around. Even Ma calls me Hockey now. Funny, isn't it?"

Her words set up little vibrations of excitement in my mind. I said, "Does your mother ever talk about the old days? That time before she came to the island? When she lived in Victoria, or Seattle?"

"Seattle? Ma lived in Seattle?"

"She never mentioned it to you?"

"Oh, no, never. See, Ma doesn't remember anything from those days. I thought we were from Vancouver, but I can't tell you why. I've never been to Victoria. Haven't been anywhere 'cept Courtenay and Comox."

The door opened a crack. Mother Harkness's face appeared in the opening. I pretended not to notice her, but raised my voice so that she could hear me. "There are people in Victoria who remember your mother. Some of them might like to see her again, but it's not important. If she doesn't want to see them, she doesn't have to."

"Are these the bikers? My daddy was a biker."

"Some were bikers, some not."

The door opened a bit more and Ma Harkness sidled in. She was still wearing the shapeless raincoat, tightly belted at the waist. Wisps of grey hair stuck out from beneath a headscarf. All her teeth had gone, and her lips were sucked together in a way that drew long hollows beneath her cheekbones. She had a faraway smile.

Addressing Hockey, I said, "Do you know a man called Fred Eade?"

Hockey was startled. "Sure," she said. "Fred was here visiting a little while back. Fred's the one promised us the insurance money."

"Fred Eade promised you insurance money?"

"Well, only if Ma would show him her tattoo. Fred said that if she showed her tattoo, she'd get insurance money."

"And this tattoo. When he saw it, was he satisfied?"

"I think so. But Fred never came back."

I said, "Marcia Harkness, the one that my friends know. She had a tattooed shoulder."

Hockey looked at her mother and smiled. "Why don't you let Mr. Seaweed have a look at it?"

Instead of replying, the old woman scuttled out of the room.

"She'll be back," said Hockey complacently.

I said, "Did Fred Eade ask for anything else, leave anything?"

Hockey thought about the question, then shook her head. "You mean papers?"

"Yes, old family pictures, documents, things like that."

"He never asked for nothing. Seeing the tattoo was all he wanted. He was only here for a bit. Him and that girl."

"Do you mean Patty Nolan?"

Hockey became animated. "Yeah, Patty. I liked her. You know Patty?"

"I was talking to her yesterday."

Hockey said, "Next time you see Patty, tell her she's welcome to come visit us again. She had us all laughing with her jokes and her antics. Maybe she'd like to hang out with us for a while."

"I'll tell her," I said, adding, "It would make my job a bit easier if you or your mother have any photographs or papers that I could look at."

Hockey raised the lid of a packing case, took out an old steel fishing-tackle box and put it on the table. Before we looked inside the box, the door opened and Mother Harkness came in. She had taken her coat off and pulled down the sleeve of a baggy polyester sweater to expose her right shoulder. I saw the strap of a grubby brassiere, bulging whey-coloured flesh. And a mottled red scar at the point of her shoulder. The red scar was the faded tattoo of a rose. Exactly where it was supposed to be.

THE AIRCRAFT BANKED, then began its descent into Vancouver International. The man in the seat next to me stirred nervously, holding onto the armrests with both hands and jutting his elbows into my side. I hardly noticed, did not even turn to look at the city of Vancouver, laid out below. I was thinking of the marvels that had come from Marcia Harkness's fishing-tackle box. It had been full of Hunt-family documents and photographs. I saw Alison's and Marcia's birth certificates. There were pictures of both women as babies. There was a receipt for one of Marcia's boarding-school uniforms, doctor's prescriptions. Faded sports ribbons. A real ivory comb with missing teeth. An old celluloid doll with missing arms. The picture of a tall, slender young man wearing a PPCLI uniform. Marcia Harkness had no idea who the soldier was, but I knew. It was Calvert Hunt.

I RENTED A WRECK and drove it south from the airport toward the Peace Arch border crossing. At White Rock I turned off. The rest home I was looking for was perched on a hillside overlooking Georgia Strait.

A nurse escorted me to Mrs. Coulton's room. The old lady was in a rocking chair, placidly knitting and watching TV. Outside, the sodden boughs of a Japanese cherry tree waved in the breeze. Patrick Coulton's widow put the knitting on her lap and clicked the TV off with her remote. My visit was expected. After introductions the nurse left us. Mrs. Coulton extended her hand. I took it gently, careful of the fragile bones beneath liver-spotted skin. Her hair was white. She looked serene, content.

Speaking with a soft Canadian-Scottish burr she said, "I asked Nurse to bring Paddy's things up from storage, but there isn't much left to show you. When Paddy died I sent most of his stuff to the Salvation Army." She pointed to a side table. "There's his old logbooks and his expense books. I kept them because I thought the government might want to have a look at them. You know what the government's like."

I said, "Have you remembered any more about the things we spoke of on the telephone?"

She shook her head. "Paddy was always very close-mouthed about his work. Didn't bring his troubles home, not like some. He never had much to say anyway. More of a thinker than a talker was our Paddy. He hated it when they made him retire. Policing was his whole life. That's why he went into the private investigations. It gave him an interest. Life's no use if you don't have an interest."

I said, "Paddy was a good cop. Over 30 years with the Vancouver PD."

"That's right. Before that, Paddy did three years in the navy. He liked the security and the benefits. When he retired officially, he had a good pension, Paddy did, which is why I can live here now, comfortable with my TV and my knitting. Old Paddy never did retire properly, though. He kept on messing about with this and that until the end. But you're just being polite. You want to talk about that girl who went missing in Nevada. The reason I remember it was because it was one of the cases where Paddy took me along. When we could, we mixed business with pleasure, so to speak. He was running around in the desert, doing his work, while I was in the casinos enjoying myself." She had a faraway smile. "Paddy was Scottish too. Always close with his money. Not that he was mean. Paddy didn't have a mean bone. But still it was nice that he could get paid to go to Reno."

"Can you remember what year that was?"

"Let me see. It'd be 1985 or 1986, I think. I know it was before young Marion was born."

"Marion?"

"My granddaughter. She's top of her class at Kwantlen College."

"Did Paddy find what he was looking for in Reno?"

"Oh, bless my soul, I can't tell you, Mr. Seaweed. He never said a blind word to me about it if he did." She pointed to the logbooks. "Why don't you have a look in them. Take 'em with you if you want. Maybe you'll find something to help you. I can't make head nor tail of 'em myself."

After studying Paddy's books for a few minutes I wasn't able to make head nor tail of them either. Entries were written in a private code. Cases were referred to by number instead of name, and I was unable to find a key. But now I knew for certain that Paddy had traced a missing woman as far as Reno. Would a cop as dedicated as Paddy, following a fresh trail, fail to find her?

CHAPTER SIXTEEN

It was three in the morning when I parked my Chevy on Foul Bay Road. A white half-moon watched me through scudding clouds and illuminated piles of leaves raked onto boulevards. A slight wind sent down more leaves as I approached Calvert Hunt's new security gate. It was locked, of course; I had to climb a stone wall to get onto the grounds. As I went up Hunt's driveway a family of raccoons emerged from the rhododendrons and scurried single file across the lawns. One halogen lamp, shining from a pole, lighted up Ribblesdale's main front entrance. A smaller lamp, its light half-diffused by thick ivy, shone above a second-storey fire escape.

It was very dark outside Charles Service's office. I found a suitable pane in a leaded-glass window, masked it all around with sticky tape and dislodged it with a stiff blow of my elbow. The glass bowed into the room with a sharp crack, but the tape prevented it from rattling onto the floorboards. I backed away from the house and watched from a distance. The house remained as silent as before; no lights came on. I waited five minutes, went back to the window and reached inside for the bronze catch. The window opened easily.

I climbed inside and with my flashlight checked Charles Service's cabinet. It was a substantial metal cube, as big as a clothes dryer. The lock was too tough for an amateur safecracker like me, so I went looking for its key in Service's desk.

Somewhere deep within the big house, stairs creaked. I switched my flashlight off and felt a little buzz of adrenaline as soft footsteps crossed the floor above. In the ensuing silence I heard the faint hiss of water running through pipes. After a moment the footsteps retraced their route.

Service's desk had seven drawers but the safe key wasn't in any of them. I checked the filing cabinets, but they were locked and I didn't know how to open them without making a racket. I went back to the desk again, removed the drawers, one at a time, and felt around in the spaces behind. Eureka! The keys were hanging from a cup hook screwed to the back of a drawer.

One key opened the big cabinet. It contained half a dozen small deed boxes and six large, flat, neatly wrapped packages. I slit a package open with my pocket knife and found what Victoria's detective squad had wasted five years looking for — the paintings removed from the walls by the gang that killed Harry Cunliffe.

I spent a few minutes removing traces of my visit, but couldn't do anything about that broken window. The pane was partially concealed behind curtains, though. Maybe Charles Service would notice a draft or find the broken window and think that raccoons had done it. Maybe there really is a Santa Claus.

I SLEPT LATE. While shaving, I thought about food. It had been days since I had lived a normal life. Meals and sleep had suffered, and now I needed a decent breakfast. I could always go to Lou's, have the usual eggs and bacon. Shoot the breeze with Bernie and Chantal, listen to Lou's latest beef. No, I wanted something peaceful. The case was solved. Wrapping it up shouldn't take long. And with any luck Chief Mallory would be so pleased with my efforts that he'd restore funding to my neighbourhood policing scheme.

Outside Mom's Café, boats bobbed in the swell. A strong south-westerly whistled through the rigging of that old Atlantic fishing trawler. Winter was coming apace. The nautical dreamers were still loading stores aboard their rusty ship. I envied them their coming trip to sunny Guatemala. I went inside the café and ordered corned-beef hash with poached eggs and multigrain toast.

Somebody tapped my shoulder. It was Captain Bloggs.

"I see in the newspaper that they arrested the dame what killed Fred Eade," the captain said by way of introduction.

I invited him to join me and said, "Patty Nolan? The police have her in custody, but she didn't kill Fred Eade."

"Think so, eh? If it weren't her, why did she run away?" Without waiting for my reply, the captain added, "But just the same, it's a helluva way to go. Fred was no great shakes but he deserved better than being shot like a dog."

"Who doesn't? But a guy like Fred, he always led with his chin, did things the hard way. Maybe things went wrong when he was a kid and he was pushed off balance. Got his feet set on a certain path and never was able to get off it."

The captain snorted derisively. "Hogwash. You make your own luck in this life. I get tired of hearing how people turn out bad because society was mean to 'em." The captain pointed outside. Black smoke was pouring from the rusty trawler's smokestack. He said, "You take them poor lubbers over there, for example."

I said, "What about them?"

"They've made two attempts to get that rustbucket to Guatemala. Once they got as far as Race Rocks before they had to be towed home by the Coast Guard. Once they steamed three hours before they found out their bilge pumps don't work. Now they're at it again. Sailing at first light tomorrow for Guatemala. Non-stop. That's what *they* think."

"Well, they're stubborn, Captain, give them that."

His jaw worked from side to side. "Stubborn, hell. They're just dumb. Instead of learning from experience they'll go out, get drowned and blame fate. Them folks is bound and determined to commit suicide and there isn't a thing anybody can do to stop 'em. They'll wind up on a lee shore somewhere, mark my words, and that old tub will make a reef for the fishes to play in."

My breakfast arrived; I started to eat.

The captain said, "Did you ever hear from Taffy Jones?"

"Nope," I said. "But that reminds me of something. Look at this."

I dug in my pocket, found the photograph I wanted and showed it to the captain.

The captain said, "Why, that's young Harry Cunliffe."

"Right. Wearing a beard. I didn't recognize him at first."

"No? Well, maybe not. But you didn't know him like I did."

A black-hulled schooner came into view around the Coast Guard station. The schooner's skipper pushed down his helm and headed in for the marina. Captain Bloggs stood up, fastening the shiny brass buttons on his pea jacket as the schooner's crew lowered sail.

"I've got to run," Captain Bloggs said. "That fellow will be looking for a place to tie up."

THE LOT BEHIND SWANS was full so I parked on Fisgard Street and strolled to my office, hoping to catch sight of the curvaceous Halvorsen. No such luck. I unlocked my door and went inside. At that moment a battering ram smashed into me. I went hurtling across the room till I hit a wall and fell. When I tried to get up there was an automatic pistol just inches from my nose.

Charles Service was holding the pistol in one hand and stroking his shoulder with the other. "Sorry about that, Seaweed. Bit clumsy, but I'm taking no chances with you." He spoke in an ordinary conversational tone.

"What the hell is all this?" I said, reaching for my chin and feeling a thin trickle of blood where I had bitten my lip.

"Stop! Move and I'll shoot!"

I knew he wasn't fooling, but I was awkwardly half-twisted. I told him so and he let me ease myself around very slowly till I was sitting with my back against the wall.

Service watched this intently. When I was settled he said, "Don't move again."

"Sure," I said. "Maybe this time you'll finish off what you started earlier."

Service narrowed his eyes. "I don't understand. Started what?"

"Are you denying that you shot me from that roof across the street?"

His lips twisted in a sneer. "If I had, we wouldn't be having this talk. You'd be dead."

Service sat on the edge of my desk, swinging his foot, resting the gun on his knee. I said, "Is that the gun you used on Fred Eade?"

He thought this over and said, "Yes. It's old, but I keep it oiled. I thought of using it on you yesterday, actually."

"Actually?"

"Actually. But Phyllis Williams came into my office. She didn't know it, but she saved your skin."

"Tell me something, sir. Is that the gun you killed Harry Cunliffe with?"

Service's polite mask slipped and his face worked with the effort of concentration. "How did you find out?"

"You gave yourself away."

His unblinking eyes were dull and opaque. "No doubt, but how?"

"I know how, and I know *why*."

"You know why I killed Harry Cunliffe?"

I ignored that question and said, "When did Calvert Hunt change his mind about wanting to reconcile with his daughter?"

Service moved impatiently. "What difference does it make?"

"Let's just say you're humouring a dying man."

"Yes. It's a simple question of priorities. Either I take care of you or I go to jail." Service's self-assurance showed in his unfurrowed brow and easy conversational tone.

I wanted to disturb his cocky confidence. "But you didn't have that rationalization when you killed Harry Cunliffe. Greed made you do it."

"I was needy, too. I needed money, still do. Lots of it."

"And you know how to get it. Cocaine's expensive, of course."

Service nodded, appearing genuinely sorrowful. "It was a rash act. I liked the boy, his father is an old and valued friend. That's why nobody suspected me. Shooting Fred Eade, on the other hand, gave me intense pleasure."

"You're wrong about one thing, sir. I've suspected you since day one. Proving it was another matter. There never was a florist's van, was there?"

"I can see that you're going to tell me everything, aren't you, Silas?"

"Only if you want to hear it, sir."

"And stop calling me *sir*, for God's sake!" snapped Service, irritated at last.

I managed a grin. "Sure, why not? There never was a florist's van."

Service shook his head. "You were on the Cunliffe case for one day only, then were taken off. I know you're not that clever."

"I was taken off the case because Victoria's chief detective inspector didn't want a muddy-booted savage clattering across Calvert Hunt's beautiful hardwood. It was a high-profile case. If there was any glory going, the DCI wanted it all for himself. But that's incidental. You killed Harry Cunliffe because he went to Ribblesdale with proof that Alison Harkness, Hunt's presumptive heir, was alive and well and living in Nevada. I know that for years you've been spending huge amounts of money on cocaine and on Sarah Williams. I suppose you've been looting Hunt, have you?"

"Yes, there's no point in denying it now. I have to admit, you're smarter than I gave you credit for."

I noticed Service's gun. It was a police-issue Glock and I wondered how he'd obtained it. I said, "So you killed Harry. Somewhere prior to that you saw an Aboriginal driving a florist's van. For reasons known only to yourself you railroaded that hard-working honest driver into the hoosegow. Poor guy. That florist-van story was entirely fake, a red herring. The missing paintings added weight to your tale, gave an apparent motive for the robbery. Yeah, the DCI bought it. It looked as if Harry Cunliffe blundered onto the scene of a robbery and it was his bad luck to get blown away. But you removed those paintings yourself and hid them."

Service's eyes were remote. "Yes. I concocted that story on the spur of the moment, but it worked."

"Right. There was only one Aboriginal driver working for a florist in Victoria. He was in custody in less than a day. The case against Scow was entirely circumstantial. Victoria's detective squad wasted a lot of time trying to find those stolen pictures. All the time you were laughing up your goddam sleeve. The DCI became convinced that Harry Cunliffe was shot by accident, just an armed robber's stupid blunder. So that's the background.

"Now let's talk about Calvert Hunt's wife. After meeting and speaking with the gracious Phyllis Williams, Mrs. Hunt's sister, I can understand that Marcia's mother was a woman who'd carry a grudge."

Service nodded. "Yes. Calvert's wife *and* Phyllis were a fine pair of bitches. From Mount Royal, of course; they were thoroughly upper class. That's why Calvert married her. She was his intro to polite society. I don't know how Calvert tolerated her, but he did. He made a billion dollars in industry but was powerless before his spiteful, domineering wife. When Marcia turned out to be as determined as her mother, it was just a matter of time before bombs went off on Foul Bay Road. Marcia was kicked out and disowned. Calvert Hunt went along with it."

"But later Calvert had a change of heart? Ordered that Marcia be found and brought back, correct?"

Service nodded.

I said, "You hired Patrick Coulton. Coulton didn't report directly to Hunt, he reported to you. Coulton was an experienced detective. Marcia hadn't been missing long. I think he traced her and told you where she was." I moved my shoulders slightly.

Service pointed the pistol at me and said, "You're doing all right, so don't spoil it now."

"You never told Calvert that Marcia had been traced. You paid Coulton off."

"Now you're guessing," said Service.

"Maybe. Anyway, a couple of years after Coulton found her, Marcia was dead. Killed in a freak accident." I stared him in the eye. "Correct me if I'm wrong."

"You are substantially correct. Actually, Coulton made two separate investigations and was successful on the second try. He found Marcia in 1985, I think. Maybe '86. In the main, you're right. I must congratulate you."

Service was smiling again, enjoying my story. I decided to shock him and said, "You kept everything secret. Coulton was paid off and sent home. But Coulton had delivered a golden goose. Now you knew where Marcia was, you kept tabs on her. When Marcia was killed, you saw a way to loot Calvert's estate."

Service's smile vanished.

I said, "That's when you set up that dummy heiress on Hornby Island."

"That's impossible! You can't know that, damn you!" Service was visibly shaken. Colour had drained from his face. He said, "What else do you know?"

I stretched my legs a bit. "You were Hunt's lawyer, his confidant. You knew all about his last will and testament, probably wrote it yourself. You knew how much Hunt money was sloshing about. What you wanted was a piece of it."

Service swallowed a couple of times and nodded.

I said, "Calvert Hunt has no direct heir. Most of his fortune would go to charity. Was there anything in it for you, the faithful retainer?"

Service's face smoothed to blandness. "No. Calvert thinks I've been adequately compensated for my devoted service. After his death I have to shift for myself. The house and a million or so would go to the Williamses. The rest of Calvert's assets would vanish down an enormous charitable sinkhole."

"You didn't like that idea very much so you set up a phony heiress and plunked her down on Hornby Island to wait for the day when you could produce her at maximum benefit to yourself. On that day, no doubt, you'd also produce a second incontestable will."

Service looked pleased with himself. "It's true, I've been robbing old Calvert for years. I have his absolute trust and, frankly, the old man isn't as sharp as he used to be. But hoodwinking him was one thing. Concealing my little peccadilloes from auditors after his death would be more difficult, hence the imposters. Once I get myself declared their legal guardian, I'll be home and dry."

"You maliciously and unnecessarily wrecked an innocent man's life and you murdered two others, but apart from that I almost admire you, in a way. In a way. What you did took long-term planning and must have cost plenty over the years. That tattoo on the phony's shoulder was a nice touch."

"I'm glad you like it. The woman on Hornby is a real drug fatality, by the way. She'd blown her brains out with drugs. I found her in Vancouver and set the scam up. It was a bonus that she had a daughter about the same age as Alison, but I could have faked that detail if necessary. The phonies were two lost souls living in an east-end women's hostel. I set them up on Hornby Island and gave them bits of identification in case I ever needed to produce them in a hurry. I had the woman tattooed by the same artist who did Marcia."

"That was more or less the way I saw it, but there was a big foul-up.

In fact there were two foul-ups. Things happened that you didn't anticipate," I said slowly, spinning the story out. "The first foul-up involved Fred Eade. Fred had run into the phony Marcia Harkness on Hornby Island. He thought she was Frank Harkness's wife. But what he didn't know, at first, was that she was supposed to be a rich man's daughter. Fred forgot about Marcia until he saw the advertisement I put in the papers. That's when Fred decided to get clever. He had me tailed. The tail was a fat man driving a stolen green Toyota. His name is Sidney Banks. Sid followed me to Ribblesdale and, I assume, reported to Fred. Fred Eade was then able to put two and two together. Now he knew, or thought he knew, who Marcia Hunt was. But Fred Eade was a two-for-a-quarter grifter. He wasn't satisfied with a nice reward. Oh, no. He got clever and tried to steal the golden goose. Am I right?"

Service leaned forward a bit. "Yes. Fred Eade went to Ribblesdale and tried to get to Calvert Hunt directly, but that's impossible. He had to go through me. When I found out what he wanted, I had to shut his mouth."

"You shut his mouth but you botched it. As I just told you, Fred didn't have his own car. Sidney Banks drove him around when necessary. You thought that Fred was acting alone."

Service drew his eyebrows together, but his gun still pointed menacingly.

I said, "It didn't suit you to produce your phony heiresses at that point. So you went down to the *Ocean Reaper* and found Fred drunk. You killed him. When I went down to the boat I almost ran into Sidney Banks, who had just discovered Fred's body."

Service gave a reluctant nod. "I should have waited until I knew more. If I'd known about Fred's accomplices I might have done things differently and allowed the women on Hornby to be revealed then. I've killed, but I'm not insane. I can't keep killing people, can I? But I didn't know about Fred's accomplices, so he had to die." He frowned and said, "I suppose Patty Nolan told you all this?"

I shook my head. "Patty's in the dark about most of it. She knew that Fred had tried some funny business with you but didn't know exactly what. Not at first. She knew where the phony Marcia was, though. Patty wouldn't tell me everything I needed to know because she was afraid of getting in deeper than she was already. All she wanted was a little money so she could hire a lawyer. Your luck was still holding, Charlie boy."

"It isn't luck entirely is it? Don't you think that my scheme was well managed, in the main?" Service's voice had a plaintive quality.

I shrugged. "But to proceed, sir. Harry Cunliffe ran into the genuine Alison Harkness in Nevada and guessed who she was. Just how he made the connection I'm not sure. Harry was Calvert's godson, knew a lot about the Hunt family. Presumably the real Alison knew enough about her mother's history and unwittingly divulged enough clues about her true identity. But Harry was discreet. Instead of telling Alison what he suspected, he came back to Victoria and told *you*."

Service said, "Yes, Cunliffe's running into Alison was a million-to-one shot."

I studied his face and shook my head. "I'm a poker player, sir, so I know something about odds. Harry's finding and meeting Alison was a long shot, but it wasn't a million to one. Reno is a popular destination for Victorians. Alison met people from B.C. all the time. She knew that her own mother had been born in Victoria and had no reason to keep it a secret. She probably told several people over the years. She finally met somebody who made the right connection. But when Harry came to you with the news, you panicked and killed him like a rat."

Service's gun hand had drooped, but at my words he raised it and aimed at my head. His hand shook as he said, "I did not panic, you bastard. I'm warning you, don't provoke me."

The telephone started to ring. I said, "Want me to answer it?"

"Shut up, don't move."

It pealed five times. The caller listened to my message and left his own. It was Alex Cal, the fake street jiver. We heard Cal say, "We been watching your movements, motherfucker, and we know you are back in this fair city. We got another silver bullet with your number on it waiting for you." The phone clicked off.

Service laughed out loud. He said, "You have just heard the voice of Providence. Get to your feet now. We're going for a ride. You are going to walk out of this office with me. Don't try anything fancy or my first bullet will put a hole in your spine. The next will kill you. I'm a desperate man. I'm ready to shoot you on the street in broad daylight, taking my chances that I can escape afterward."

Service's luck was still holding. If the lawyer killed me, Bernie Tapp or Denise Halvorsen would undoubtedly find Alex Cal's recorded message. Jiggs Murphy and Alex Cal would take the rap.

I climbed to my feet. Service said, "Turn around and face the wall. Place your toes four feet from the wall and lean forward until your hands touch. Stay there while I check your pockets." Service jammed the gun muzzle to my neck and frisked me till he found my Glock.

He pocketed the semi-automatic and stepped back. "All right, Silas, don't do anything rash."

"I won't, believe me."

"Good. Take your belt off and unzip your fly. Then put your hands in your pants pockets and keep them there so they don't fall down. If we meet anybody en route who knows you and wants to speak, don't answer. Is that clear?"

It was clear.

We walked outside. The streets were busy and the sight of two men walking close together went unnoticed. Chantal, walking her strut, saw me coming and plunked herself in my path. When I tried to duck around her she grabbed my arm and said, "Hey, Silas, you better watch out. Alex Cal is gunning for you."

"Thanks, Chantal," I said, feeling Service's gun prodding my spine. I edged past her.

Mystified by my attitude, Chantal put her hands on her hips and stared after us, shaking her head.

I said, "There's trouble, Mr. Service ... "

Another sharp jab shut my mouth and we walked in silence to Service's Lincoln, parked on Pandora Street. The lawyer fumbled with his car keys for a moment, but, changing his mind, he said, "Where's your car?"

"One block over."

"We'll take it instead of mine."

The lawyer shoved me. We crossed the street and went down Fan Tan Alley into Chinatown. My Chevrolet was parked outside Don Mee's restaurant. Service got me to open the Chevy's passenger-side door and slide behind the steering wheel. He got into the passenger seat and said, "You're going to chauffeur me along the waterfront, Silas. A nice little scenic drive."

When I fastened my seat belt, Service laughed but made no comment. Following his instructions I drove along Wharf Street, went slowly past the Empress Hotel, then kept going along Government Street until we reached Dallas Road.

"Which way?" I asked.

"Turn left. Go along the waterfront."

"Then what?"

"You'll see. Get moving."

But we were delayed for a minute. A covered horse-drawn sightseeing wagon was lumbering past with a cargo of tourists. The driver was extolling the beauties of historic Victoria. As the two plodding horses pulled slowly by we heard the driver's amplified voice say, "In a minute you'll see the ancient breakwater at Ogden Point, built by British engineers in the year 1862 ... " The sightseers, huddled in thick red blankets, looked bored and cold.

Service fidgeted at the delay. I said, "Where are you going to do it, Service? In Hunt's garage?"

"Shut up!"

The wagon creaked past. I turned left onto Dallas Road. There were fewer cars here. Suddenly Service said, "She was wrong, that girl. Ogden Point breakwater wasn't built in 1862."

I gave him a quick glance. Perspiration beaded the lawyer's forehead. His gun, pointing at me until then, was aimed at the floor. I accelerated slowly as we passed Beacon Hill Park. To divert Service's attention I said, "I'll tell you how I tumbled to you, if you want."

"All right, tell me."

We were doing 70 kilometres an hour now, but the lawyer was staring at me avidly when I said, "It was when I got back from Nevada and we met in your house. I gave you some photographs."

"I know, I know!"

We were up to 75 and slowly accelerating. I said, "Those pictures, do you remember whose they were?"

"Of course I remember. There were pictures of Marcia and Alison and what's her name? Effie. And one of Harry Cunliffe ... " The lawyer stopped speaking as realization struck home. "So that's it, that's how you knew?"

"That's right. You acted as if you didn't recognize Harry in his beard, but it was unbelievable. The people who knew Harry well all recognized his picture. But there's more. You told the police that when Harry Cunliffe was murdered you were working in your office. You heard a shot, went to investigate and found Harry dead, shot, lying in the lounge. Then you looked out the window and saw a florist's van disappearing down the driveway, but it's all bullshit."

"Is it?"

"You know it is. First of all, your office is at the back of the house. The quickest way from your office to the front door doesn't even go through the lounge."

I had Service's undivided attention now. He said, "I never told you that I ran through the lounge first. What I said was — "

"Yes, yes," I interrupted. "But if you *had* gone through the lounge first, and *if* Harry had been dead, it would have stopped you. Any ordinary person encountering a dead or dying man would stop whatever they were doing and try to render assistance as a first priority. After all, young Harry was supposed to have been a friend of yours. But that doesn't matter. What's important is, there's no way you could identify the driver of any vehicle *leaving* Ribblesdale. The only thing you could see would be the back of the driver's head, if that."

Service was expressionless.

I said, "Did you tell Alex Cal and Jiggs Murphy that I was going to Seattle?"

"Possibly," he said. "I might have let it drop."

We were doing 100. Service was still completely engrossed in my tale when I slammed on the brakes at the road bend near Clover Point. The Chevrolet's faulty passenger seat jerked forward, Service became airborne and his head slammed against the windshield. With my left hand I spun the steering wheel around, trying to negotiate the corner. With my right I reached for Service's gun, but the lawyer's arm was twisted at an unnatural angle. I lost control of the car. The careering vehicle mounted the sidewalk and smashed through steel railings on two wheels. My foot was still jammed on the brake, and I was still fighting for Service's gun when it discharged with a roar. Then the Chevrolet went spinning and rolling down a grassy bank toward the beach. Held by my seat belt I felt the world revolving while, next to me, Service was being alternately hurled to the roof and thrown down across the seats. We spun a few more times until the Chevrolet came to rest on its side.

A couple of joggers rushed forward and dragged open the driver's side door. They did not see the misshapen bundle lying across the back seats. I was hanging in the seat-belt straps but my rescuers quickly undid the buckle and hauled me out. Gasoline fumes seared my nostrils.

We moved away from the wreck. Somebody was saying, "Anybody else in there?" when there was a loud explosion. A giant black-and-yellow fireball rose into the air. Intense heat drove us back. Soon the fireball had gone but a black cloud lingered over the wreck, and oily flames licked through smashed windows.

Somebody said, "You're hurt."

I brushed my cheek. "It's nothing. I bit my lip, that's all."

I pulled my head back and closed my eyes and felt cold rain washing down my face. Feeling slightly dizzy I pushed my through the crowd that had gathered and walked up the slope to Dallas Road. My ears rang from the explosion, but I could hear seagulls screaming as they hung in the air above the beach. Waves crashed against the seawall below Ross Bay cemetery, where soon Charles Service's remains would undoubtedly lie.

Before I reached the road, police and ambulance sirens were wailing. But I wasn't ready to speak to my colleagues. There were things I had to take care of first. After that, I'd call Bernie Tapp.

CHAPTER SEVENTEEN

Jiggs Murphy was doing his rounds. He went to the Purple Pony, where he spoke to a few women and allowed them to buy his drinks. Later he drove downtown in his Buick.

I was waiting for him under the marquee outside the Monterey Inn, killing time with Chantal and three teenaged hookers who were sheltering from the rain. The hookers were telling me about strippers — how much *they'd* enjoy being paid to roll around in the nude on bearskin rugs under hot spotlights instead of hustling their sore little asses on Victoria's chilly streets.

Chantal — who at 25 was the senior woman — said she'd heard that strippers made $1,000 a week. Another girl agreed, saying, "Sure they do, if they put out as well."

Their discussion ended when a dirty Buick nosed up to the Monterey's curb. All four women vanished.

I was pretty sure that Jiggs and Cal had tried to kill me, but I needed to be certain. After all, I'd been pretty sure that George W. Bush would never be elected to a second term.

Jiggs Murphy parked in a three-minute zone, locked the Buick and, grinning after the fleeing girls, stepped onto the sidewalk. He was buttoning a tweed sports coat over his fat drinker's gut when I said, "Hold it, Jiggs."

His mouth dropped open in surprise and he grabbed for an inside pocket, but I was too quick. I smashed Jiggs's nose with my right fist, then buried my left in his belly. Jiggs, sucking air through his bloody nose, folded at the waist like a carpenter's ruler. My knee came up and hit Jiggs in the face. I grabbed the tail of his sports coat and ripped it up until Jiggs's head was covered. His arms were trapped. My knee came up again. Jiggs quit struggling. When I stepped back he collapsed.

A young couple came out of the Monterey Inn arm in arm. They stopped to watch me as I rolled Jiggs onto his back and frisked him. I pocketed Jiggs's automatic, turned my head and barked, "I'm a police officer. If you're smart you'll clear off before the paddy wagon gets here."

The woman tugged her partner's arm and they scuttled off into the wet night. I found Jiggs's car keys, bundled the comatose pimp into the Buick's trunk and drove off in it. The whole incident had lasted less than two minutes.

When Jiggs Murphy woke up in a lonely section of Beacon Hill Park, he was handcuffed inside the Buick's trunk. I shone a flashlight in his eyes and said, "Somebody put a bullet in me a few weeks ago. Was it you?"

I waited 10 seconds. When Jiggs still hadn't acknowledged my question I reached down, grabbed his broken nose between my finger and thumb and gave it a sharp twist. Jiggs screamed.

I said, "Am I getting through to you now, pal?"

He mumbled something. I leaned forward and said, "You got something to say?"

"It was Alex, not me," Jiggs moaned. "It was his money you stole."

"Now tell me, exactly and sincerely. Where can I find Alex Cal?"

The reply was slow in coming. When I reached for his nose again, Jiggs muttered an address. I slammed the trunk shut on him.

ALEX CAL LIVED AT ONE of Victoria's ritziest addresses — a penthouse suite in the Viceroy Hotel on Victoria's Inner Harbour. It was late when I entered the hotel, looked around the deserted lobby and crossed to the elevators. My windbreaker was soaked, the knees of my Levis were stained with blood. The desk clerk, busy with his accounts behind the reception desk, didn't even look up. The elevator door opened and I got in.

I wanted Alex Cal dead. Every time I saw a young crackhead or 14-year-old meth freak, I thought of him and my hatred grew.

The hotel had seven floors, but, as I discovered, the elevator would not ascend to the penthouse without a special key. Lacking the key, I had to get out at the sixth floor. Cement stairs stretched up and down the emergency escape route. At the penthouse level I encountered a locked steel door.

Downstairs again, the Viceroy's public rooms and restaurants had closed for the night. I concealed myself in a corner and watched. The night clerk was still bent over his accounts. A minute passed. Then five minutes, ten. I began to wonder whether Jiggs was going to survive in the Buick's stuffy trunk. Maybe he would run out of air, suffocate. I didn't care very much.

A man wearing a black hat and overcoat came into the hotel. He had a white silk scarf around his neck, but for some odd reason had oversized basketball shoes on his feet instead of polished black shoes. A woman in a fur coat and carrying an electric fan was hanging onto his arm. They were both very drunk. The clerk looked up, grinned and reached for their room key. The couple thanked him with the grave courtesy of people who know they are drunk but are trying to conceal it. They staggered across the lobby, got into the elevator and were whisked away. The clerk left his post and went through a door behind the desk.

I snatched a penthouse key from its pigeonhole and got into the elevator. I tried the key in the elevator's penthouse actuator. It fitted. This time I rode all the way up.

At the penthouse floor, an unlocked glass door led onto a roof garden. Outside, a low ornamental iron railing and trees growing in pots partially screened one penthouse suite from its neighbour. I climbed the railing and looked through windows into Alex Cal's dimly lit apartment. The faux embers of a gas fire glowed red. A black cat came out of Cal's apartment and walked straight toward me. The cat mewed, rubbed itself against my ankles, then darted out of sight. The suite's sliding glass patio door was ajar. I took a deep breath and went inside.

Etta James' voice came softly from hidden speakers as I moved around. I saw a big kitchen with a breakfast area, a formal dining room, a bathroom with a Jacuzzi smelling of bath oils. I had to smile. Cal and I enjoyed the same kind of music. I hoped he wouldn't be enjoying it much longer. Thick carpets cushioned my footsteps. I was startled when the cat reappeared. It began to cry, so I picked it up and stroked its silky back. The cat shuddered and dug its claws into my sleeve. I kept stroking until the cat stopped mewing. My heart was racing when I put it down and watched it stalk away.

I was reaching for the bedroom's doorknob when it suddenly moved. I threw myself aside and heard the soft pop of a silenced pistol as I dropped behind a high-backed sofa. Then all the lights in the room came on and Alex Cal was revealed. I could see him, but he didn't immediately see me. His massive figure was completely naked. The gun in his hand would have been entirely concealed in his big fist if not for its extended silencer.

The pimp said softly, "Come on out, whoever you are, or I'll come find you."

Grinning, Cal advanced into the centre of the room and turned slowly, pointing his gun straight ahead. I picked up a heavy brass table lamp. When Cal's back was turned I hurled the lamp at his head, but it missed and smashed against a window. Cal dropped to his knees, facing the window, and fired a shot blindly as I came out of cover, running. I dived onto his back and tried to seize the gun, but the pimp's body was oily and wet from his recent bath and my grip slipped. His gun went skittering across the floor. The pimp was as strong as he looked. He rolled forward, broke free and dived for the pistol. I kicked the gun away, but Cal grabbed my leg and heaved me off balance. I made a wild grab and caught him around the waist. We crashed to the floor together. A blow exploded against my left ear, lights danced inside my skull. I let go the pimp's waist and reached higher, trying to pin his arms, but Cal was too strong and too slippery. He delivered another blow, this time to my upper arm, and pulled free again. He made another lunge for the gun, but I kicked him hard in the chest and followed through with a punch to Cal's head. A jolt of paralyzing pain radiated up my arm when my blow landed. Cal shook his head. He seemed a bit dazed and backed away from me without the gun.

I faced him from a distance of six feet. My right hand was useless, possibly broken, but the pimp was hurt too.

Cal said, "All *right*, motherfucker. Your time has come. You are going to be put away."

"You called me a motherfucker once too often and hurt my feelings, you bastard."

The pimp grinned. "Man's feelings get hurt by words, just imagine what's in store when I start torturing your body. Me and my friend, the Irish man … "

I strode forward, set my feet on the carpet and swung at Cal's stomach, but the pimp swayed aside and his counterpunch hit my upper arm. Then the two of us were locked together.

The pimp's skin was covered with perspiration as well now; I could not get a proper grip. My arms were being pinned and, at the same time, both of us were aware that either of us would bite the other's neck or ear unless pressure were constantly applied with the side of the head. The pimp gave a sudden heave. I went limp. My sudden lack of resistance sent us crashing, me uppermost. This time the pimp's head smashed down on the floor and at the same moment my knee smashed into his groin. Cal was out cold.

I stood up, trembling, nursing my mangled right hand. It was already blue and swollen. Etta James still sang in the background, Victoria's night sounds drifted in through the broken window.

There was no alarm, no angry telephone ring, no interfering neighbour arriving to complain about the noise. The cat had watched it all from a window ledge. It mewed once. When I dragged Cal out of there it was sitting on its haunches, unconcernedly grooming itself.

THE DEEP-SEA TRAWLER was named *Treasure Island*. That drizzly dark night its rusting blemishes were invisible. I imagined it slicing through the North Atlantic, dragging mile-long nets across the Grand Banks, fishing for cod and halibut and redfish. But the *Treasure Island* was old, the glory days of the Banks were over. This trip to Guatemala was the old trawler's last chance to prove itself before ship breakers cut it up.

The ship had no lookout. No doubt the crew was ashore, celebrating its coming departure. A diesel generator thudded away in the engine room, a thin plume of steam issued from a pipe behind the ship's funnel. There was a small hatch on the *Treasure Island*'s foredeck. I swung the hatch cover back and went below. Down there it smelled of tar and twine and salt and fish oil. Brand new fishnets lay on the floor, still bundled the way they had come from a net-maker. There were bits of old canvas, baskets, empty buckets and brushes down there too — and plenty of room to hide a couple of gagged and trussed-up pimps.

I heaved Alex Cal and Jiggs Murphy aboard the *Treasure Island* one at a time, wheeling them across the floats on a two-wheeled dolly that I found in the ship's fo'c'sle. I dumped the pair of them down the hatch without too much care. Nobody saw me close the hatch on them except for a few bedraggled seagulls hunched on pilings. How long would the pimps remain imprisoned before somebody found them? Maybe they wouldn't be found at all. For a little while Chantal would be able to keep all her earnings. There'd be a sharp jump in the price of street drugs — until other hustlers moved in to fill the vacuum.

I spent the rest of the night dozing in Jiggs's Buick, monitoring the police band and looking out to sea, until the *Treasure Island* slipped its moorings and struck out for warm southern seas.

CHAPTER EIGHTEEN

Denise Halvorsen was puzzled, but she waited until Lou refilled our coffee cups before saying, "I still don't understand it all. Tell me again why Charles Service set up those phonies?"

I said, "Service knew that the Hunts would never allow Frank Harkness to inherit their wealth. But Service figured that if, after Calvert Hunt died, he produced a poor, sick, brain-dead woman and 'proved' that she was Marcia, then he would apply to be declared her legal guardian. It was all set up. He was the Hunts' trusted lawyer and I doubt there'd be any serious objections from anyone. Service could continue to loot from Calvert Hunt's enormous wealth. Service's plan was well thought-out. The evidence that he provided to the phonies was real. The things in that fishing box were items that Service had taken from Marcia's old nursery. The master stroke was that rose, tattooed on the phony's shoulder. Nobody would recognize this imposter, but they wouldn't deny her claim."

"Maybe. But what if the real granddaughter showed?"

"There was only a slight chance of that happening. The legitimate Marcia had turned her back on Victoria, and besides, neither Joan Alfred or Alison knew anything about the Hunt family or its money. Joan had no wish to investigate her brother's past. There was too much ugliness. No, Service's scheme was perfect, a mixture of good planning and good luck. And think of the payoff for him. By his own admission he'd been looting Hunt for years. With phony heiresses parked at Foul Bay Road, the looting would have continued."

"All right. How about DNA testing? Service couldn't fake that."

"Good question. DNA wasn't a factor when Service set the scam up originally. It must have given him a few sleepless nights."

Halvorsen said, "So it was greed that drove Service?"

"No. Cocaine was driving Charles Service," I said. "He was a complicated man. He probably loved Iris Naylor. That didn't prevent him from jilting her to romance Sarah Williams. And when Service stole those paintings, he couldn't bear to destroy them."

"But he killed the son of his friend!"

"Harry Cunliffe's chance discovery of Alison in Reno was going to destroy Service utterly. He panicked. Harry paid the price."

Outside Lou's café, Chantal patrolled in the rain, twirling a big umbrella. I said, "But the story ended well for Calvert Hunt. When he met Alison and Joan he was overjoyed. Marcia's death was one thing. Discovering that he has a granddaughter has given the old man a new reason to live. It's also given him a chance to give Alison the love he ought to have given Marcia."

"So, a story with a happy ending."

"Happy for some people. Not for Iris Naylor. She really loved Service. It's going to be a long time before she recovers from the shock of knowing she loved a murderer."

"Sarah Williams. What about her?"

I took a sip of coffee. I said slowly, "I'm not sure what kind of relationship Service had with Sarah. His death doesn't seem to have disturbed her too much."

"And that young Native man, Jimmy Scow. He served years in prison for a crime he didn't commit."

"Jimmy's been vindicated and he will be fine now. He hired Sammy Lofthouse to sue the city for wrongful arrest. I understand they're arranging an out-of-court settlement."

"Well, you did a great job."

"Yeah? Well I was highly motivated."

Denise went out.

That's when Gottlieb came in. He leaned over my table and said testily, "*She* can run, but you can't."

"Gottlieb! I'm pleased to see you."

"Lying prick. I've been looking for you all week. What's the matter?

Do you want this earth dwarf theft kept in the family? Or do I have to call Stolen Property?"

"Stolen Property? What are you going to say to them? That you tricked some poor sap out of a million bucks and got sore when he returned the compliment?"

"I paid good money for that manikin," Gottlieb said in rising tones. "Do you have any idea how much it cost me to get that wall fixed?"

I told him to sit down. Gottlieb didn't want to sit down. He wanted to hit somebody, preferably a Coast Salish neighbourhood cop.

Lou put a quarter in the Wurlitzer. Frank Sinatra started singing "Nancy (with the Laughing Face)." Lou knows it always makes me blue — I don't know why he does it.

Gottlieb said, "Sheesh, Silas. Your hand's all swollen. What happened?"

"Broken bone. I jammed it in a door."

"Or between somebody's thighs."

"Gottlieb," I said. "That's vulgar."

"Vulgar? I'll tell you what's vulgar. You and that thieving bastard Gregarious George are vulgar. You make a right pair. George won't talk to me either. I saw him on the street yesterday. He saw me coming and took off. Just like that Halvorsen dame."

"So you saw George. But what exactly did you see?"

Gottlieb pondered for a moment. He said thoughtfully, "George was sober. Clean and sober. Funny. It never registered till this minute."

"That earth dwarf, it's changed George's life. Twice," I said. "First it turned him into a drunk."

"Once a drunk, always a drunk."

"He's just got himself a seiner job. George is going commercial fishing up in the Queen Charlottes."

"That's if George isn't in jail, sharing a cell with you," Gottlieb said. He lowered his voice and hissed, "I'm not kidding, Silas. If I don't get that dwarf thing back, I'm raising a big stink."

"George hasn't got it anymore. He couldn't give it to you even if he wanted to. Which I can assure you he doesn't. But as it happens, I know where it is."

"Where is it?"

"If I tell you, will you listen politely?"

"Sure. I'm a businessman. There's no sense getting litigious if you don't have to."

"It's a long complicated story."

"Well I ain't got all day, so cut it short."

"I came into a windfall recently," I said. "Four thousand that I found in an alley. That's nothing to a man like you, Gottlieb, but it's a big deal to me. I wasted some of it on a noble or a childish impulse, depending on your point of view. The rest of the money, well, for a while I didn't know what to do with it."

"You should have asked me," Gottlieb said.

"I asked Chief Alphonse. The chief suggested I spend the money on a Black Tamahnous ceremony for Gregarious George. I thought that was a great idea. We sent for Little Sam."

"Little Sam, the medicine man?" Gottlieb said sarcastically.

"That's the one. He's small, but he's big. We gave Little Sam the money and told him what we had in mind. Little Sam's had a lot of experience in these matters. But working with guys like Little Sam, you've got to be patient. What happened was, Little Sam decided to fast."

"Fast my ass," Gottlieb said. "You're talking fast but you haven't told me nothing yet."

"Little Sam has a place where he goes to visit his tamahnous, up near Spectacle Lake. After going without sleep and fasting for two days and two nights, Little Sam saw a red woodpecker, a powerful spirit. The earth dwarf had sent it to him. Little Sam tried to catch the woodpecker, but the woodpecker flew away past Little Sam's right hand. Not the *left* hand, note, the right hand. It was a sign. Little Sam told Chief Alphonse. Chief Alphonse put the word out. Every Salish chief from Seabeck to Comox showed up in the Warrior longhouse to see what would happen next. We had two special invited guests as well, Effie Yokwats and Jimmy Scow."

"What *did* happen next?" Gottlieb said.

"Nothing much. Not at first. To strengthen himself for his ordeal, Little Sam ate two soft-boiled eggs and drank one cup of coffee. Little Sam then sent for Gregarious George. George showed up as pissed as a newt. Little Sam asked George if he was ready to stop drinking. George said he wanted to, but he was sick, he couldn't help himself. Little Sam took George's hand and the pair of them spent the best part of an afternoon alternately bathing in the sea and doing sweat-lodge medicine. When Little Sam thought that George was ready, he led him naked into the Warrior longhouse and made him sit close to the fire. After some dancing and rattle-shaking, Little Sam and Gregarious George went out on a lengthy medicine-ghost journey with your earth dwarf."

"They took my earth dwarf on a lengthy journey?"

"In a manner of speaking. Little Sam prefers to say that the earth dwarf took *them* on a journey. The point is, Gottlieb, that earth dwarf belonged to the land of the dead. Its home was in the east, across a river. Did you know, Gottlieb, that there is a fork in the road to the land of the dead?"

"No. I *do* know there's a fork in Lou's cutlery drawer."

"The left fork is a short road. It's the one travelled by people who die suddenly. Here's something else you may not know. Salish dead people are all ghosts."

"That explains a lot."

"Dead people live the same kind of life as people do here on earth, except everything is backward. When it's day here on earth, it's night in the land of the dead. When it's high tide here, it's low tide there. And so on. Ghost houses are the same as ours, ghosts hunt and fish and eat things just like we do. Little Sam told us that Gregarious George had died two years ago but had never been buried. George's body stayed here, but his spirit had gone to the land of the dead and brought back the earth dwarf."

"George told *me* that he found the earth dwarf on a beach."

"Whatever. It was time for the earth dwarf to go back home where he belonged. Because Gregarious George had made such a lengthy business of dying, it would now be necessary for him to take the long *right* fork to the land of the dead. The big question was, would George come back alive? Nobody knew. In the entire history of the Salish people the only similar case involved a Snohomish boy, back in the 1890s. *He* came back alive."

"You're pulling my leg, Silas."

"Think so?"

"You're pulling somebody's leg. Maybe your own."

"That's provocative, Gottlieb."

"You tell George that if I do catch up with him, he'll be leaving the land of the living."

"Are you going to be polite or do I leave here and go home?"

"What have you got to go home for?"

I scowled at him.

"I'm sorry, Silas. I guess I'm a bit uptight. Keep talking."

"To get to the land of the dead, Little Sam and George and the earth dwarf had to cross two rivers, the first very swift, which was bridged by a fallen tree. The side from which Little Sam and George approached the second river was slow-running but a mile wide. The farther side had a high bank on which Salish ghosts live. This river was crossed in a canoe. Men and women ghosts were having a Red Tamahnous potlatch and enjoying themselves at the top of the bank. Little Sam and George wanted to join these ghost people, but when they tried to climb up the bank they kept slipping back. Ghost people lowered ropes to help them. The earth dwarf went first and got up safely. When Little Sam and George tried to get up the bank, the ghost rope kept breaking. The ghost people shouted to Gregarious George, 'Does your wife know that you came here today?' George said, 'No.'

"The ghost people told George to go back home to his wife and stop drinking. They did not want him in the land of the dead just yet. All they wanted was the earth dwarf. George could come back to the land of the dead when he was older."

"So that's where my earth dwarf is?" Gottlieb said. "In the land of the dead?"

Now Frank Sinatra was singing "Fly Me to the Moon."

"That's right," I said. "That earth dwarf is on private Salish property. It's the only privacy we have left. Ask anybody."

Gottlieb went out of the café, shaking his head and muttering.

I was just about to get up and leave myself when Patty Nolan came into the café. She was as surprised to see me as I was to see her. I invited her to sit at my table, and after some hesitation she did so.

I asked her how she was doing. She grinned at me and said, "I'm broke, Sammy Lofthouse is riding my ass for money and I don't have no place to stay. Otherwise, things are great."

"Need something to eat? It's on me."

"Sure. They do an all-day breakfast here?"

I waved at Lou. When he came over he refilled my coffee cup. Patty ordered bacon and eggs with sourdough bread and decaffeinated coffee.

I said, "If you had money, what would you do with it?"

Patty didn't hesitate. "Get the hell out of Victoria. This place is jinxed. I can't sleep on Fred's boat no more 'cause I keep seeing him. Dead. I imagine him lying there dead, you know?"

"What about Hornby Island? Hockey Harkness would love to see you again."

"That'd be great. Hang out in the fresh air. Pick oysters. Who knows? I might even find a place of my own on Hornby, make a new start. Stranger things have happened, right?"

I took Charles Service's crumpled blank cheque out of my wallet, wrote Patty's name and some numbers on it and folded the cheque in two. I shoved it across the table and said, "Here's a cheque for you, Patty. Don't look at it till I leave. You'll find out if it's any good when you try to cash it."

I paid for Patty's breakfast and went out.

I WAS STANDING on Black Rock. Below me was the sea, and the Warrior Reserve, and all that was left of once-great forest. Douglas firs and hemlock trees and red alders and willows grew thickly up the slope, concealing our longhouse and my little cabin. Lights twinkled in the darkness, branches swayed in an onshore wind. Ted Crow Chance's big seine boat rode at anchor in the bay — a shadowy outline against the loom of Colby Island. Ted's diesel had thrown a crank so he was still uselessly tied up while the rest of our Native fleet — 20 boats — had sailed north.

I stripped off my clothes and dived off the rock. The inky water was icy cold. I started swimming and kept at it until I stopped thinking about anything except physical survival.

At midnight I fell into bed and slept.

ABOUT THE AUTHOR

Stanley Evans' previous novels are *Outlaw Gold* and *Snow-Coming Moon*. He and his family live in Victoria, British Columbia.